A GOOD MARINE'S MURDER

Other Books by David C. Corbett:

"Abaco Gold, The Maravilla Connection"
"Shield of Lantius"

A GOOD MARINE'S MURDER

DAVID C. CORBETT

READERSMAGNET, LLC

A Good Marine's Murder
Copyright © 2018 by David C. Corbett

Published in the United States of America
ISBN Paperback: 978-1-947765-78-8
ISBN eBook: 978-1-947765-79-5

All rights reserved. No part of this publication may be reproduced, stored in a retrieval system or transmitted in any way by any means, electronic, mechanical, photocopy, recording or otherwise without the prior permission of the author except as provided by USA copyright law.

No lines, parts, and quotations were taken from other books or any previous publications.

The opinions expressed by the author are not necessarily those of ReadersMagnet, LLC.

ReadersMagnet, LLC
10620 Treena Street, Suite 230 | San Diego, California, 92131 USA
1.619.354.2643 | www.readersmagnet.com

Book design copyright © 2018 by ReadersMagnet, LLC. All rights reserved.
Cover design by Ericka Walker
Interior design by Shieldon Walker

"For Donna, who's support is never ending."

DEFINITIONS

<u>A</u>

    ACRO—A pilot's abbreviation for "aerobatics.

<u>B</u>

<u>C</u>

    CAD—A small explosive device found in a pylon (see pylon below).
    Cherry Picker—A very large crane, used to pickup an aircraft from the ground and move it to another location.
    CANX—To cancel.

<u>D</u>

    DD-175—A form used by aviators to file a flight plan.
    DDI—Digital Data Information
    DME—Distance from the plane to a selected radio beacon.

<u>E</u>

<u>F</u>

<u>G</u>

    G's—Short for "gravity." Our body is normally at one (1) G, or gravity. When a pilot pulls G's, he can load the plane and his body up to as high as 7 to 9 G's.

H

Head—The toilet and/or where the toilet is located, aboard a boat.
HUD—Heads Up Display

I

IFF—Identification Friend of Foe; a radio type signal set by the pilot and sent from the aircraft to a radar controller on the ground. The code allows this controller to identify the aircraft for navigational separation purposes as well as determine if the aircraft is friend or foe.

J

K

L

M

MCAS—Marine Corps Air Station
Military Time—Military time starts at 0001 and runs to 2400. Thus, 1 AM is 0100, 1 PM is 1300, 8:45 PM would be 2045, and so on. The Army, when referring to time would say, "thirteen hundred hours," while the Navy and Marine Corps would simply say, "thirteen hundred."

N

NADEP—A huge facility which can rebuild an aircraft from the wheels up. MCAS, Cherry Point has a NADEP.
Nozzles—The AV-8 (all models) have four exhaust nozzles, two of which are located on each side of the plane, approximately midway aft. These nozzles can be vectored

fully aft (up and away flight) to 90 degrees down (hover mode), and finally to a position where they face forward, or 98 degrees from fully aft. The 98-degree position is called the "breaking stop," and used to slow the aircraft down in flight or on landing.

O

Ops—Abbreviation for "Operations" or the G-3, at Wing/Division level, and known as the S-3 at squadron level.

P

PAD—A small area (possibly as small as 75′ X 75″), normally, made of metal, where a Harrier can make a vertical landing.

Pylon—A finlike device, located under either wing, used to attach auxiliary equipment or weaponry (bombs, rockets, etc.) to an aircraft. Most fighter/bomber aircraft have multiple "pylons" under each wing.

Q

R

Radial—A compass bearing from or to and aircraft.

S

Six-By—A large truck, with six wheels. Normally, seen with the cargo area covered with canvas.

Squawk or Squawking—To transmit a certain required IFF code. (See IFF)

T

Tarmac—A bituminous binder, similar to tar macadam, for surfacing roads, air port runways, and parking areas. In aviation language, the tarmac is where squadron aircraft are parked.

U

V

W

X

Y

Z

PROLOGUE

THOUSANDS OF WHITE washed trees, their limbs long forgotten memories, stood like bleached bones reaching for the heavens. The ground surrounding the drying skeletons still appeared racked with open wounds. These were the harsh reminders of Hurricane Irma's strength and the time when that monumental tempest had torn and ripped the land to shreds several years before. All of South Florida still bore the scars from Irma's fury, and the radar approach lane into Patrick Force Base, where the massive storm had been at its worst, was no different.

The pilot, on final approach to Patrick, took no notice of the ground. He was concentrating on flying his aircraft to a safe landing.

Sitting behind the stick was a United States Marine Corps major. The plane? An AV-8 Harrier II. The small fighter bomber, its four nozzles set at sixty degrees, settled at a rate of six hundred feet per minute, and was now passing the outer boundary of the air base. The major was not alone. He had a wingman, but they had separated while passing ten thousand feet, some twenty miles from the airfield. They were executing individual approaches under the guidance of an Air Force radar controller, who comfortably sat sipping coffee in the radar room located in the bowels of Patrick's, Base Operations.

Landing, the bird settled with a heavy thump on its center lined main and nose wheels. Spindly outriggers, mounted mid-way on both wings, bowed slightly under the pressure of a light cross wind. The pilot smiled at his well-executed landing and commenced taxiing for Base Ops located under the field's control tower. A blue "Follow Me" truck dashed in front of the aircraft's nose, and the two civilians manning the vehicle indicated they would lead him to a parking area. He selected his nozzles to forty-five degrees down, the proper angle for taxi, and began following the truck. A cloud of spray followed the Harrier just below the hot nozzles. The field's runway and taxiways were covered with puddles from a recent summer thunderstorm. Patrick AFB was at the southern end of Thunder Storm Alley; an area transit pilots liked to avoid during August days, particularly between the middle hours of dawn to dusk. Reaching the tarmac at the base of the tower, the truck stopped, and the passenger jumped out to provide hand signals for the Harrier's final parking. The man, a Cuban, was middle aged and short. His skin was mahogany brown, his muscles knotted in cords, and his dark eyes darted rapidly in all directions. The major, looking at the man signaling for a left turn, thought his taxi director could well pass for an armored tank, if only he'd had tracks instead of feet. He followed the powerful civilian's hand and arm gestures into his proper parking spot, waited until the man reappeared from under his wings, where the wheels were chocked, and then shut the engine down.

Once the Harrier was silent, its engine wind milling with the breeze blowing across the expansive parking mat, the major threw a leg over the canopy rail, and began climbing down the steps built into the Harrier's fuselage. His feet safely on the ground, he stripped his flight gear off, and hung it on a pylon under the left wing. He retrieved his fore and aft "Marine Green" cover from his right, flight suit leg pocket and placed it on his head. He smiled at the human tank.

"Fill'er up and check the oil," he said, smiling at the dark-skinned man.

"I'll see to it, sir," the man said, returning the smile.

The Major started walking across the tarmac to Base Operations. His wingman had just cleared the runway, and began following the same blue truck, which had sped off once the Cuban's feet had hit the cement. The second aircraft would be parked next to his own, and having given the code words, "Fill'er up and check the oil," to the human tank, both birds would be used to stash several bags of pure cocaine.

Less than an hour passed before the two pilots had filed a flight plan, on a DD-175, for Marine Corps Air Station, Cherry Point. Returning to their birds, after eating a quick sandwich bought from a vending machine, they gave a cursory once over to their aircraft, climbed aboard and started their engines. The tank assisted in their start cycles and checks, and pulled the wheel chocks when they were ready to taxi. It would be less than two hours until their wheels touched down at Cherry Point, on a hot Sunday in August.

ONE

"Kill him!"

At the other end of the line there was a long pause. "Jesus, Mr. Bolivar, I've known the man for over twenty-five years. We were lieutenants together in Viet Nam for Christ's sake. How can you expect me to kill him?"

"That's not my problem. It's yours!" Raoul Bolivar smiled into the phone. The grin held no mirth. His lips curled at the corners of his slender face with the malevolent knowledge of what must be going through the mind of the man at the other end of the phone line. "You've got men working for you up there, let them handle it. Make'm earn some of the money I've been paying them."

"Mr. Bolivar, please don't make me do this. He only came to me a couple of hours ago, and he's not even sure what he's got. Let me do some poking around before you make a final decision."

Raoul's small smile changed to the leer of one who wields power with the authority of a blacksmith's hammer striking an anvil. "I said, kill him. If you can't stomach the job, then I'll send some of my boys north. You don't want me to do that, now do you? I can assure you there will be more deaths than that of your trouble maker. Get my drift?"

"Are you threatening me?" There was real concern in the man's voice.

"Take it any way you damn well please. You're nothing but a white honky trying to get rich, as far as I'm concerned. Now do what you're told, and do it quick before I really get pissed." Raoul slammed the phone back on its cradle and smiled with genuine pleasure. "I love it when I've got some damned whitey over a barrel," he grinned at the two men sitting before him.

Colombian born Raoul Bolivar, at the age of thirty-three, was a man of significant stature. Standing six foot four in his stocking feet, his mulatto skin was the color of cream chocolate, and his dark eyes shone with Latin fire. He'd been a minor hit man for the Martz drug cartel when he was fifteen, and had risen steadily in the organization until, in nineteen eighty-eight, he oversaw most of the production of raw cocaine for the cartel's head, Alberto Martz. Though the Martz Cartel was a small organization compared to that of Columbia's major drug syndicates, it none-the-less produced and shipped enough coke to the United States to make many men, such as Bolivar, very rich. The bottom fell out of the Martz organization in nineteen eighty-nine when Columbia's president, Virgillio Barco Vargas, a political liberal, declared war on drug traffickers. One of the first cartels to suffer its assets being seized was the Martz family. Raoul, through individual initiative, escaped arrest and returned to his home in Medellin to begin the creation of his own cartel.

It only took Raoul two years to establish himself as one of the most important figures in the drug world, and now he sat in a plush home office in Miami, Florida. The house was more a mansion than a home. Its location, overlooking Biscayne Bay, placed it among the highest land values in Miami. His fortune exceeded anything his old boss, Martz, could have dreamed. The cartel had tentacles entwining every continent, and his ruthless command of this empire was feared by other cartels as well as the most sophisticated law enforcement community. Raoul Bolivar was a man to be respected, and his word was law. When he said, "Kill him," he meant, "Do it yesterday."

Behind a desk in Havelock, North Carolina, sat the man to whom Raoul had given orders. His back was rigidly straight in the leather chair in which he was sitting, and he stared with blank eyes at the phone he still held in his hand. His mind swam with the need to make a decision. He knew beyond any doubt what Raoul meant when he had implied there would be additional deaths, should he choose not to obey the command. His family would be the targets. He could not put them in jeopardy, any more than he would place his own life on the line.

He used his right forefinger to press the phone's disconnect, then released the button and began dialing. He would have to follow Raoul's orders. It was his life or the life of Colonel Adams. There was no real choice at all. The phone began to ring.

"VMAT-203, Flight Line, Staff Sergeant Todd speaking. Can I help you?"

"I'd like to speak to Sergeant Reddock."

"Just a minute, I'll get him for you."

Several minutes passed with nothing but the phone humming gently in his ear.

"Sergeant Reddock."

"Do you know who this is?"

"Yeah. Whacha need?" Reddock asked with the anticipation of money in his pockets.

TWO

COLONEL JACK ADAMS sat on a wooden bench in VMAT-203's flight equipment section. His face was lined with thought, and his blue eyes reflected troubling inner concerns. He had just finished briefing with the operations officer, Major Tom Beasely. The flight was to be an instrument refresher, and that meant he would have no wingman to worry over. He would fly alone in a single seater. Normally, Adams would have briefed for a back seat ride in a tandem-placed bird, but today he would not have a student in the front cockpit. A student who would try damned hard to kill his instructor while attempting a vertical landing on the South Pad, one of the three Harrier pads located on Marine Corps Air Station, Cherry Point. This morning he just wanted to add a couple of hours in his log book. He hadn't been able to fly as much since he had taken over as the Second Marine Aircraft Wing's Operation Officer…more commonly called G-3. The job required more time behind a desk than at the controls of his first love…the Harrier. The Harriers of VMAT-203, the Marine Corps' premiere training squadron, were there to teach young pilots to fly the only true single engine V/STOL aircraft in the world…the McDonnell Aircraft, AV-8B, Harrier II. He had transitioned from A-6 Intruders, into the Harrier four years earlier, and he needed this hop to keep his flying skills sharpened.

Jack stood, a worried look on his face, and opened his metal, flight gear locker. Taking out his G-suit, he began zipping the waist band around his mid- section, and thought about the quandary concerning him for several days. Something was very wrong within the Harrier community. It had nothing to do with the standard obstacles he faced every day. These entailed such things as too much flight time required for the allotted money given the Wing by the Navy, the high accident rate Second MAW was presently experiencing, and the too many deployments scheduled for the number of squadrons and personnel available. No! This was a problem which had him disturbed not only about Second MAW, but for the reputation of the entire Corps.

He shook off the dark thoughts plaguing him, and finished struggling into his torso harness, a tangle of webbed straps which would fasten him to the ejection seat and parachute once he was seated in the aircraft. Grabbing his helmet, he started walking for the door and the Flight Line working spaces.

"Have a good flight, Colonel," a Lance Corporal yelled to him as he passed out of the locker room.

"Thanks! I will," Jack yelled back.

As he left Flight Equipment, he forgot about the disturbing concerns which had successfully kept him awake for the past several nights, and thought only of flying. The ability to compartmentalize thoughts was something every fighter pilot learned early in his career. If a jet pilot was to stay alive, while dashing about the heavens at better than the speed of sound, he had to learn to lock extraneous thoughts away in their own "mind box" while at the controls.

Stepping up to the long, angled desk in the Flight Line shack, he picked up and read the past discrepancies on Double Nuts. Harrier Zero Zero, known to the squadron as Double Nuts, had been assigned him by the Duty Officer while he briefed. He took his time, closely reviewing the past ten flights for any information another pilot or maintenance personnel might have thought important enough to note about the airplane. Satisfied the AV-8B would fly; Jack signed the "yellow sheet" and officially took possession of the plane. By placing his signature on the "yellow sheet," he became responsible for its preservation on the ground as well as in the air.

Leaving the paperwork behind, Adams stepped quickly toward the sunbathed flight line. The sky was cloudless, a welcome relief after several days of pouring rain. The hot, steamy August afternoon made him sweat profusely inside his cocoon of flight gear. Just as he cleared the enormous hangar doors, a young corporal fell in step with him, taking his helmet.

"Afternoon, Colonel. Great day for a flight," the plane captain smiled. "She's all ready to go. Preflighted her myself."

"Thanks. I'm looking forward to getting airborne."

The two walked steadily down the center of a long line of Harriers…their noses pointing at each other from either side. Double Nuts, with two large zeros-painted in white on the nose and tail, was located six planes down the left side of the line. As they approached, Adams noted a sergeant closing an engine panel on the aircraft's starboard side.

"I thought you said she was ready to go?" Jack asked the plane captain beside him.

"She was. I don't know what Sergeant Reddock is doing."

Adams stepped up his pace, struggling against the forty odd pounds of flight gear he was wearing, and intercepted the sergeant just as he was leaving the bird. "What's up? Something wrong?"

Startled, Sergeant Reddock looked squarely into the colonel's face, "No sir! Nothing's wrong. I just wanted to double check some earlier work one of my men did this morning," the lanky, brown eyed, sergeant answered. "I'm finished now." He flashed a crooked smile. "Have a good flight," he finished, and began retracing Adams' foot steps to the hangar, his short, uncombed hair ruffling slightly in the afternoon breeze.

"Yeah, I will. Thanks," Adams said half-heartedly to the retreating figure, and turned to start his preflight, while the corporal climbed the boarding ladder and began readying the cockpit.

Adams always believed an aircraft signed off as "up" and ready for flight by a good plane captain was enough for him to trust the bird ready to take airborne. It was an "old school" thought. Not at all what today's youngsters were being taught, he realized. They regarded an extensive preflight as part of the job. Jack was a "kick the tires, light a fire" preflighter. He finished circling the aircraft just as his plane captain took the final ground rung on the ladder. As the corporal stepped away, Jack started up. Reaching the top of the ladder, he gave a cursory once over of his ejection seat. It looked like all the right parts were connected and he swung his right leg over the cockpit's railing and wedged himself down into the seat. Leg restraints secured and his lap belt and shoulder straps tightened, Jack began his prestart check list. His fingers tripped over switches while his eyes darted around the side consoles and instrument panel. His experienced eye ensured everything was as it should be before he torched off the big Rolls Royce F402, dual spool, axial flow, turbo fan engine capable of producing 23,400 pounds of thrust. It never ceased to amaze him that an airplane as small as the Harrier, only forty-six feet long, with a wing span of a mere thirty feet, could have stuffed in its confines an engine so huge. It made him wonder at his own sanity. The mere thought of sitting in a cockpit of an aircraft composed of nothing more than an engine, fuel, and armaments was not something a reasonable man might consider conducive to a long and productive life. Regardless of his thoughts, for the next two hours, the tiny fighter/bomber, capable of airborne exploits no other airplane in the world could begin to accomplish, was his to enjoy.

In less than five minutes, Jack was ready to start a fire in the burner cans of his ride for the day. Signaling his plane captain with two fingers circling in the air, he closed the canopy, checked the fuel shutoff handle "on," his throttle "off," and hit the start switch. The aircraft began to shudder as the engine electronically activated its start cycle. Jack brought the throttle around the horn to the idle detent and scanned his gauges, which began to twitch, then rise as systems slowly came on line with the engine's spool up. He paid particular attention to the JPT (Jet Pipe Temperature) to ensure it did not rise above five hundred and forty-five degrees centigrade, indicating a HOT start. A hot start could mean a fire, and a fire on the flight line could mean nothing short of a major disaster.

The start was normal, and the engine settled into a rumbling idle at twenty-six percent. Satisfied his motor was running normally, Jack began the after start checks. It took another ten minutes for him to complete setting up his Inertial Navigation, Digital Data Information, Communications, and Heads Up Display systems. When he was convinced the aircraft was functioning within limits, he signaled once more to the corporal on the ground. The two then completed the exterior examination of the bird, using hand and arm signals to relay information back and forth to each other. By the time Jack had completed all the ground checks and was ready to taxi for the runway, he was soaked in his own perspiration. Raising his helmet's visor, he wiped his dripping brow with a chamois he always carried in his lower G-suit pocket. Stuffing the rag back in its pocket, he placed his fists together, thumbs out, and gave a jerking motion for the wheel chocks to be removed.

"Mars base, Double Nuts is taxiing," Jack radioed to VMAT-203's readyroom.

"Roger, copy," Adams' headphones crackled. "Have a good flight."

"Roger that. Switching to ground."

Jack turned his attention momentarily to his radio controls on the DDI, and switched to Cherry Point's ground control. "Ground, Mars Zero Zero. Taxi one. No information," he spoke into the mike inside his oxygen mask.

"Mars Zero Zero, understand no information. Cleared to taxi to warmup area one. Duty runway, three two. Altimeter, two niner, niner two, temperature eighty nine degrees Fahrenheit," the tower's ground controller answered.

Jack eased the throttle forward, dumped the nozzles to ten degrees and moved out of his parking spot under the supervision of his plane captain. He did a brake check, causing the fighter to nod gently on its front wheel and strut. After checking his nose wheel steering, he turned left and headed for the taxiway. The customary salutes between plane captain and pilot ensued as he left the flight line. Once on the taxiway, he turned left and headed for warm up area one, located in front of Base Operations and the tower. He closed and locked his canopy, tightened his oxygen mask firmly on his face, lowered his visor, and switched to tower frequency.

"Tower, Mars Zero Zero. Position and hold."

"Mars Zero Zero, cleared position and hold runway three two."

"Mars Zero Zero, roger."

The Harrier taxied onto the huge hub of the world's largest Marine Corps air field's Center Mat. Cherry Point's Center Mat, composed of several acres of concrete, is where the four major runways of the air base begin as well as end. Viewed from the air, the field looks much like a wheel, the Center Mat being its hub. Jack carefully checked for other aircraft that might be approaching from his right, the landing end of runway thirty-two, and taxied into the takeoff position. He made one final scan of his instruments, checked his nozzles aft, and started his final takeoff checks.

STO stop set fifty-five, Jack thought to himself as his hands did the work of setting the short takeoff stop which would limit the amount of nozzles he could put down during takeoff. He set his trim zero, zero, and two degrees nose down for his ailerons, rudder, and horizontal stabilizer respectively. His selected STOL flaps, as he turned in his seat, looking over his right shoulder at his wing, to note the appropriate flap droop, that little extra flap extension so important to a short takeoff roll. He was ready to go!

"Tower, Mars Zero Zero, ready for takeoff," Jack told the tower operator.

"Mars Zero Zero, you're cleared for takeoff, runway three-two. Wind three one five, at fifteen."

"Roger, cleared for takeoff."

Jack jammed the throttle to its maximum power. The engine roared into life, trying to accelerate to its full capacity in less than three seconds. Just as rapidly, Adams pulled the throttle aft to the idle position, stopping the acceleration at fifty-five percent. He did this three times in rapid succession, clearing the big 402 of any problems it might have during such a rapid spool up. He double checked his STO stop set at seventy degrees, and shoved the throttle forward a final time, stopping the RPM at fifty-five percent. Holding the brakes, to stop the aircraft from leaping forward, Jack moved his left hand to the nozzle lever located just outboard of the throttle. He yanked back on the lever, dumping the nozzles to fifty-five degrees, his proper STO angle. The four nozzles moved as fast as his hands, and Jack swiftly checked his duct pressure, and then moved the nozzles to ten degrees. Perhaps fifteen seconds had passed when he engaged his nose wheel steering and shoved the throttle to the stops. As he released the brakes, the aircraft literally leapt forward, gaining speed at a tremendous rate. In less than five seconds, Jack had flying speed. He'd rolled a scant three hundred feet when he slammed the nozzle lever to the STO stop. Double Nuts jumped into the air!

Airborne, Jack slowly began moving the nozzles aft, allowing the aircraft to gain additional flying speed. He raised the gear, cleared his STO stop, and accelerated to three hundred knots… his climb speed. Perhaps thirty seconds had passed since he had released his brakes, and already he was clearing the airport's outside boundaries. After a quick scan of his instruments, Adams switched to the Wing's training area radar controller.

"Twilight Control, Mars Zero Zero, airborne, passing three thousand, requesting clearance into training area Bravo."

"Mars Zero Zero, cleared into Bravo. Squawk 2654, and monitor 268.8."

"Mars Zero Zero, roger. Squawking 2654, and monitoring button fifteen."

His radio check-in complete, Jack headed for the training area over North Carolina's Pamlico Sound. He leveled off at seven thousand feet and allowed the aircraft to accelerate to four hundred and fifty knots. Jack planned to start his hop performing some aerobatics. The acro would give him a few minutes to loosen up and do some "real flying" before he entered the instrument pattern.

In the radar controlled instrument pattern he'd do nothing but execute a series of boring TACAN and radar controlled approaches. Planning to start with a loop, Adams shoved the throttle to ninety-five percent, allowed the bird to accelerate to four hundred and seventy-five knots and eased the stick back into his lap. Double Nuts felt the four G load on her wings, and the nose started to rapidly move above the horizon.

Jack held the four G's, as the aircraft climbed through nine thousand feet. The Harrier's nose began to approach the vertical as it passed through twelve thousand feet. Jack, intent on doing a perfect loop, was startled by a nearly inaudible "pop" deep within the bowels of the aircraft. The pop was followed by a rapid deceleration of the engine. Double Nuts was now over the top and upside down. Jack, realizing he had an emergency in progress, jerked the throttle to mid position, moved the stick to the left, and released the G's. The aircraft righted itself as he tried to ascertain what his problem might be. The engine continued to decelerate to idle.

Jack moved the throttle forward, hoping to get a response from the motor. There was none…the RPM remained at an altitude idle of twenty-eight percent. The fighter's throttle produced no response from the engine. Adams realized he could be in real trouble. He was heavy with fuel, much too heavy to try a landing, even if he were directly over a landing field.

"Twilight, Mars Zero Zero."

"Mars Zero Zero, go ahead."

"Twilight, I've got an emergency up here. The engine won't accelerate above idle. I'm presently on the zero two-seven-degree radial at thirty-six miles, heading two-seven zero, descending through ten thousand."

"Mars Zero Zero, roger, we have you. Please advise intentions, and say souls aboard."

Double Nuts was losing airspeed and altitude, regardless of what emergency actions Adams took. He hit the fuel dump switch, trying to lighten the aircraft which might provide him more gliding range. He settled his speed at two hundred and thirty knots, allowing the bird to fly at its optimum glide angle, but there was no way he could make the thirty miles back to Cherry Point and he knew it. Adams made his decision.

"Twilight, Mars Zero Zero. One soul aboard. I'm dumping fuel and heading for land northeast of Oriental. Once I'm over land, I'll turn the bird back toward the sound and eject. Request you launch the Angel for me."

"Roger, Mars Zero Zero, we'll have the rescue helo airborne. Good luck!"

"Thanks, I think I'll be needing it."

From the beginning of the emergency, Jack had remained calm and professional. Now, the full realization of ejection hit home. Throughout his flying career, Jack had lived by a set of Adams' laws, one of which was "stay with your bird as long as you can." His premise for such a law stemmed from the understanding that as long as the airplane was flying, there were three things going for the pilot: One: the plane. Two: the ejection seat, and Three: the parachute. As soon as the ejection handle was pulled there were only two items left to be relied upon, the seat and the chute. His odds, Jack felt, diminished with each action, and in the end, relying only on the chute cut the chances of survival pretty damned thin. He liked the idea of staying with his airplane.

The stricken aircraft passed over land as it dropped through five thousand feet. Adams started a slow one hundred and eighty degree turn, trimmed the aircraft to maintain its airspeed, and radioed Twilight.

"Twilight, Mars Zero Zero. I'm out of here. Do you have a good fix on me?"

"Roger, Mars Zero Zero. Again, good luck!"

Adams did not respond to Twilight's last communication. He was passing four thousand feet and wanted out. His aircraft had given up on him; it was time for him to give up on it. Reaching between his legs, he grabbed the ejection handle, forced his back and head against the seat, and pulled the yellow and black striped handle.

He'd been prepared for the ejection blast and was stunned when the handle flapped loosely in his hand and nothing happened. For the first time since the emergency had started, Colonel Jack Adams was afraid. The plane's nose dropped when he'd let go of the stick. The stricken bird was now passing two thousand feet and accelerating through three hundred and twenty knots.

"Twilight, the God-dammed seat didn't work. I'm going to try again."

Jack grabbed the stick and gave it a yank, let go, and pulled the ejection handle with every ounce of strength he could muster. Nothing!

Again the nose dropped. Now the airspeed was pushing over three fifty, and there was a scant thousand feet before the bird came to an abrupt stop. Jack, surprisingly composed, knew it was over for him. He thought of his family and all he would be missing. The Harrier II known as Mars Zero Zero struck the earth at four hundred miles per hour, at an angle of fifteen degrees nose down, and exploded into a flaming fireball.

THREE

Oaks and pines sagged under Carolina's heat and humidity. For the past three days rain had plummeted the ground, taxing the drainage facilities of the small towns surrounding MCAS Cherry Point. Farmers, normally happy to have rain in August, were shaking their collective fists at the weather gods. Their fields were nothing more than dark slush waiting to eat a tractor foolishly brought to work the soil. Marines struggled against the heat, working on a variety of military fighter bombers lining the Point's flight lines. Pilots hurried through their engine start check lists. They were rushing through all of their flight line procedures in order to close the canopy, gaining welcome relief from the air conditioning provided by the jet engines' heat exchanger.

Colonel Dan Breakheart, call sign "Cuda," short for barracuda, turned the key to his office door and wiped the sweat running in rivers from his forehead. He was returning from a late O-club lunch with his best sidekicks, Snake and Ragman. Bob "the Snake" Burns and Dave "the Ragman" Brower had spent their time together discussing the upcoming Hancock Creek Regatta. The three were avid sailors, and each owned sailboats over thirty-five feet in length. Cruising, racing, and messing about on boats was their second love after flying. They had known each other longer than Breakheart cared to remember. The three met shortly after the Marine Corps purchased its first Harriers from the British government in nineteen sixty-nine. The airplanes had arrived from England in mahogany crates, requiring their entire assembly be accomplished on the hangar deck of the newly formed V/STOL squadron. In those first months of the AV-8As, no one was sure just what the newest Marine Corps aircraft could accomplish airborne. The British had been flying the AV-8A for several years, but their usage was almost exclusively in the low level regime…routinely flying as low as fifty feet over the German countryside. This was perfectly understandable, considering the Brit's European mission to defend against a Russian onslaught across the Iron Curtain. Very little experimentation with the use of the nozzles airborne was thought to be necessary by the Royal Air Force. On-the-other-hand, the Corps viewed the ability to vector the four nozzles while up and away as a possible enhancement to the Harrier's capabilities as a fighter. It was a new exciting world for the soon-to-be friends. A time when a little of the old "barnstorming" days of flying returned for a brief period. Learning to fly and experimenting with the Harrier had fused a friendship bond among the three which was impossible to break.

The meat loaf lunch had been delicious, and lively conversation among the three made time slip by rather quickly. It was now fourteen hundred, well past the time Breakheart would have normally returned for an afternoon's work as the Second Marine Aircraft Wing's Safety Officer.

Deeply tanned, Colonel Breakheart stood five feet eight inches, if he stretched for the height, and tended to be on the pudgy side. Weight had been a problem since his childhood in the small Florida, Gulf Coast town of Sarasota. To overcome the flab plague and to maintain a fit one-hundred-and-eighty-pound Marine appearance, he ran three miles every day it didn't rain. Breakheart did not run in the rain. In fact, he thought those who did had more than likely lost a small portion of their brain housing group. The pavement pounding was meant to burn off the extra calories ingested from eating or the occasional alcoholic hook. Removing the fore and aft piss-cutter from his blond head and throwing it on his desk, he strode to his office windows overlooking the Center Mat. His pale blue eyes, which were quick to shine with cheerful good humor, scanned the Center Mat and runways. Two Harriers were holding short for takeoff, and an A-6 was braking to a stop from a landing. He turned to his desk, noting the pictures and bits of paraphernalia scattered about the office. The items on the wall and sitting on the tables of his office reflected Breakheart's career of twenty-seven years. There were F-8 Crusader and A-4 Sky Hawk models, as well as several pictures and models of Harriers. In a place of honor on the wall across from his desk, was an array of plaques and pictures of the Cobra, AH-1J helicopter in flight. Several of the wooden commemorative items had the word MARHUK inscribed on their surfaces. MARHUK stood for Marine Hunter Killer, an operation Breakheart had been involved in during the last year of the Viet Nam war. He had only flown the Cobra helicopter for eighteen months, then had returned to the Harrier when his combat tour was over. Though helicopter time in a fighter pilot's log book was, Breakheart thought, worse than syphilis in his medical record, he displayed the MARHUK plaques with the honor they rightly deserved. It was a comfortable office, not as large as some he had used in the past, but it suited his needs.

Breakheart moved to an overstuffed, leather executive chair and sat down behind his desk with a sigh of resignation…paper work had to be done. He began rummaging through the stack of accident reports he had gladly left two hours before. Picking up an open file, he'd just begun reviewing the latest A-6 accident account when there was a rap on his door.

"Come," Breakheart called.

The door cracked open, and Sergeant Luts stuck his head into the office. "Sir, the general is on the phone. Line one."

"Thanks."

Colonel Breakheart picked up his phone and put it to his ear, "Yes, sir, Colonel Breakheart here. Can I help you?" he asked formally. The "yes sir" had a definitive southern drawl.

"Cuda, get your ass over to my office right now. We've got a problem on our hands," General Geise said in a tight voice.

"What's the trouble?" Breakheart asked, immediately thinking who he might have pissed off recently. He was forever letting his mouth get him in one predicament or another. General Geise called him his staff's "Firebrand."

"I'll explain it to you when you get here, but I can tell you we have a Harrier down. I'll see you in a minute," Geise said, and hung up.

Christ, what now, Dan thought as he retrieved his cover and placed it neatly on his head. He walked into the hall separating his office from that of his enlisted staff and yelled to Sergeant Luts that he was on the way to the Wing Headquarters. He hurried down the double flight of stairs, retrieving his sunglasses from the left arm pocket of his olive drab, NOMEX flight suit. His car, a black Pontiac Firebird, sat in the parking lot directly in front of the plate glass doors of Base Operations. Breakheart climbed into his black leather upholstered automobile and started the 5.7 liter engine.

Breakheart had bought the manual shift, six speed Firebird a year after his wife had shut the door to their house for the last time. It was a gift to himself. A "thank God she is gone, though she's taken almost everything but the three boys with her" offering. Colonels in the Marine Corps *did not* get divorces, and the fact his had been finalized six months before he went before the board for promotion to general did much to relieve him of the pressures of putting a star on his shoulder. He was slightly bitter about the lack of promotion, but not to any real degree. His career had been rewarding and fulfilling. More importantly, he enjoyed what he was doing. Over the years, Breakheart had earned a reputation as one of the finest fighter pilots the Corps had to offer, and now, in his capacity as Wing Safety, he was considered to be a persistent accident investigator. Over the last two years, he had solved two accidents most of his contemporaries regarded as unsolvable. One of these had taken over six months to come to a viable conclusion, and the hours spent investigating, contemplating, and deducing what had occurred would have filled a normal man's work year. Breakheart was proud of his Corps, and it showed in everything he did.

It took five minutes to reach the three-story, brick building which housed Second MAW headquarters, as well as that of MCAS Cherry Point's commanding general's staff. The large structure had been built during World War II, and though its facade was timeless, once inside anyone could tell by the design it reflected another age. Second MAW, Major General Jonathon A. Geise's office was located on the first floor of the east wing. Breakheart pulled the Firebird into a parking space reserved for senior staff officers and entered the east wing's front door. Turning right, he paced down the hall lined with pictures of past Wing Commanders to the anteroom leading to his boss' office proper.

"Afternoon, Chief," Breakheart spoke to Colonel Keller, the Wing's Chief of Staff. "What happened that has the General so upset?"

"Good afternoon, Dan. I think I'd better let him fill you in. But I hope you don't have any major plans for the next couple of weeks," the Chief answered.

"Oh great! Sounds like I'm in for another stint in the boondocks digging pieces of airplane out of the mud. Who was it?" Breakheart asked with concern, as he stood in the doorway to the Chief's office.

Colonel Keller did not get the opportunity to answer. A young First Lieutenant, dressed in starched camouflaged utilities with creases so sharp they could cut a finger, interrupted their conversation.

"Colonel Breakheart, the General will see you now."

Breakheart turned to follow the Lieutenant to Geise's outer office which held his aide, driver, and secretary. The secretary was a female staff sergeant whom he knew from his two years as

VMA-542's commanding officer. She had been one of his finest avionics' technicians, and he had promoted her twice meritoriously.

"Hey, Sergeant Gilbert," Breakheart said, noting that the sergeant could well be on the cover of Vogue Magazine. She was a beautiful woman. Beyond her natural good looks, she was one hell of an avionics' person as well. Now she worked directly for General Geise…a real feather in her cap.

"Hi, Colonel," Gilbert answered Breakheart, as she rose to knock on the General's door.

"Get him in here," the booming voice of General Geise echoed through the large office spaces.

Breakheart slipped by Staff Sergeant Gilbert, giving her a smile that said, "His bark is worse than his bite," and moved into the large office of his boss. The Commanding General of the Second MAW enjoyed a work space lined in dark wood paneling. In the corner, to the right of the main entrance, stood the Wing's Colors on either side of a large American Flag draped with battle ribbons. Covering most of the wall space behind the General's desk hung a display of plaques representing all of the squadrons attached to the Wing. Against one wall was a comfortable seating area with a sofa, two overstuffed chairs, and a large coffee table. A white oak desk sat in the far end of the spacious room, the expansive top of which was cluttered with papers and files. To the right of the desk stood a trophy case filled with memorabilia of every sort, all of which dealt with the Wing's accomplishments. Next to the cabinet was another door, now open, which led to Brigadier General Gene Blake's office, who was the Assistant Wing Commander.

Rising from his leather executive chair, General Geise said, "Come in Dan, come in. Sit down and pour yourself a cup of coffee."

Breakheart moved to the sofa, waving away the need for coffee and stepped in front of General Blake. Breakheart excused himself to the senior officer. Blake was the antithesis of Geise in every respect. Where Geise was a big man with a real tendency to be overweight, Blake was small and wiry. The Commanding General displayed a gregarious personality, one reflecting wit and laughter which endeared the balding general to his men throughout the thirty years he'd served in the Corps. He was a man whom Colonel Breakheart admired as a commander as well as a person. There was no higher compliment he could give a fellow officer.

On the other hand, Blake was one of those individuals who had been promoted to rank at the utter amazement of those he lorded over. Where Geise was fun-loving, an excellent pilot, well respected in the F-18 community as one of their best aviators, Blake was a braggart. He could talk for hours about his prowess behind the controls of an AV-8, an airplane he had only been flying for the past three years. In fact, he couldn't fly his way out of a paper bag and everybody knew it. Blake, a Cobra helicopter pilot throughout most of his career, had been the executive officer of HMA-239 when Breakheart had been force-transitioned out of AV-8's and into the AH-1J Cobra, in nineteen seventy-one. He had not liked the self-inflated major then, and thought even less of the general he was today.

General Geise eased his bulk into one of the overstuffed chairs, shook his head sadly, and said, "Cuda, it's Jack Adams. He crashed about an hour ago northeast of Oriental. He didn't make it."

Breakheart let the words sink in. He and Jack Adams had been friends for years. "How?"

"We're not sure about anything except that the ejection seat didn't fire. He tried to eject, but the damned thing didn't work. We know that much from his last transmission to Twilight. That's why I want you to do the investigation," Geise said, his voice softening to a low roar.

"Has Sally been notified yet?" Breakheart asked, thinking about the petite blond who had prepared many a meal for him and his family over the years.

"The Chaplin and I will be going over just as soon as we're done here," Geise answered. "God! I hate this part of the job."

"You said you wanted me to do the investigation," Breakheart stated. "You know I can't do that as the Wing Safety Officer. Conflicting interests."

"Yeah, I know. Tell the Chief to cut orders making you Special Staff and assign Lieutenant Colonel Barry from Logistics to be your temporary replacement as Safety. How soon can you get started?"

"Hell, I'm already on my way. I'll have to run home and leave a note for my boys, but if you could arrange for a Huey to fly me to the accident site, I'll be there within an hour. You know I like to see the scene of an accident as soon as I can after it happens."

"Right!" Geise turned to General Blake and stood, "Gene, arrange for the chopper. If you need me, I'll be with Jack's wife." With those final words, Geise closed the meeting and moved back behind his desk, gathering his cover for the trip to the Adams' home.

Both Breakheart and Blake stood with their boss…Breakheart to relay the message to the Chief and Blake to return to his office. Before leaving, General Blake elbowed Breakheart in the ribs.

"Hey, Cuda, when this is over are you going to go one-on-one with me? I want to show you how a real pilot flies a Harrier," Blake gibed.

The taunt was a standing invitation the general gave Breakheart every time he was unfortunate enough to be in his presence. One which he thought to be humorless and without warrant of answering, particularly this afternoon. He found the remark to be crass and unfeeling. But, as a good colonel in the Corps, he kept his mouth shut, thinking to himself what a jerk Blake really was.

Breakheart left the Headquarters building after conveying the change of staffing orders to the Chief. Leaving the parking lot, he turned left on to Roosevelt Avenue, the main thoroughfare through the base. Roosevelt Avenue began at the main gate, in the middle of the town of Havelock, and extended easterly until it dead ended at the Navy Boat Docks. While driving the ten minutes to his home in officer's country, Breakheart used the car's cellular phone to call his office. He told Sergeant Luts to have his 782-gear ready to take to the field and to double check that the canteens were filled with fresh water. He wondered for the thousandth time why "field gear," such as belts, shoulder packs, and canteens was called 782-gear.

Once inside his quarters, a spacious home with four bedrooms and a spectacular view of the Neuse River, Breakheart wrote a note to his teenage sons, explaining he would be late and to fix their own dinner. That taken care of, he went to the front hall closet and took out an old, battered pair of flight boots. These he slipped on in exchange for the brightly polished ones he wore on a daily basis. The worn leather of the older pair was reserved for investigative work…where mud, muck, broken aluminum, and burned composite, graphite fiber crunched under their heavy rubber soles.

Breakheart took a last look around the house to make sure the boys would have what they would need for the night, then hurried out to the waiting Firebird. By the time he arrived back at Base Ops, a Huey helicopter, its blades spinning, was waiting for him. Locking his car, he ran for the double doors leading into Base Operations, bound up the two flights of stairs to his office and grabbed his 782-gear from Sergeant Luts. With little more than a "thank you" left behind, he started for the stairs once more, taking the steps two at a time. Breakheart made the helicopter pad, yanking off his piss-cutter and stuffing it in his leg pocket on the fly. In less than a minute, he was ducking under the whirling blades of the helo and scrambling aboard with the help of the aircraft's plane captain. Once seated, the plane captain, a Lance Corporal, handed him a helmet. He slipped it on and plugged the headphones into the black cord dangling from the overhead. Then, fumbling slightly in his haste, he found the seat's restraint belt and fastened it tightly around his waist.

"Do you know where we are going?" Breakheart keyed his mike and asked the pilots sitting in their cockpit bubble.

"Yes, sir," the pilot answered, while the co-pilot gave a thumbs up. "We got a DME and radial from Twilight just before you boarded. Are you set to go?"

Both Breakheart and the plane captain gave a thumbs up, and the Huey's engines began to wind their way to a higher pitch. He could hear the pilots talking to the tower, asking for clearance for takeoff, and they were suddenly airborne. Passing low over the

Center Mat, the chopper took up a northeasterly direction while gaining airspeed. They flew over the Neuse River and headed easterly down its northern shore until they reached the small river town of Oriental. There, they turned inland. Five minutes later they were over the crash site.

"Fly over and around the site at about three hundred feet. I want to get a good view of the crash before we land," Breakheart keyed his mike and instructed the pilot.

"Roger," the lieutenant at the controls answered, and took up an orbit over the downed Harrier.

Colonel Breakheart viewed the devastating scene below. Already there were Marines from VMAT-203 cordoning off the crash area. Breakheart knew there would be a five-man accident investigation team poking at the wreckage, one of whom would be the squadron's Safety Officer. He also knew they would be expecting a Colonel to take charge of their team. Major Bill Dyke, Stray Dog to his friends, had been 203's Safety Officer for almost two years. He was well aware of the requirement to have the same ranked officer as Colonel Adams, or higher, as the Accident Board's head.

The helo continued to circle. Breakheart began cataloguing the scene and firmly filing it in his memory. Double Nuts had crashed in a cultivated field expanding over thirty acres. He could see several Marines standing over a charred hole which was, undoubtedly, the plane's initial impact point. It was a blackened pit scored into the earth by an aircraft striking the ground at a high rate of speed. The hole was located directly off and to the east of a small, one lane dirt road which rose several feet above the surrounding plowed field. Though there was nothing growing in the huge field, Breakheart thought that it had probably been recently planted with beans. He knew beans were one of the primary cash crops grown in this part of Carolina. Parts of the Harrier were scattered, fan shaped, from the impact point. Larger hunks of engine, wings, tail plane, and fuselage could clearly be seen from his vantage point aboard the helo. These larger pieces were strewn as far as a quarter of a mile from the dark pit, and Breakheart knew it was going to be tough to reconstruct what had gone wrong. The one thing he couldn't find, as they circled, was the ejection seat. He silently prayed that 203's advance party had already located the seat and removed it from the area. He didn't want to see his friend's broken body. It was horrifying enough when you didn't know the dead pilot, but when it was a man you had known for years, it made holding one's stomach down almost impossible.

Having made mental notes concerning the direction the aircraft had been flying just prior to impact, the overall layout of the crash site, and the general distance the wreckage had been thrown on impact, Breakheart spoke to the pilot. "You can take her down now. Thanks."

The lieutenant flew his bird low over the road, indicating his intentions to land. Marines scattered in both directions down the dirt ruts, clearing a landing area for the helo to set down. The approach was smooth and the landing nothing more than a slight bump when the skids struck earth. The Huey's engines throttled back to idle. Before Breakheart unstrapped his lap belt and slid the helmet from his head he relayed a message to the pilot.

"Lieutenant, keep her running. I'm going to send the photographer to you so that he can get some airborne pictures."

"All right, sir. Do you want me to wait for you after he is finished?"

"Yes, please. I don't know how long I'm going to be, but shut her down and wait," Breakheart instructed.

Now disconnected from the intercom, Breakheart leaned forward into the cockpit, he smiled and gave a thumb's up to the two men sitting in their straight-backed seats. "Thanks," he mouthed, and jumped out the side door.

"Am I glad to see you, Colonel," Major Dyke said, running forward to greet Breakheart. "We've got a mess here, and we haven't found Colonel Adams yet."

"Why not?" Breakheart asked, his fears confirmed.

"Because we can't get out in the field. All the rain we have been having the past few days has created a quagmire of the area. Step off the road and you sink up to your knees in mud. I don't know what we are going to do. We think he is over near that ditch," Dyke said. He pointed to a drainage trench cutting across the field, beginning a hundred yards from the road and running perpendicular to it. "He's got to be in that mess somewhere or we would have seen him in the field."

Breakheart thought for a moment. "Yes, you're right. If the seat had been in the field I would have seen it while I circled in the Huey. Okay, our first priority will be to find Colonel Adams. Have you got communications set up with home base yet?"

"Yes, sir. What do you need?"

"Tell them to send as many packing pallets as they can load on a six-by and get it on the road ASAP. I want to get Colonel Adams out of here before nightfall. In the meantime, if we have any spare tents, canvas, or sheets of plastic let's use them to start constructing a ramp across the field as far as we can. Your men did come with the necessary equipment to spend the night, didn't they?"

"Yes, sir. We've got enough troopers to help plot the crash site as well as maintain twenty-four-hour security," Major Dyke answered.

"Okay! Get your men hopping and then gather the Accident Board here with me. By the way, have you got good enlisted men from each maintenance shop to help?"

"Yes, sir! Gunny Hicks gathered the best men he could before we left. Hicks is conscientious and really knows his stuff. Do you want him to meet with the rest of the team?"

"See to it, and Stray Dog, one more thing. I'm sure the Base Photographer is here, isn't he?"

"Yes, sir. He is standing by waiting to board the Huey. I figured you would want some airborne shots of the area," Dyke stated.

"Great. Get him on over here so he can take his pictures. We'll need him again when we find Colonel Adams' body. And, Stray Dog, I'm glad I'm working with you on this one. It is going to be rough, I'm sure of that."

"Same goes for me, Colonel," Dyke said, then spun on his heel to carry out the instructions he'd been given.

Several minutes later, men were busily looking for items that could be used to forge a ramp across the muck. Six men broke from the melee and began trudging their way toward Colonel Breakheart, arriving in a silent group behind him. Dan was in deep thought, scanning the muddy field as if it were a place of a recent battle. All he knew for the moment was that Jack's ejection seat had not worked, and that his friend was dead. But over the next few days he would find out why. The answers lay scattered in a farmer's bean patch, and he would dig them out one piece at a time.

As Breakheart stared at the muddy field, Major Dyke tapped him lightly on the shoulder to gain his attention. Turning from his thoughts, Dan turned to faced the men with whom he would work closely for the next several days, weeks, or months; whatever it took to discover the reasons why a Harrier had crashed; killing its pilot.

He knew, though he felt heavy of heart over Jack's death, that he had to detach himself from the grief of losing a friend and approach the accident as if the death meant nothing to him at all. Only in that way could he rationally evaluate the evidence this team of his brought forth. He recognized all of the board members, even as Major Dyke introduced them. They were a small contingent from VMAT-203's instructor base, each a captain save for Major Dyke and Gunny Hicks.

"Our first priority," Breakheart began addressing his team," will be to find Colonel Adams and get him out of here. After that we will begin our investigation proper. I don't think we will get much done today, at least not out here, but I will expect to meet with you back at the squadron later tonight…say around twenty-two hundred. Hopefully, this field will dry up some overnight and tomorrow we can begin digging through the wreckage. One thing I want to make perfectly clear to each of you, and Gunny, you're to make sure every man of yours knows it as well. I don't want anything moved until it has been catalogued and located on a grid. Is that clearly understood?" He noted the head nods and went on. "My guess is, we'll find most of the aircraft in the hole. It appears to be about twelve feet deep and slightly longer than the plane. From the looks of the crater, I think she nosed in around twenty degrees nose down, but we'll determine that for sure later. I'll give you a full briefing on what I'll expect from you later this evening. Remember, the sooner we get this wrapped up, the sooner you all will be flying again, because nobody is to be on the squadron's flight scheduled until I give the say so. See you tonight. Dismissed."

The small band broke up and headed toward the action taking place down the road. A stretch of field was being breached with tarps, and soon men would be able to make their way into the ditch. Stray Dog remained behind.

"Anything I can do for you, Colonel?" He asked.

"No, nothing right now," Breakheart answered. "I think you had better ensure you will be able to get a camp set up before dark. The board members will stay until we find the body. On the other hand, the security team and anyone else you deem necessary had better plan on camping here for a while."

"I've taken care of it," Major Dyke replied. "We'll set up camp on a dry spot located near the entrance to the field. The squadron's logistics officer has arranged for meals to be delivered three times a day from Cherry Point, and port-a-potties will be in place by night fall."

"Sounds like you have done this before," Breakheart smiled at his companion.

"Too many times for my liking," Dyke said sadly. "You would think you'd get used to it, but I never do. In fact, it just gets worse with each one."

"I know what'ya mean," a somber faced Breakheart drawled. "Let's wander over and see how they are coming with the bridge."

The two officers walked slowly to the area where men were busily stretching anything that could help breach the muck leading to the ditch. By the time they arrived, tarps and spare tents, along with pallet boards and freshly cut brush, had made a path twenty foot short of the thick underbrush lining the trench. Time was now the enemy. It was already pushing deep into late afternoon, and full dark would be on them in less than two hours. Breakheart wanted to get the body loaded in the waiting ambulance before the use of flashlights became necessary. Having seen what a body can look like after a crash of this sort, he knew his crew would more than likely must search not for just Jack, but for body parts. As they watched, the final distance was spanned, using three sheets of plywood intended for camp construction. Breakheart joined the men struggling over the crude walkway to the ditch.

Several enlisted men were already searching the sides of the deep furrow before Breakheart and Major Dyke stepped onto the comparably dry ground of the ditch's sides. The remaining members of his team followed in silence. There was little talk now that the ditch was accessible. Every man knew the grisly task of finding the downed pilot was one that required few words.

"Oh God! I've found him," a mournful cry echoed through the evening's silence. "Over here."

The young corporal stood, his right arm held high indicating his position, fifty yards down the slimy trench. He was yelling and backing away from the sight at which he was pointing. Without warning, he turned and doubled over in agony, belching out the contents of his stomach on the wet mud. Two other men arrived before Breakheart, and both followed their comrade, grunting in misery several feet from the bloody mass of flesh that had once been a human being. Dan tried to harden himself against what he knew lay ahead, but nothing could have prepared him for the awful sight laying in the mud.

Mars Zero Zero had struck the muddy bean field at better than four hundred knots. On impact the bolts restraining the ejection seat to the floor of the tiny cockpit had given way, allowing it to be propelled, seat and occupant, through the front windscreen…metal frame, half inch glass and all. His body had been severed into four major sections. The body part Breakheart now looked upon was what remained in the twisted, broken ejection seat. It was no more than a torso without a head. The legs were cut off below the knees, and there were no arms. Blood covered the stump of what had once been a man and ran down the crumpled metal of the ejection seat, dripping sluggishly on the ground. Breakheart hitched a step backward, spun around and threw up yellowish bile. He could not be macho, even if he tried.

Wiping the ropey slime from his chin, he said, "Okay, get the corpsmen over here along with the photographer. Keep everyone else away until we remove the body."

Men stopped where they were. Though the grisly sight aroused their interest, it was enough to be ordered not to approach the remains. Four corpsmen labored their way across the tarp-covered mud with a stretcher piled with sheets and a rubber body bag. Behind them, a sergeant followed with a camera he had used to take airborne pictures minutes before. The small entourage made its way to Colonel Breakheart, looking to him for further instructions.

"Sergeant," Breakheart said to the man caring a bag of photographic equipment, "take your pictures and standby. We'll be finding more body parts, and I want their position photographed as well."

The sergeant stepped forward, slipping on the muddy bank of the trench and began taking his pictures, stopping to vomit only once. When he indicted he was through, the corpsmen began gently removing the torso from the seat's restraint straps. Carefully, and with as much dignity as possible, they wrapped the body stump of what had once been Colonel Jack Adams in a sheet, and then slid the bulk into a rubber body bag.

"Okay, show's over," Breakheart said quietly. "Let's start looking for the rest of the body. When you find something, give a yell for me and the corpsmen."

It did not take long before the remaining parts of Jack's body were found. At least the larger pieces of legs and arms. The head was apparently not intact. Jack's smashed helmet contained shards of skin and bone, but nothing more. Breakheart knew from experience that his crew would be picking up chunks of what was left of the pilot's head for the next couple of days. They would locate meaty, grey matter by the sound of buzzing flies. The tiny winged creatures would surely gather as they always did in times such as these. Breakheart had been there and done that. The scavengers always gathered after an accident…the human type as well. It was a grim fact, one that went with the territory of probing into the cause of an aircraft crash.

By the time Jack Adams' remains had been located and transferred to the olive drab ambulance with its white circle and red cross painted on its top, night had begun to cover the muddy field. Flashlights wove pale chalky lines through the gathering darkness. Men silently came from the ditch, crossing the tarp covered mud to their camp site. Tents began to spring from the ground as if canvas seeds had been planted during the sun's warmth and now emerged from the ground to greet the moon's baleful light. The ambulance, loaded with its grisly remains, left for Cherry Point's hospital, where an autopsy would be performed on what was left of the body. Colonel Breakheart surveyed the flurry of activity and called for Major Dyke and Gunny Hicks.

"Gunny, are you all set here?" Breakheart asked the senior enlisted man.

"Yes, sir, we've got everything under control. The six-by arrived with the load of pallets. We'll use some of them for our camp. I imagine you'll want the bulk of them tomorrow to move across the field."

"That's right, Gunny. I'll have the squadron's logistic officer double check on the hot meals, particularly tomorrow's breakfast. I appreciate your help. If there is anything you need, anything at all, you let me know, ya hear?"

"What about the Accident Board members? Do you still want to meet with them tonight? It's getting late." It was Major Dyke who asked.

"Yes. I'm heading back to the Point now in the chopper. I've got to brief the General on what we've found, but I'll see the board at twenty-two hundred as planned. Do you want to ride back with me in the helo?"

"No thanks. I've got my car," Major Dyke responded, "I'll see you at the squadron." With his final remarks, he saluted Breakheart, and walked off to join the other officers making up the team.

Breakheart nodded to the Gunny and began to walk back to the waiting Huey. The helicopter's crew had waited patiently for their passenger. As they saw him making his way toward the helo, they began preparing the bird for flight. By the time Breakheart had strapped in, the aircraft was already shuddering under takeoff power. The flight back to Cherry Point was uneventful and Breakheart sat quietly in the rear of the small aircraft thinking about his comrade, Jack Adams. They had been good friends, and it was now, while flying through the night, that he said his goodbyes. He knew he, and others like him, would gather at the O-club bar one evening soon and give Adams a proper send off, but for now he just thought silently.

Once back at Base Operations, Breakheart climbed the stairs to his office and let himself in. He hit the light switch and picked up the phone to call his home. He talked briefly with his oldest son, Bill, explaining the situation and telling him that he would not be home until after ten. That accomplished, a very tired Marine Colonel headed to the Wing's headquarters for a talk with his boss, General Geise. Geise and Breakheart had been through this type of ordeal before, and Breakheart knew the Wing's commanding general would not go home without first hearing from him. It had been that way since he had investigated his first accident for the general over a year ago.

"It was bad, I mean really bad," Breakheart said to General Geise, sitting in the general's office. "I guarantee it will be a closed casket funeral. Plus, the investigation is going to be very difficult, at least until we get the Harrier out of the field. You just can't imagine how muddy it is out there, but we'll get it done. I've got my first real meeting with the board this evening, and we'll be in the field first thing in the morning."

"What's your initial reaction to the accident scene?" General Geise asked. From past experience, he trusted Breakheart's gut reactions.

"I don't really know. It's strange, but I've got a rotten feeling about this one. It just doesn't make sense. I mean…sure, fighters crash because something goes wrong, but to not have the seat work is very strange. We've never had a SJU-4/A seat not get the pilot out. Sure, there have been guys who pulled the handle too late or too low and didn't make it, but not to have it fire at all…that's an entirely different matter. From the description Twilight Control provided Major Dyke about Jack's radio transmissions just prior to the crash, my guess is he had a throttle problem of some sort. Of course, we won't know for sure until I can locate the engine and fuel control, but that's what it sounds like to me."

"When do you think you'll have the plane out of the field and back here?" Geise asked, quietly. The big man was in a somber mood, created by Breakheart's briefing.

"I've got no idea. If we don't get any more rain, probably three or four days. If the field gets any muddier than it is now, God knows how long it will take. Maybe weeks!"

"Okay. Thanks, Dan. If you need help from my end, don't hesitate to ask. Just try and clear this thing up as fast as you can."

"How is Sally taking it?" Breakheart asked with genuine concern, running his hand through his uncombed, blond hair.

"Not good, but she's a trooper. Most wives who have been married to fighter jocks as long as she has know this thing can happen. Still, she is in pretty bad shape. You know, they all go through that "strong-silent, I'm going to be brave" period. My wife is with her now, and will stay with her until the rest of her family can get here."

"Damn it all to hell, why does it always seem to happen to the 'good guys'? It's never the jerks like Ar…" Breakheart started to say Blake, but stopped short of saying the Assistant Wing Commander's name.

"Like Blake," General Geise volunteered, with a grin.

"You said it, General, not me. Sir, with your permission, I've got to go. I've got the meeting with my board in about a half hour, and I'd like a chance to wash up before I go."

"Take off, Cuda. And thanks for stopping by. Give it your best shot," General Geise said, ending the meeting.

Breakheart left the darkened Headquarters building after spending fifteen minutes in the head, washing the grime from his face and hands. He drove to VMAT-203's parking lot, located a block from Base Operations. The squadron's flight line was silent and the parking spaces mostly deserted. The CO had shut down 203's flight operations soon after the accident occurred. Breakheart looked into the clear night sky, seeing an aircraft making its final approach to runway thirty-two, its position and anti-collision lights shining brightly against the star-studded blackness. To his left, far down the flight line, a Harrier was cranking up for a night hop. One of VMA-542's birds, thought Breakheart. He walked across the parking lot and mounted the stairs leading to VMAT-203's administration and operations spaces.

The Harrier training squadron was the largest single flying unit in the Marine Corps. Its hanger, which housed not just the maintenance work areas and the hangar proper, but the day-to-day work spaces of the staff as well, sprawled for over an acre and a half. The second deck accommodated the offices of the squadron staff, known as "S" sections. The S-1 (Administration), S-2 (Intelligence), and S-4 (Logistics/Supply) were situated at one end of the long hall, while the S-3 (Operations) took up the remainder of the other end. Breakheart turned left as he entered the hallway and headed for the readyroom.

VMAT-203's ready room was unique from that of its sister squadrons, if for no other reason than sheer size. Ready rooms were normally the size of a high school classroom, but 203's could make two such enclosures. Used as a gathering spot for officers and for meetings requiring a large space, the ready room sported a coffee pot, something rarely turned off, and the duty officer's desk. During flight operations, a duty pilot sat behind the semicircular counter littered with flight schedules, telephones, and weather reports. Under the stained, plexiglass table top resided radios and additional phones which linked the duty officer with airborne Harriers as well as the tower. The entire wall behind the counter was taken up by a plastic-covered board depicting the day's flight schedule. A quick survey of the board, by anyone with understanding of the meaning of the scribbled grease pencil marks covering the plastic, could ascertain how the flight schedule was progressing for the day.

Breakheart noted immediately that the Duty Officer's schedule board had the word "CANX" boldly written across the entire board as he walked into the room. His accident team members were already gathered, sitting in the straight-backed chairs that took up most of the room's floor space. He took them in at a glance, only half noticing the huge pictures of Harriers adorning the walls of the large room. Major Dyke was sitting at a small table next to the passageway wall. He and Captain Tom Evans were playing Acey Duecy, a standard ready room dice and board game. Every squadron in the Navy and Marine Corps must have an Acey Ducey board, thought Breakheart as he nodded to Stray Dog.

"Let's get started," Breakheart said quietly, interrupting the ongoing conversations of his team.

He walked to the front of the room, stepped up on the small platform, and began wiping clean the blackboard which covered the forward most wall. "This won't take long. I just want to get some things straight between us before we go charging into the fracas."

As he began speaking, the five officers gathered themselves in front of him, settling down in the leather covered, carrier readyroom chairs normally reserved for the commanding officer and his senior staff officers. "Tomorrow we'll start digging Double Nuts out of the ground. But before anything is disturbed, I want every major hunk of aircraft plotted on a grid. Major Dyke, I'm placing you in charge of making the grid. Please make it large enough so we can make an analysis from it at a later date." He looked squarely into Dyke's eyes, to burn home the need for a good grid plot. "Most of you," Breakheart stopped speaking and looked directly at each board member, "know me, and my reputation in this business. I expect 110 per cent from each of you until we have the final report on paper. Any questions so far?"

There were none, and Breakheart continued.

"I approach an investigation of an accident by looking for those things which could not have caused the crash, rather than what did. Put another way, we eliminate what couldn't have caused the aircraft to go down, and then we know for sure what did." He turned to the blackboard behind him, and picked up a Mark-A-Lot pen and began writing.

> Engine
>
> Hydraulics
>
> Flight Controls
>
> Fuel Systems
>
> Electronics

After writing these major aircraft systems on the board he turned and said, "We'll look at each one of these systems in detail, deleting each as we can. I know right now it sounds like the engine gave up, but the reason it went bad is what we are here to find out. As for the ejection seat, though it will be part of our accident report, I want to handle it separately. The damned thing didn't fire, and we've got to find out why…NOW! The entire Harrier community will want information on the seat as soon as we can possibly get it to them. Captain Harris," he singled out a ruddy-faced, dark-haired team member, "I'm putting you in charge of getting the seat to the rework facilities seat shop first thing tomorrow morning. I want a preliminary report by tomorrow night. Do you understand?"

Captain Harris said, "Yes, sir."

"Good. Now for the rest of you, you'll want to wear your grubbiest flight suit to muck around in that field. Plus, everyone in the field is to wear gloves. Carbon graphite fiber can be rough on exposed skin. We have the pallets to use as islands, and we'll scatter them across the field in the morning. Stray Dog and I will begin work on the pit, where I think we'll find the bulk of the airplane. But, from the Huey I could see the first couple of compressor sections in the field about a quarter mile downstream from the hole. We'll want those hauled out as soon as the field dries up some. The other pieces can be brought to the road only after they have been properly plotted. Most importantly, I don't want anything, any gauge, handle, switch, or dial moved before its setting has been properly logged. I want to know what every gauge read just prior to impact, and the same goes for switch and handle positions. Is that clearly understood?"

Heads nodded the affirmative, and Breakheart went on. "Finally, we will meet here or somewhere in the squadron area each night. The exact time will be decided on a daily basis, when we finish at the site. Hopefully, we'll only need to have evening meetings until we get the plane back here in a hangar, but don't count on it. You married guys had better warn your brides that you are going to spend some late hours here. That's all I have for this evening. I'll be driving out to the site at zero six-hundred if anyone needs a ride." No response. "Okay then, I'll see you tomorrow." Breakheart closed the meeting.

FOUR

THE BLACK FIREBIRD slowed from fifty-five to thirty, as it entered the riverside village of Oriental. Topping the bridge over the town's harbor, Breakheart could see a small forest of sailboat masts rolling gently under the pressure of a light wind surge. The boats were swinging in open water on moorings or docked at a marina located in the very heart of downtown. The Neuse River sailing community, from New Bern to Minnesota, created much of Oriental's economy, and it was a favorite place for Breakheart and his boys to sail for a Sunday seafood lunch.

Breakheart had left 203's parking lot at zero six hundred on the dot, just as he had indicated the night before. Now on the road, he was reviewing in his mind last night's conversation with Snake. He had called his best friend when he had gotten home the night before. It had been late, but it was not unusual for either friend to call the other when something was troubling them. The fact Jack's ejection seat hadn't fired was reason enough to have Breakheart's mind stirring with misgivings. The two friends talked for fifteen minutes, getting no closer to the answer than Breakheart had before he'd phoned. They both agreed the seat must have been really messed-up not to have at least fired the initial rocket stages, and neither could understand why. Now, as the sun was peeking its way above the Carolina pines, Breakheart was on his way to the accident site.

He arrived twenty minutes later, just as Major Dyke was briefing the enlisted working party. The men who would accomplish most of the dirty work required in the sorting out and dragging Zero Zero's wreckage from the muddy field. The Major used many of the same words Breakheart had emphasized to the Accident Board the night before. There were twenty men dressed in heavy coveralls. Much too heavy, considering the extreme heat and humidity. Adding to the bulky clothing was Marine issue webbed gear with two canteens and a first aid kit hung to the belt's eyelets. Most had thick leather gloves stuck in a pocket, or were holding them in one hand. The men listened intently to Major Dyke. Some of these men had rummaged into the broken remains of an aircraft before, but for a few it was new experience. Stray Dog was making sure they all understood the importance of their mission, and the absolute necessity of not disturbing the location or position of anything they might find. When he was finished with his men, Major Dyke walked over to Breakheart.

"They're ready, shall I get them started?" Stray Dog asked of the colonel.

"Have you made sure there are pallets stationed throughout the field? I don't want them mired in muck all day long. They'll need a dry spot to relax once in awhile."

"Yes, sir. Gunny Hicks had the men working at first light making dry paths with plywood and brush throughout the field. It didn't take long once we got the first couple of pallets in position. Besides, the field is drying slowly," Stray Dog answered.

"Right! Yeah, go head and get them started. Where is the rest of the board?"

"Most of them are already in the field. I've put Captain Borgeding in charge of the overall plot, and Harris has already loaded the seat on a six-by and headed back to the Point. The only thing left is the hole. Are you ready to get grubby?"

"You've been busy, Stray Dog," Breakheart smiled at his second in command. "Good job!"

While Dyke gave his final orders to the waiting Marines, Breakheart walked to the rim of the blackened hole where he hoped to find the remains of a broken AV-8. Reaching the pit, which was surrounded by ten enlisted men ready to start digging, Breakheart peered into the oozing mess of wet earth and JP-5 fuel. The stink of jet fuel was familiar, but over powering. The men standing over the gaping cut in the ground each had a shovel or small entrenching tool in their hand. Gunny Hicks stood on the hard surface of the dirt road, overlooking his men and the hole.

"Good morning, Colonel," Hicks said, saluting smartly. "We're ready if you are."

"Let's get started then," Breakheart said, removing a tape measure from his over sized breast pocket. "We'll measure the hole first. I want its length, breadth and depth. Once we have that, and a compass sighting to confirm the heading the airplane was on just before it hit the ground, we'll start digging. Okay?"

"Yes, sir. Here, let me get the measurement for you," Gunny Hicks answered, taking the tape from Breakheart. "Hey, Jones. Get over here and measure the hole for the Colonel," Hicks growled at a young Private First Class.

Fifteen minutes of struggling in the fuel soaked hole and Jones reported the measurements to be thirty-five feet long, seventeen feet, six and a half inches wide, and twelve feet, ten inches deep. The plane struck the ground on a heading of one seven five degrees, magnetic.

The pit was littered with small bits of aircraft, wiring harnesses, and engine blades, but no major pieces, such as portions of the fuselage or wing, were visible. Breakheart felt sure they would find most of the remaining aircraft buried in the hole. Although, he knew the aircraft had broken up on impact from his airborne view of the field the day before. The hunks of engine compressor and turbine stages he had seen from the chopper and the fact the ejection seat left the cockpit violently enough to destroy his friend's body, clearly indicated the plane had ripped itself apart with its vicious collision with terra firma. From the burnt soil and brush surrounding the hole, he judged there may have been an instantaneous explosion as well.

With the measurements recorded, Breakheart gave the order for the digging to begin. Carefully, men slid over the rim, picked a spot, and began excavating. They dug not with vigor, but rather as if they we working for a lucky anthropologist exhuming an ancient city. The ground was meticulously scraped with a shovel before it was sunk into the soft earth. Then, when a shovel full of dirt had been cleared from it surroundings, it was slowly and carefully sifted for aircraft remains. If a cockpit instrument or gauge could be found, they were careful not to disturb the setting it showed on impact. Each man knew one of those gauges might tell the entire story of what might have caused the accident. It was slow, tedious work, and the sun's heat, steaming off the newly planted field, made it all the more grueling.

Breakheart watched the progress in the pit for the better part of an hour, then told Major Dyke and Gunny Hicks he was going to walk the field. Stepping off the road's hard surface, he sunk above his ankles in mud.

"God damn it all to hell, why does every Harrier have to crash in such crap as this?" he said to no one in particular. He was venting frustration, and those nearby realized his need to do so.

Breakheart spotted one of his board members fifty yards away and started sloshing in the captain's direction. He stopped several times, looking at blackened segments of what was now left of Mars Zero Zero. A two-foot hunk of the tail plane lay half buried and torn approximately twenty-five yards from the impact hole, and on the same bearing the plane had crashed. Breakheart kicked at the twisted carbon fiber noting its small size. He thought, for the first time, that they might not find a lot of the Harrier in the hole. It was evident from what was left of the tail plane, there had been one hell of an explosion on impact. Normally, this would not be the case, but when he gave the actuality of the matter thought, he realized he'd never investigated an accident where the bird had been full of fuel. Double Nuts had not been airborne for more than ten minutes, and the full internal fuel tanks must have detonated like a bomb when they ruptured, he thought.

He continued toward the captain, and found more evidence suggesting a massive explosion. Bits and pieces of charred metal, no larger than a finger, covered the area like so much confetti. He reached the spot the captain and two troopers were recording on a plot sheet.

"What have you got here?" Breakheart asked.

The captain, known to Breakheart only by his call sign "Troll," looked up from the clipboard he'd been studying intently. "I'm sorry, sir, I didn't hear you walk up. He didn't salute, and there was no need too. They were in the field, working, and that made the normal greeting unnecessary. "We're plotting what looks to be a portion of the right wing. Sir, I think the airplane exploded on impact. There are millions of fragments scattered everywhere you look, and nothing much bigger than your hand. This hunk of wing is one of the largest pieces of airplane we've been able to locate."

"Yeah, I think you're right. I just hope we'll be able to find the engine and fuel control, and there is enough left of both to glean some good solid information from them. Keep up the good work," Breakheart instructed as he moved on across the bean field.

Breakheart noted areas of the field were being roped off, as he was sure Major Dyke had instructed. Squares of fifty to one hundred feet were being laid and numbered. The plotting would revolve around each of the squares. Within each of the roped areas, two or three camouflaged-clothed men wandered with clipboards and poking sticks. The sticks were used to gently prod and poke bits of metal, noting its position and what it was thought to be. By noon, not only had the sun become unbearably hot, the field, now resembling a huge checker board, and was alive with tiny human pawns moving slowly from square to square. Breakheart called a stop to the digging and searching, and ordered his men to take a couple hours out of the steamy heat for lunch. Earlier, around eleven hundred, a pickup truck had delivered sack lunches and six, twenty gallon thermos cans of Kool-Aid. The men didn't hesitate at the request from their colonel, and began straggling into the camp area, grabbed a lunch sack, and found themselves a place to fall into a heap of soaking sweat.

Breakheart asked Major Dyke to join him for lunch at a small, country town restaurant ten miles back toward Oriental. The eatery was called "Charlie's" and was reported to have the largest hamburgers in North Carolina. Dyke agreed, and the two set off in the Firebird. Lunch was spent discussing the morning's findings and the decor of the establishment. The restaurant was festooned with pictures ranging in diversity from a signed picture of The Blue Angles flying the F-11s, to smiling fishermen holding stringers filled with red drum. Between swigs of ice tea, they decided they had found nothing of any real importance in the muddy field, with the possible exception of determining the aircraft had exploded with tremendous force. So far, only the first couple of compressor stages had been found and plotted, and the only thing Breakheart could learn from the massive engine sections was that it had been running at low RPM when the aircraft hit the ground. He could ascertain this meaningful reality from the curvature of the blade tips… bent opposite to the direction of engine rotation. Several hundred compressor and turbine blades had been found, both on the field and in the hole. Most confirmed his conclusion, the engine had been running until the very last, and exploded like a bomb on impact.

The burgers were indeed the grandest Breakheart had ever seen. Special buns were prepared in the kitchen just to handle the nine-inch hunk of beef covered with fried onions. They were delicious, and the two men ate, breaking their silence only twice to request more tea from a pretty red headed waitress. When the last of the fries and sandwiches disappeared, Breakheart asked to compliment the chef, who came to their table and was delighted by the generous remarks given by both men.

By fourteen hundred, the bean field was again filled with working Marines. Already covered in black mud, which stuck to their clothing like glue, they began their labors from the morning's stopping point. Sergeant Reddock was in the field as well. Gunny Hicks, in his effort to pick the best technicians from each maintenance shop, had made the request for Reddock. The sergeant was known for his knowledge of the F402 engine, and under normal circumstances, would have been the perfect choice. However, Double Nuts' accident was not normal. Reddock, a small man, but one who lifted weights to increase the definition of the rope-like muscles swelling on his arms and chest, appeared to be as involved in the search for debris as all the other Marines in the vast field were. He was, however, looking for a specific engine part...the Dual Wound Resolver, commonly called simply the Resolver. It was just forward of this critical segment of the engine that he had attached a spring and a locking device just prior to Colonel Adams' flight, and if he didn't want some very hard questions asked of him, these attachments had to be removed. His search for the Resolver carried him over the entire field, anywhere engine parts had been reported by the various teams working within the roped areas. During lunch, he'd listened carefully to the conversations of his fellow squadron mates and had even asked outright about the location of various engine elements. This was not thought to be unusual, as he was the senior F402 mech in the field. It was through one of those conversations he'd learned of a large section of the engine lying in the ditch, not far down the trench from where the Colonel's body had been found. After lunch, his overall trouser pockets stuffed with tools, he joined his companions and disappeared into the ditch.

Captain Reggie Hamilton got out of his car, having eaten a ham sandwich, with extra mayo, he'd made for himself before leaving his BOQ room that morning. Assigned to the squadron's standing Accident Board just a month before Zero Zero went in, this was the first time he'd been involved in the investigation of a crash. He didn't like it! As he strapped on his web gear, from which hung his two canteens and a first aid kit, he thought of how he should be flying, not plowing some damned bean field looking for twisted metal and burnt gauges.

Hamilton had chosen Harriers right out of Flight School, they were the reason he signed his name on the dotted line with the Marine Corps and not the Air Force. From the moment he'd first seen an AV-8A flying at an air show in his hometown of Kissimimee, Florida, Harriers became the center of his life. After graduation from the University of Florida, he signed on with the Marines to become a Naval Aviator, and to fly Harriers. He loved his work, and had been with 203 for six months. Before that, he'd spent his first two year tour with VMA-542, the Tigers. Now, he was an instructor, teaching men not unlike himself.

Reggie's assigned search area was on the far side of the field, some three quarters of a mile from the actual crash site. He, and his allocated enlisted men, found little, but what they had, were much larger pieces of aircraft than those found near the impact area. As he stepped from the road into the mud he decided to cut across the field using the relatively firm ground the ditch provided. He hadn't walked the ditch that morning, primarily because he did not want to come across any more of the Colonel's flesh, which some members of the team suggested would still be clinging to the ground. Now, however, the thought of slogging his way through three quarters of a mile of mud overcame his squeamishness. He headed for the ditch.

Sergeant Reddock crawled up the side of the ditch, cautiously stretching his neck to peer over the gentle rise. He scrutinized the field, marking where activity was taking place. He saw no one near, and thought he would have time to make the necessary adjustments to the hunk of engine lying at the bottom of the trench beneath him. He slid back down the bank, took a pair of dykes from his left leg pocket and leaned over what was left of the right side of the crashed airplane's engine. He began cutting away something attached to a stainless steel rod entering the Resolver's housing.

"Sergeant, just what in hell do you think you're doing?" Captain Hamilton asked, as he walked forward to get a better view. "You know you're not supposed to mess with anything in the field."

Reddock spun around, a surprised and guilty expression drawn tightly from eyes to mouth. "Ah,... Well you see, sir, I just wanted to have a look inside. I am the engine shop's representative you know," he stated, gaining composure.

"I don't care if you are Christ Almighty, you have no business opening anything in the field. We'd better go talk to Colonel Breakheart."

"But, sir, I haven't changed a thing. We don't need to see anyone. I'll just go about my job. Okay?"

Hamilton thought for a moment. "No! I don't think so. Come on with me, and that's an order." Hamilton turned to begin the trudge back down the ditch to the road, expecting Reddock to follow.

"No, sir," Reddock said in a bone chilling voice, the gap in his teeth showing clearly. "In fact, I don't think we'll be going anywhere."

The sergeant swung the heavy cutting dykes with all the strength he could muster, hitting Reggie Hamilton squarely on the right temple. The captain went down like he'd been shot at close range by a 12-gauge shotgun.

"At least you won't, you stupid, smart-ass fuckhead. Not now, not ever!" Reddock swung the dykes once more then again, crushing the dark haired man's skull like a melon.

The Adrenaline pumped through Reddock like he'd been mainlined with drugs. His mind worked furiously. He took several deep breaths to clear the images of being caught and executed for murder, then began to devise a workable plan of action. Crawling up the bank once more, he saw that he was virtually alone. Good, he thought, I'll hide the body until tonight. By then I'll know what to do. No problem, his mind spun answers to the immediate dilemma. He knew this area had been plotted earlier in the morning and there was little chance of anyone scouring it again until they were ready to start moving aircraft debris out of the field. He dragged the limp body of Captain Hamilton to the engine section he'd been working on, then went through the captain's pockets. Furiously, he began digging a shallow cavity under the engine, having rolled it on its side. The ground was soft, and it took little time to have a depression deep enough to slide the captain's body into. He quickly covered Hamilton with a thin layer of dirt and rolled the engine back on top of him.

Again, he climbed the ditch to view the area. No one was near. He was sure no one had seen his dirty work. He moved out of the ditch and joined three other Marines two hundred yards a way. Tonight, he thought, I'll move the body. Already, a plan was formulating in his mind, and he knew he could take care of the problem.

Colonel Breakheart stood at the bottom of the hole, his boots and flight suit soaked in mud and JP-5. The stench, wafting from the broken earth, was overwhelming, but he and the other men continued to sort through the dirt like so many moles. Pieces of aircraft lay around the hole, bits dug out of the ground throughout the day. Surprisingly, nothing of any size had yet been found. Breakheart had been sure they would find the bulk of the airplane buried in the hole, but so far, that had not been the case.

"What do you think, Gunny? Are we wasting time digging here?" A discouraged Breakheart asked.

The Gunny was just ready to answer, when a young Private First Class digging at the rear of the hole yelled, "I've got something big here. I think its part of the aft fuselage."

Several Marines rushed to help the private, and within minutes, a large portion of Double Nuts' fuselage was beginning to show under the muck. It was a segment of the airplane from frame fourteen to the just forward of the tail section. It was soon obvious to Breakheart, it was the bottom half of the plane and did not include the engine. Apparently, when the aircraft exploded, the engine and top half of the fuselage were blown clear of the hole. That meant anything which might prove useful to the investigation was more than likely scattered in the muddy field, and not in the hole. Nonetheless, he would have his men continue to sift the hole.

"Gunny, we'll need a cherry picker out here to move this out of the hole. Do we have one here with us yet?" Breakheart asked, knowing the answer. Gunny Hicks had proved to be very resourceful.

"Yes, sir. It arrived around thirteen hundred. It's parked behind the camp site. Shall I have it move this," he pointed into the hole, "now?"

"Yeah! You go ahead and get it out. I'll radio the squadron for a flat bed truck. We might as well start moving Double Nuts' bigger pieces to the Point. Before you move it, however, take a compass sighting along its center line in the hole. That should tell us within a couple of degrees what the actual flight path Double Nuts was on when it hit. At least, it should be closer than the sighting we got from just the hole. Oh, by the way, I've arranged to use the south section of 203's hangar for our lay out, so tell the driver to take it there for us. See to it for me, will you?" Breakheart started climbing his way out of the hole.

While the Gunny gave orders for the removal of the fuselage, Breakheart slowly began walking toward the camp. His mind working on the accident. So far he had nothing to go on except the explosion and the fact the engine had been running. Normally, he thought, an eyewitness would have been useful, but not in this case. He already knew something had gone wrong with the aircraft, and nothing a witness could tell him would add to the investigation. As he walked, Major Dyke fell in step with him on his left side, a half pace behind.

"Sir, we have the grid completed. Do you want to join me for a general inspection of the area?"

"Yeah, let's do that. Maybe we'll stumble across something that will give us a hint of what happened. Have you heard anything about the seat from Captain Harris?"

"No nothing, but we'll probably see him at this evening's meeting. By the way, we'll have to use one of the briefing rooms for our get-together tonight. The Squadron is flying a night schedule. Will that be all right with you?"

"Sure, no problem," Breakheart answered. "I think we'll start picking the smaller pieces out of the field tomorrow and moving them back to the Point. From the looks of it, it will probably take us the remainder of the week to clear the area. Has anyone talked to the owner yet?"

"Wing legal has been in touch with him. He seems to be a nice guy. He told legal he doesn't plan on suing the government, but he does want his bean field cleared of as much metal as we can possibly find. The metal left behind apparently fouls up his farming gear when he tries to harvest or plow."

"Well, we'll sure as hell try to get as much out of here as we can. Get in touch with him for me, and tell him we'll give him a call when we're finished. That way, he can inspect his property before we leave. I'll call Wing and have a lawyer here as well, that way we can have all the paperwork completed while all parties are gathered in one place."

"Sounds good to me, but we've got another problem," Major Dyke offered. "The newspapers are stacked up like cord wood just short of our camp. Security is holding them at bay, telling them there is a chance there are explosive devices still in the field. It's a half truth, since we haven't found the wing pylon CADs yet, but sooner or later we'll have to let them in for their shit-ass pictures."

"God! I hate reporters. They blow everything way out of proportion, and every time I give them a statement, they take my words out of context. Let's see," Breakheart looked at his watch, "it's sixteen thirty now, I'll talk to them after we finish walking the field."

Both men fell silent as they paced across the expanse of the crashed airplane's remains. It took them an hour to view what they thought necessary, and when finished, they had nothing new to add to what they already knew. Taking his leave, Stray Dog stepped off to talk to Gunny Hicks, and Breakheart headed for the reporters.

The gaggle of men and women waiting for him at the camp represented more than just the local newspapers. There were reporters from as far away as Raleigh, and TV camera crews from two networks. As he approached, they began getting cameras and tape-recording equipment ready.

Before any of the crowding media people could open their mouths, Breakheart said, "I'm Colonel Dan Breakheart. I have the dubious pleasure of being the senior officer in charge of the Accident Board. Now, I will answer all the questions I can, but I expect you to report exactly what I say and not place words in my mouth. Nor do I want to see or read copy which is taken out of context so you people can dramatize the accident for journalistic and monetary gain. Is that understood? If any one of you feel I'm being unreasonable, then the interview ends right now. I've had enough dealings with the media to know you can screw up things beyond recognition, and I don't want that to happen here."

The reporters assured him they would do as he requested, though Breakheart retained serious doubts. Reporters, both newspaper and TV, rarely reported a story truthfully. Perhaps the unruly breed might attempt validity in their account, but when it came to military matters, they seldom understood the complexity of events and, therefore, fabricated as they deemed necessary.

For the next forty-five minutes, Breakheart answered questions with as much diplomacy as he could muster, and did a taped interview with the TV crews. By the time they were satisfied they had enough for a story, and sufficient gore to please their readers, they packed their kits and drove off in a cloud of dust. It was approaching six thirty, time to shut down for the day. He walked to the pit, where he found Gunny Hicks was just finishing loading the broken fuselage section onto a flatbed.

"Gunny, call in your men. Let's call it a day. I'm leaving now for the Point, but if you need anything I'll be in the squadron area later this evening. And, by the way, thanks for the good work. Please pass the same to the men for me. I'll want talk to them personally before this thing is all over."

The Gunny said his goodnight, and continued to oversee the loading. He thought about Colonel Breakheart, and decided he liked the man. The Colonel remembered to compliment the Marines working for him.

Breakheart crawled behind the wheel of his car, and took one last look at the accident site. Starting his engine, he slipped the Firebird into gear and headed for Cherry Point. An hour later he drove into his driveway off Jefferson Drive, noting the beat-up yellow station wagon he'd given the boys when he'd bought his sports car.

For the next hour, he showered the grime from his sweaty body, changed into a fresh set of utilities, and sat down to talk to his sons for a few minutes. The boys, ages thirteen, fifteen, and sixteen were use to their father being gone for long periods. When their dad was not on a two or three week deployment or overseas for a year at a time, he was forever tied up with his work. Most times, at least during the week, their paths crossed at the breakfast table and in front of the TV late at night. In between, they were pretty much on their own. The weekends were theirs. *Dreamer*, the family's thirty-seven foot, cutter sloop was where the Breakheart men got together and raced or cruised. Dan felt sorry about not spending more time with his children, but Marine Corps duties always seemed to come first. Everything was a crisis in the Corps, and every new contingency should have been taken care of the day or week before. Work ate his time like a hungry bear, sopping the hours like honey.

By the time he stood at the doorway to General Geise's quarters, ringing its multi-toned doorbell, it was well past twenty hundred. Built in the nineteen forties, Geise's quarters were palatial in comparison to most housing on base. Architecturally designed to resemble a southern plantation home of old, the white, two story house was festooned with Greek like columns supporting the front porch. The immaculately kept grounds were tended by a gardener who visited weekly, and from his efforts, the yard was alive with flowering color during the summer months.

Breakheart, not concerned with the house looked like, rang the bell once more. He had to be at 203 by twenty-one hundred. Time was short, but he wanted to brief Geise on the day's findings. The door opened and a pretty brunette of around forty-seven answered the door.

"Hi, Dan. Come on in. John," referring to her husband, Jonathan Geise, "is waiting for you."

"Thanks Marge. It's good to see you. It's been awhile. How are you?"

"I'm fine, and you?"

"Super. How is Sally holding up? I haven't had a chance to stop by yet, but I will make a point to tomorrow."

"She is doing as well as to be expected, and her family arrived this afternoon," Marge answered, just as her husband walked out of the living room.

"Hey, Cuda. What's up? Anything new?" The big general asked in his booming voice.

"No. Sorry! Nothing much to tell you, except I'm sure the aircraft exploded violently when she hit. There aren't many hunks of aircraft over the size of your arm. We did find a part of the fuselage in the hole. It should be on its way back to 203 as we speak."

As Breakheart was answering, they moved into the living room and sat down in front of an oriental carved coffee table which looked to be a small acre in size. Marge Geise, left the room, returning almost immediately with a brandy decanter and two snifters. She filled the snifters to the halfway mark and handed them to the men, excused herself and disappeared a final time.

"I hope to have some information on the ejection seat when I debrief my team tonight, but nothing beyond that." He took a swig from the glass, and let the fiery liquid burn down into his throat. "Damnation, this is good stuff," he smiled at the general, and continued. "Tomorrow I'll stop by Twilight Control and review the transcript of the tape of John's last radio transmissions, but I don't think I'll get much from them. As far as I know, all he said was he was experiencing a problem with his engine, not what the cause of the emergency was."

"Yeah, that's what I've heard as well," the General replied. "Just for your information, the memorial service will be held the day after tomorrow at fifteen hundred. Do you think you'll be able to break away long enough to attend?"

"Of course, sir. John was a good friend. I'll be there. Breakheart took another long pull at the brandy, draining his glass. "I've got to run, sir. The team will be waiting for me as it is." He stood to leave.

"Okay, Dan. I'll talk to you tomorrow."

"Roger that," Breakheart said, gathering his utility cover from the end table he'd set it upon. "Thanks for the brandy, and please say goodby to your wife for me." With his parting words, he passed through the door and headed for VMAT-203.

He hurried up the stairs to 203's readyroom and asked the Duty Officer where the Accident Board was meeting. The lieutenant behind the desk pointed to briefing room two, and rogered an aircraft's check in at the same time. Breakheart made for the designated briefing room.

No sooner had he opened the door to the small room than he knew something was wrong. The faces and hushed voices foretold of something dire, and Breakheart didn't need dire.

"Jesus Christ, what the hell are all the long faces about?" Breakheart asked.

Major Dyke moved from his chair, making room for the colonel. "You're not going to like it," He said. "You had better sit down, sir."

"Damn it, I don't like it already, and you haven't given me a clue yet."

"It's the seat," Dyke said flatly. "I think I'd better let Captain Harris tell you about what he's found so far." He nodded to the captain.

"Well, what have you got?" Breakheart asked, his eyes boring into those of the captain's.

"Sir, I picked up the seat early this morning. We loaded it in the back of a pickup and brought it straight to the NADEP's seat shop. They were expecting us, as they had heard about the seat not firing, and had three engineers standing by to tear it apart when we arrived," Harris began.

"Good job. Go on," Breakheart said.

"Well, it didn't take very long to find out why the seat didn't fire. The firing handle had been disconnected, or had never been connected in the first place."

Dan Breakheart stood, knocking his chair against the wall. "You're telling me, the God damned ejection handle was disconnected. How in God's name could that happen? I'll have somebody's ass on a pogo stick for this. I can't bloody well believe something like this could happen. Not with all the quality assurance checks done on an ejection seat prior to its installation into a bird." He was mad, red faced mad, and his outburst had the others in the room cringing at his words. "What else did you find, anything at all?"

"Yes!" Captain Harris spoke tentatively. "The device used to hold the first stage rocket from firing while a technician attaches the handle was installed. Either the seat was placed in the airplane that way, or someone tampered with it prior to Colonel Adams' flight."

"Well, have you talked to the seat mechanics who last performed maintenance on the damned thing. What have they got to say about it?"

"I've talked to the men in the squadron's seat shop," Major Dyke interrupted, trying to remove some of Breakheart's wrath from his captain. "They assure me the seat was installed intact, and all quality assurance checks were performed. I viewed the paper work along with Captain Harris. It all appears to be in order."

"When was the seat last out of the aircraft for inspection?" Breakheart asked in a calmer tone.

"Fifteen days ago," Dyke answered.

Breakheart, his eyes barking hate and discontent, was silent for a moment. "Sabotage! Are you suggesting Double Nuts was sabotaged prior to Colonel Adams' hop?"

"Not necessarily *his* hop, but, yes I believe the seat was incapacitated intentionally, and it was done after the seat was installed in the bird. Why? I have no idea, but it appears to be the case."

"If what you are suggesting is true, one of two things follow," Breakheart said quietly. "One, the seat was fooled with for no reason other than to have it fail should anyone need its use. Or, two, it was sabotaged for Colonel Adams' flight, and that would mean whoever disconnected the firing handle had to know the airplane was going to develop an ejection situation."

"You're right, of course," Dyke mulled. "But it doesn't make sense. Why on earth would anyone want to kill Colonel Adams? Hell, he wasn't even attached to the squadron, and only flew with us, maybe, three or four times a month."

The other members of the board sat listening to the two senior officers. Captain Harris stirred in his chair uncomfortably. "Sir." He spoke to Breakheart. "What you're suggesting is premeditated murder. If that's the case, someone in 203's maintenance would have to be the murderer. Someone who knows a lot about the Harrier."

"Yeah, I know," Breakheart replied. "The thing is, we have got to find out what made Double Nuts crash, then we might have a lead to the man who fucked with the plane. More importantly, this is no longer just an accident investigation. We've got to bring Naval Investigative Service, NIS, into this as well. He paused, "Harris, have you ensured the seat's security?"

"Yes, sir! It is locked in a wire cage located in the NADEP's seat shop."

"Good, I'll have NIS over to look at it tomorrow morning. You be at the seat shop before it opens and don't let anyone else mess with it. I doubt NIS will be able to lift fingerprints or any other information of value off of it, but we don't want to take any chances. Hell, maybe they will get something for us to work on. In the meantime, Stray Dog, you take the team to the field and start loading the plane for transport back here. I'm going to do some footwork here in the squadron tomorrow. By the way," Breakheart changed the conversation, "where is Captain Hamilton? I thought I made it clear I wanted the whole team here for these meetings."

"I don't know," Major Dyke answered. "His car was still at the site when I left, and no one, at least none of the team members have seen him since earlier this afternoon. He probably had car trouble returning to the Point. He's a good man Colonel, I'm sure there is a good reason why he isn't here."

"Okay, but tell him not to let it happen again, or at least call and let us know what he's doing."

"Yes, sir, I will," Dyke replied.

"One final thing before we breakup. I don't want any of this seat thing out of this room. I mean not your wife, dog, or best friend. What we have talked about in this room stays here. Is that clearly understood?" Breakheart looked from member to member, receiving a head nod from each. "Okay then, I'll see you here tomorrow night, and by the way, you all are doing a fine job. Keep it up!"

The meeting ended on that note, and the officers walked solemnly from the small briefing room, each going his separate way. Breakheart walked directly to the Duty Officer and asked for the key to the Commanding Officer's office. He went straight to the office, unlocked the door and turned on the overhead light, picked up the phone and called NIS. The conversation continued for fifteen minutes before he returned the phone to its cradle. He then called General Geise, arranging for an early morning appointment. Preparing to leave, he stopped and returned to the telephone, making a call to Major Bob Burns.

"Snake, I need to talk to you," Breakheart said into the phone. "Can I meet you at the club?"

"Hell yes. I'm on my way pally," Burns answered. "See you there in about thirty minutes."

"Right, and thanks," Breakheart said, hanging up the phone for the third time. He left the office, locking the door behind him. After returning the key to the Duty Officer, the worried colonel headed for the officer's club.

While the accident board met in VMA-203's operation's spaces, Sergeant Reddock was busily devising a plan to remove Captain Hamilton's body from the ditch. He'd eaten a hot meal. The spareribs had been only luke warm, served from vats filled by the cooks at Cherry Point's chow hall, but overall, it was a satisfying meal and a welcome respite from the long day's activities. He'd sat talking, joking, and eating with several other Marines whom Gunny Hicks had chosen to remain overnight. Earlier, while the sun's rays still gave light, he'd made a point of locating Hamilton's car. It was a fire engine red Corvette. The 'vette was the envy of many of the enlisted men attached to the squadron who thought it would bring the local gals to their knees…if only they could afford such an automobile.

The car was parked under a stand of pines not far from VMAT-203's bivouac site. He had removed a set of keys from the captain's body before covering the remains with damp dirt under the engine section. Now, all he had to do was wait until the camp slept.

FIVE

RAGGED SNORES GENTLY rolled across the tent. Of the five Marines, four slept the sleep of the dead…one lay awake on his cot. The night heat made the tent uncomfortably warm, and Sergeant Reddock lay atop his sleeping bag bathed in his own perspiration. Not all the dampness was caused by the heat. He fidgeted in worry, as he stared at the tent's ceiling and listened to the hum of the trailer-mounted generator providing power to the camp. He was worried about the time. It was already one in the morning, and his tent mates had only recently drifted off to sleep. The poker game started not long after chow had been served at eighteen hundred, and the young troopers had continued their game until midnight. The sergeant knew it would take him at least three hours to execute his plan, and he needed to be back in camp before the camp began stirring with day's first light.

He listened to the sounds of sleeping men for a moment longer, then assured his companions were indeed dead to the world, sat up on his cot. Noiselessly, he slipped into his utilities, the only clothes he had in the field, and jammed on his cover. Tugging on his boots, he grunted quietly, hoping he would still have enough time to get rid of Hamilton's body before his tent mates awoke for breakfast.

Then he gathered a flashlight and two large black garbage bags he'd taken from supper's chow truck. He glanced at his sleeping companions then slipped out of the tent. He knew the Gunny had posted guards on either end of the dirt road before dark. The sentries stood watch on a two on, four off schedule, and their timetable did not make a difference in the execution of his overall scheme. However, he hoped not to be moving during a change in shift. Regardless, while he remained near the camp, he would take his time and be very careful.

Reddock walked through the sleeping camp and onto the road, cognizant of the corporal on his right. The glow of a cigarette illuminated the night like a bright firefly, and Reddock estimated the guard to be fifty yards away…walking toward him. *If I hurry*, he thought, *I'll be well in the field before he gets to the camp.*

Sergeant Reddock's stomach crawled across the road. Then, in the relative safety of the bean field, he moved into a low squat, duck-walking his way carefully to the ditch. He reached the trench without being spotted, and in the confines of the ditch, straightened up, and began walking unencumbered to the engine and the dead Hamilton. He used his flashlight sparingly, and when he did, his fingers covered the lens with his left hand so only a bare ray of light shone. Reddock found the body easily, still covered with the F402, and began to dig. The digging really was no more than scraping the light covering of dirt from the remains. In less than ten minutes, he had Hamilton uncovered and began stuffing the stiffening body into one of the plastic bags. The entire corpse would not fit, but by stuffing the captain in head first, and then doubling the body over, he was able to get both plastic bags around Hamilton. The bags would provide a smooth surface on which to drag the body over the muddy field.

Replacing the engine into its original position, Reddock began the long trek to Hamilton's Corvette. The ditch could not be used. To drag the body through the ditch meant he would have to use the dirt road and pass by the guard, and that was something he definitely did not want to do. He struggled with the dead weight up the side of the trench, slipping twice, letting Hamilton slide roughly back to the bottom. The third time, sweat pouring from his face, and his sinuous arms aching from exertion, Reddock made it to the top. He took several deep breaths and tried to regain his initial composure. Now the real work starts, he thought to himself.

Reddock began dragging the body across the field, paralleling the road. It was grueling work. The water-soaked field provided little footing, and the heavy weight he was lugging behind hindered every step. It took the sergeant an hour to cross the field and enter the relative safety of a piney woods. Once clear of the open stretch, he sat down heavily on his burden.

"You're a pain in the ass," he said to the black plastic bag. "You stupid son of a bitch. Why in hell did you have to come along when you did? If you'd stayed clear, I wouldn't have to drag your fucking body through this crap."

Renewing his resolve Reddock stood, grabbed the bags, and began the trudge through the woods. In some ways the going was easier, except the bag and body kept catching on branches and downed limbs. Not having to worry about the sentries helped, and the sergeant made good time, reaching the red Corvette at four a.m.

Reddock silently thanked the captain for backing his car off the hard topped road a short distance from where the dirt ruts leading to the field began. The auto sat ten feet clear of the pavement. He unlocked the passenger's door with the keys he'd taken from Hamilton's flight suit pocket when he'd buried him under the engine, and stuffed the body onto the leather seat. Satisfied whit his work, he walked around to the driver's side. Unlocking the door, he slipped the car out of gear, and straightened the wheel. He moved rapidly to the rear of the Corvette and began pushing. Slowly the 'vette moved onto the hard surface of the county road. Reddock trotted forward and turned the wheel to the left then resumed pushing, this time at the driver's door.

He steered the car down the road for another hundred yards, well away from the dirt road and the guard on watch. Then, and only then, did he think it safe enough to wrap himself behind the steering wheel. He started the engine, careful not to touch the brake...he didn't want to alert the sentry with the glare of red taillights, and quietly meshed the gears into first. The car idled forward as he eased the clutch and began to pick up speed.

Safely clear of being seen or heard, Reddock accelerated south down State Road 307, toward Oriental. Ten miles he drove, humming tunelessly to himself...very pleased with the way things had gone so far. As he reached the outskirts of the tiny town of Maribel, he saw what he was looking for. He knew there were many small tributaries, creeks and small rivers, feeding the Neuse, and that it would be just a matter of time until he found the right one. He pulled off the side of the road, short of a cement bridge, and left the engine running. Quickly, he began shifting Hamilton's body to the driver's side of the car. He dragged the dead weight around the front, cut the bags with a pocket knife and stuffed the young captain behind the wheel. Now he was faced with a problem. How to put a stick shift in gear without using the clutch.

"Dam it to fucking hell," Reddock said aloud into the night. "What the hell am I going to do now?"

He thought for several minutes, then made his decision. Shutting the driver's door, he climbed into the passenger's seat. He wound himself over the top of Hamilton, and found he could barely reach the clutch. The car's gear shift pinched the hell out of his balls, but he could stand that for a few minutes. Putting the car in reverse, he backed down the road for two hundred yards. Then, with the dexterity his lean frame allowed, he slowly began to idle forward in second gear. The car gathered speed, and he shifted into third. He aimed the car for the corner of the bridge where it met the road, and rolled out of the door just as the Corvette left the pavement. The 'vette rolled down the bank and into the night blackened water.

Reddock watched the car sink under the surface and disappear into creek. It took several minutes for the headlights to extinguish, but finally, they winked twice and went out. He smiled.

Sergeant Reddock spent the next fifteen minutes trying to brush away his foot prints and the car's tire marks from where he had parked. Using a fallen tree branch as a broom, he swept the area clean. Pleased with his handiwork, he started walking back to camp. His time was getting short. He'd driven further than he had anticipated, but he was in good shape, and had better than an hour and a half before light. He broke into a trot.

Reddock ran at a steady pace for five miles. He wasn't winded or tired. He held great pride in his body, and maintained his physique in prime shape, something he'd started as a boy. Suddenly, his back was flooded by the lights of a vehicle. He slowed to a walk. The truck pulled alongside and stopped.

Out of the passenger's side of the six-by, a Lance Corporal leaned out of the window and yelled, "Hey, Marine, need a ride?"

Reddock looked up at the corporal and thought frantically, answering, "Where ya going?"

"We're going out to the crash site. You heard about that haven't you?"

"Yeah! Sure. That's where I'm headed," Reddock answered.

"Hop in, we'll give you a ride," the Lance Corporal yelled back over the growling diesel.

Sergeant Reddock climbed up on the running board and opened the squarish side door. "Hey, thanks. I thought I was going to be late for morning muster. You guys are a lifesaver."

"What in hell are you doing out here at this time in the morning, sergeant?" The driver asked, noticing the rank of the newcomer.

Reddock answered, smiling a wicked, "you understand, don't you" grin. "I snuck off to visit my girlfriend. She lives in Oriental, and we had one hell of a night. If you get my meaning?"

The three laughed together knowingly, as the truck gathered momentum. Reaching the dirt road leading into the camp, the eastern sky began to brighten with pale light.

"Say guys, you won't say anything about picking me up, will you?" Reddock asked.

"Hell, don't worry about it," the Lance Corporal answered. "We won't say a thing to anyone. Will we, Charlie?"

"Shit no. I only wish I had a girlfriend I could sneak off and see when I wanted to," the driver answered. "Don't worry, sergeant, you secret is safe with us."

"Great. Say, would you pull up and let me out. I'll walk from here."

The big truck slowed to a stop, and Reddock leaped to the ground. He whispered a thanks to the two Marines who had befriended him and scrambled into the trees beside the road. Reddock made his way back to camp, which was now beginning to stir with Marines wandering sleepily to the Port-a-Potties. He slipped unseen into one of the fiberglass toilets, and stripped off his muddy utilities. Removing his rank insignia and retrieving his wallet and comb, he stuffed the used clothing down the "shit chute." Satisfied he would blend in with the morning crowd, opened the door standing in his skivvies and boots. Treading back to his tent, he gave good morning head nods to those he passed. He looked like he had just arisen from his cot to urinate like every other man in the camp.

SIX

BREAKHEART DROVE DOWN Roosevelt Boulevard heading for his morning meeting with General Geise. His thoughts were anywhere but on his driving. He was little aware of the platoon of Marines on the right side of the road. The men and women were part of Marine Wing Support Group 27 out for their morning run on the paved bicycle trail paralleling the road. Dan was reflecting on the conversation he and Snake had the night before.

The two had met as planned, and after ordering a rum and diet Coke for himself and a scotch and water for Bob, they had settled in at a table providing them with an overhead light. Breakheart produced a NATOPS manual, and placed it on the table between them.

The NATOPS manual, a Naval Aviator's bible, was published for every aircraft the Navy and Marine Corps flew. The thick book laying on the table between Dan and Bob was the AV-8B's NATOPS, and it contained, with exception of the fighter's weapon systems and use, almost everything a Harrier pilot needed to know about his plane.

Over several drinks the two men scoured the section covering the ejection seat. Together, they decided there was absolutely no way the seat could have gone into the aircraft with the ejection handle disconnected and the safety clasp still in place. Sabotage was the only feasible answer they could decide upon. The "why" was a mystery beyond anything they could think of with so little information. The conversation turned to lighter events during their third drink. Hancock Yacht Club's regatta was to take place on the weekend, and both men had been looking forward to the event for several months.

"Do you think you'll be able to forget this mess long enough to race?" Snake asked Breakheart.

"I'll make time, at least for the Saturday race. I promised the boys, and if I don't take them, there will be a mutiny in the Breakheart household. Besides, its high time I spend some time with my boys. I haven't even been home for dinner in the past two nights. They are great kids, but with no mom for the last couple of years, they need me even more."

"Hell, Cuda, what do the boys need you for anyway, when they have a godfather like me around?" Bob Burns laughed. "I mean, look at all the things I can teach them you can't."

"Right! The confirmed bachelor speaks from his pedestal on high. You have got to be kidding. What are you going to teach them? How to drink and chase women? That's about all you do well."

"You cut me to the quick," Snake smiled. "But, what the heck, they have to learn there is more to life than school and cooking their own dinners."

"Yeah, I know." Breakheart's forehead furled with genuine concern. "I have serious guilt feelings about leaving them alone so much of the time, but I don't know what else to do about the situation. Thank God they are old enough to fend for themselves, but it still bothers the hell out of me."

"Stop worrying so damned much. You'll grow old before your time," Snake retorted lightly, and slapped Breakheart on the shoulder. "Now, tell me how you think you are going to win Saturday's race. You will be in the cruising class, won't you?" Bob changed the subject.

"Listen you egotistical SOB, *Dreamer* and her Breakheart crew are going to whip up on you so badly you'll probably be ashamed to show your face on the water ever again."

"Fat chance that will ever happen. Besides, I have a near professional crew of bikini-clad damsels. If I can't win fairly, I'll cheat. I'll order my crew to take their tops off. That should distract enough skippers for *Rainbow* to surge ahead for the win," Burns retorted. "And anyway, everybody knows you couldn't sail your way out of a plastic sack. If it wasn't for your sons, you probably couldn't find your way out of Hancock Creek."

"We'll see who wins. Then when you're crying in your scotch, I'll be accepting the silver," Breakheart bantered with a smile. "Speaking of kids, I've got to get home, "He stood abruptly, sliding his chair back from the table. "If you think of anything more on the seat, get in touch with me."

"You can count on it, pally," Bob returned.

Breakheart was suddenly brought back to reality when the gong and flashing light short of the takeoff end of runway three two broke into his thoughts. An aircraft was taking off, stopping traffic where Roosevelt crossed the runway. It was a C-130, Hercules, and Dan watched as the gray transport lumbered into the sky, and turned west. Wish I was flying today instead of being tied up with this damned investigation, he thought to himself, and accelerated ahead to his meeting.

"Morning, Chief," Breakheart greeted Colonel Keller. "Is He in?" The "he" meaning General Geise

"Yes. Both of them are here this morning," the Chief of Staff answered. "The General is expecting you."

"Thanks," Breakheart said, and moved on into the general's outer office. "Good morning, Sergeant Gilbert. Will you tell the general I'm here?"

"Good morning, sir. How is it going?" Sergeant Gilbert asked, and smiled showing Crest advertisement teeth.

"Is that Colonel Breakheart out there?" General Geise's voiced reverberated from his office. "Tell him to get his ass in here."

Breakheart smiled at the sergeant, shaking his blond head in mirth. "I'm on my way, sir," he yelled back.

Walking through the door to Geise's office, he found himself looking at both generals sitting on the sofa drinking coffee. A major, who he did not recognize, sat in one of the overstuffed leather chairs across from them.

"Cuda, this is Major Collins. He's the head of Base NIS. I thought it would be a good idea for him to be in on this briefing. Is that a problem? Do we break any safety investigation rules?" Major General Geise stated and asked in one loud burst.

"No, it isn't a problem and no, we don't break any rules," Breakheart answered, and stuck his hand out to the Major. "Nice meeting you. Wish it were under different circumstances."

Major Collins rose from his seat and took Breakheart's hand. "Nice meeting you as well, sir."

The two junior officers sat took their seats facing the two generals. Separating the four men, china coffee cups and saucers sat on a highly polished table with a silver decanter filled with black coffee. General Geise leaned forward and poured himself a cup of Maxwell's best and offered the decanter around the table. Once each man had a cup in their hand, Geise opened the briefing.

"Well, Cuda. What do you have? Last night's call sounded like we've got more than just an accident. Anything more to report?"

"No, not really. Lieutenant Colonel Burns, Snake, and I talked about what might have happened for a couple of hours last night, but we couldn't come up with anything but sabotage." Breakheart paused momentarily, "I hope talking to Burns wasn't a problem?

There is no one in the Harrier community who knows more about the airplane than Snake."

"Hell no, it's not a problem," Geise answered. "I've known Snake longer than you have, for Christ sake. We flew F-4s together back in '67. If you want his help on the side, do it."

"Thanks. Anyway, we both agree the seat was correctly installed in Zero Zero, and somebody tampered with it afterwards. The big question is why. I just can't fathom anyone deliberately disabling an ejection seat."

"Probably some disgruntled Marine who feels he has a grudge against officers," Brigadier General Blake interrupted. "We'll more than likely never find the guy."

"Don't be too sure of that," Major Collins interjected. "I'm putting my best agents on this case, and if there is something to uncover, they will."

"Well, let's hope so," Geise boomed.

"I've got a theory rolling around in my head," Breakheart said. "I think we'll know more on the who, once we find out why the plane went down. If a major aircraft system was tampered with prior to Jack's flight, then it isn't just sabotage, it's murder. If the malfunction was strictly one of those things that can happen to an aircraft, then General Blake may be right."

"When will you know?" Geise asked.

"I can't answer your question yet, sir," Breakheart answered. "If I can get the bird out of the field, and we get lucky, maybe in a couple of weeks. It all depends on what we can determine from the wreckage. I've got my team moving some of the larger parts of the plane here on base today, but it could be several days or weeks before all the bits and pieces are in 203's hangar. Once I can start sorting through which systems were good or bad, then I'll have more information for you."

"Has any word gotten out about the seat?" General Blake asked.

"No," a pause, "I don't think so. I told my team to keep it under wraps. Still, the Harrier community is going to be clamoring for information about the seat. We have got to tell them something."

"I'll take care of that," General Geise stated flatly. "I'll talk to the Group Commander. We'll concoct a tale which should pacify the squadrons for the time being."

"Thank you, sir. I appreciate that. It will take some of the heat off of me and my board."

"One more thing," Geise interrupted Breakheart. "I called the NADEP's commanding officer and asked him to assign you an engineering liaison. I thought it might help to have one of theirs on call anytime you might need something."

"That's great, and could help me hurry things through while I'm working with the civilians. Do you have any idea who it might be? I'm going to the NADEP directly from here."

"No," answered Geise in his thundering voice. "But when you check in at the front reception area, he'll be waiting for you, or at least only a phone call away. In that vein, is it all right with you for Major Collins or his representative to tag along with you on the investigation?"

Breakheart thought for a moment. "Yes, I suppose so. Just so long as they don't hinder the investigators with questions they can't answer yet. I know we are on the same team, but I've got to find out why the bird crashed. That's my primary job."

"We won't get in your way, I assure you," Collins said. "However, it goes without saying, I expect you to provide any information which might lead to the saboteur."

"Of course," Breakheart responded.

"Is there anything else we need to discuss?" Geise asked. The room was silent for the first time since Breakheart entered. "Okay then, let's get cracking."

General Geise stood, and the others followed. Major Collins walked to the door and held it for Breakheart.

"Check six," Blake laughed, as Breakheart's back disappeared through the oak jamb.

The stupid bastard, Breakheart thought. He thinks he's so cute. Check six meaning he'd shot Breakheart down, or turned onto his tail without his knowledge. One day, I will fly against him and then he'll eat humble pie for the rest of his tour at Cherry Point.

Ten minutes later, after explaining to Major Collins that he would be in the NADEP's seat shop and his agents should meet him there, Breakheart was walking up to the glass, double doors of the main building of the NADEP complex.

NADEP, one of the largest Navy and Marine Corps' aircraft rework facilities, could perform every detail of maintenance on a Harrier short of actually building one from scratch. The military-industrial complex, known as the NADEP was a maze of buildings, hangars, work spaces, and manufacturing plants which spread over several square miles on MCAS Cherry Point. Although commanded by a Marine Colonel with only a small contingent of Marines, both officer and enlisted, the massive complex employed well over a thousand civilians. Almost a third of the surrounding private economy depended, in one form or another, on the NADEP. It provided jobs for workers from as far as seventy-five miles away. Viewed by one unfamiliar with its capabilities, the NADEP was awesome in every respect.

Immediately upon entering, Breakheart turned right and walked rapidly to the reception desk. He told the corporal behind the glass enclosed cage who he was, and that he needed a security badge. The corporal nodded politely, and informed Breakheart they had been expecting him. He passed him a plastic covered badge, with blue striping, and asked him to please wait for Ms. Zaffke, his liaison.

Breakheart walked to one of the several-straight backed chairs in the reception area and sat. *Lord Almighty, I'm going to be stuck with a woman engineer,* he thought. *What next?* Several minutes passed, long enough for him to begin squirming in his chair when a woman, who appeared to be in her mid-thirties, walked up to introduce herself.

Breakheart was caught completely off guard. He was expecting an overbearing woman mannishly dressed to help show her defiance and worth in the work-a-day, man dominated NADEP. What stood before him now was a beautiful woman, dressed appropriately for her function as a liaison within the confines of the working spaces of an industrial complex. Combed neatly, her brown hair casually touched her shoulders, framing a face any model would envy. The facial features reflected a woman of twenty or forty…ageless, and the blue eyes shining brightly from her suntanned face, radiated intelligence. Perhaps an inch shorter than his five foot eight inches, Breakheart could only guess what her figure might be, for she wore a loose fitting blouse and slacks. Her shoes were non gender, just good walking support. He stood, a bit shaken, as she offered him her hand.

"Colonel Breakheart, I presume. I'm Sena Zaffke."

"Please call me Dan, Ms. Zaffke. It is very nice to meet you," Breakheart managed to stutter. "Have you been briefed on where I want to go this morning?"

"I understand you want to talk to the engineers in the seat shop," Sena stated in a strong, but very feminine voice, pushing a wisp of her brown hair from over her right eye. "Shall we go?"

Breakheart rose and followed the lovely women out the double doors and across the street to a red brick building. Inside they were met by two gentlemen dressed in slacks and sport shirts. During the introductions, a Gunnery and a Staff Sergeant from NIS joined the group.

For the next two hours, Breakheart examined and discussed, with the engineers, the ejection seat Colonel Adams had tried to ride to safety. It was clearly evident sabotage had taken place. Apparently, the backrest cushion had been removed along with the survival pack which acted as the actual seat for the pilot. Once these were out of the way, a hole, two inches square, had been carefully cut in the metal back of the seat. This had provided admittance to the complicated working parts which regulated the seat's firing. The hole, though small, was large enough for whoever had done the tampering to attach the safety clip on the first stage rocket firing mechanism. Once the clip was in place, the ejection handle had been removed and the twin stainless steel cables, which would normally fire the rockets, were cut. The opening had then been carefully filed smooth and spray painted black. To the untrained eye, should anyone check, the seat's black metal back would appear normal in all respects. Having dearmed the seat, the survival pack and backrest cushion had been reinstalled and the ejection handle replaced. The seat would show no irregularities during a preflight by a pilot or plane captain. It had been conscientiously executed by someone who had knowledge of the seat, or at the very least, access to the detailed maintenance publications held by the squadron.

The NIS agents agreed with Breakheart…it had to be someone attached to VMAT-203. Though there were hundreds of men at Cherry Point who might have the knowledge necessary to accomplish the task, it would be highly unlikely they could have spent the time necessary to sabotage the seat without being challenged. Squadron maintenance personnel, they acknowledge, were much too protective of their airplanes to allow a man from another unit mess with them unattended. The agents left the meeting to begin their investigation at 203's hanger, while Breakheart instructed the engineers to keep their findings quiet. With assurance by the seat shop's engineers that not a word would get on the street, Breakheart and Sena took their leave as well.

"Why on earth would anyone dearm an ejection seat?" Sena asked with disbelief, as they waited to cross the street to the main entrance of the NADEP.

"I have no idea, but I can guarantee you one thing; I'm going to find out." Breakheart answered. During the past two hours, he had paid close attention to everything he had been told, but in the back of his mind he was very aware of Sena's presence. "There has got to be more to this than meets the eye. If you truly wanted to have an ejection seat fail, you would have to know it was going to be used. I mean, think about it. How many Harrier ejections occur in a year? Two? Three? No, something stinks about this whole thing. Do you have any ideas?" He turned to face the woman next to him.

"Me? I haven't a clue," Sena stated flatly. "But I sure hope you nail the bastard."

Breakheart smiled at her comment. They had reached the glass doors, and he stretched forward to open it for her. "I hope I do, too! By the way, how do I get in touch with you?"

Sena reached into her pants pocket and handed Breakheart a business card. "My office number is on the card. Please, call anytime you need my help. If I'm not in, I'll leave word where I'll be."

"What about your home number?" He asked, holding the card out to her.

Sena smiled at Breakheart, and took the card from his hand and wrote her home phone beside the office number. "Why, Colonel, are you trying to get classified information from me? I don't normally give my home number out to just anyone."

Breakheart laughed lightly. "Yeah, I can understand that, but I might have some overtime for you when we get the engine back here."

The smile which spread across Sena's face seemed to radiate enough heat to be felt on Breakheart's face. He smiled back, trying to produce an award winning Kevin Costner grin. She returned the card and started to move through the door. Breakheart gently touched her arm.

"Please. This may sound like I'm coming on a bit strong, but would you like to go sailing on Saturday? Hancock Creek Yacht Club is hosting a regatta, and I'm entered." He stopped short when he saw the rejecting look on the woman's face. "Look, my three boys will be sailing with us so you don't have to worry about me hitting too hard on you."

Sena's expression softened. She thought a moment and said, "Yes, I think that might be fun. Call me with the details tonight." She smiled again and disappeared into the huge building, leaving Breakheart with the feeling he'd just asked her to his first prom at Sarasota High.

Shaking off the sensation, he headed for the parking lot. Twenty minutes later he parked the Firebird in front of a yellow one-story home not unlike his own. Similar to his, the house was located on the Neuse River. Built in the nineteen fifties, the rambler was shaded with mammoth live oaks; their branches reaching over the roof providing summer shade. Pines, over a hundred years old, stood throughout the large yard, dropping needles to be raked in piles each fall. The yard was well cared for, something Breakheart could not boast. He tended to let his boys care for their yard, and it always looked less than impressive. A sign, with three inch block lettering and attached to a two-foot pipe, stood in the middle of the yard. The name in black, block letters read COL. J. B. ADAMS. Someone had draped the sign with black ribbon, which blew lightly in the breeze with a slight sighing sound.

Breakheart could hear the soft cloth over the cooing of mockingbirds nesting in the oaks. This was the elite of officer country, where the builders had not destroyed the esthetic beauty Nature provided. Junior officer's quarters were more like tract houses, where trees and all other vegetation had been scraped from the ground. It made for easier building, but even now, forty some years later, the trees and shrubs looked stunted in comparison to the magnificence of this section of officer housing.

Breakheart recognized several of the cars parked in the driveway. They belonged to men like himself…officers in the brotherhood of flying jet fighters. More than likely, he thought, the wives were using the automobiles this day. The women hovered around a fallen comrade's wife like bees stripping spring flowers of their pollen. It was the way of things; a natural support group to help the wife of a dead husband cope with the trauma of death. Marine Corps wives stuck together much as their husbands did, and it was at times such as these they were at their very best.

Getting out of his car, straightening his fore and aft cover on his head, an action he seemed to do unthinkingly, Breakheart thought the women cared for each other differently than the men did. Pilots went to the bar and toasted a fallen friend, with beer or whiskey, saying good bye to him by laughing an afternoon away in remembrance of his abilities and good qualities. Women, consoled each other. Both systems worked their magic…removing the hurt and emptiness.

Breakheart knocked on the door, which was answered immediately by Mrs. Geise. She smiled in recognition and invited him in. He removed his cover and stepped into the foyer. He could see several women sitting in the expansive living room. The atmosphere was subdued, but not quiet. Conversation, though muted, could be heard. From his right, coming down the hall leading to the bedrooms, Sally Adams walked swiftly into Dan's arms.

"I'm so glad to see you, Dan," Sally said with conviction.

"Are you okay?" Dan asked, pushing her gently away so he could look squarely into her eyes.

"Yes. No. Hell I'm about as screwed up as a person can get. I just can't accept that Jack is gone. It's not fair. It's just not fair." She hugged Dan closely again, tears welling at the corner of her blue eyes. "He was such a good pilot; even you have told me he was a good pilot. What happened?"

"Sally," again Breakheart pushed her gently away. "I don't know yet, but you can be rest assured I'll find out, and when I do, I will be honest with you. No cover up to make you feel better. I'll tell you the truth."

"Oh Dan, "Sally stepped back a step, "I know you will. I'm so glad you are conducting the investigation. I trust you."

"I'm sorry I haven't been over to see you sooner," Breakheart said quietly. "I've been tied up with the accident. This is the first chance I've had."

"I know, Dan, and I understand. I'll be okay. You just find out what in hell happened to Jack. That will be the best thing anyone can do for me now."

"Thanks for understanding, "Breakheart said.

Sally took his arm and lead Breakheart into the kitchen. "Do you want a cup of coffee or something? Lord knows there is enough food, cakes, and cookies to feed an army."

"No, thank you," Breakheart answered, looking at the mountain of casseroles and sweets lining every square inch of kitchen counter space. Sally wouldn't have to cook for a month, he thought. "I can't stay. I've got to get back to the field. I just wanted to look in on you, and to ask if there is anything in the world I can do?"

"No, I'll be okay. Just find out what happened. Will you be at the memorial service tomorrow? General Geise is going to give the eulogy."

"Of course, I'll be there," Breakheart said sadly. "You can count on it." He walked to Sally once more and took her in his arms. "I know it isn't much consolation, but remember Jack died doing what he loved doing most in this world. He loved to fly, and there is no better way to go than at the controls…if it has got to be. You know all of us, those who strap on jets, would rather die with our hand on the stick than die of a prolonged bout with cancer or something equally as terrible."

Sally smiled a thin smile up at Breakheart. "Dan, you are an incurable lout, but I love you anyway. There is nothing romantic about death, no matter how it comes."

Breakheart hung his head slightly, "I know, but if you fly, you have to look at death that way or you would never start the engine."

"Christ, I know!" Sally said, with an exasperated tone. "I lived with a jet jock for twenty-two years. Now, go on, get out of here and find out what happened to my Jack." She gave Breakheart a soft shove toward the front door.

Breakheart did not resist the shove, but grabbed Sally's hand and squeezed it knowingly. "I'll see you tomorrow if I can," he said, and walked to the door.

Sally watched him for a moment then said, "Wait a minute, Dan."

Breakheart stopped and turned to face her once more.

"Before you go, will you please make a point to stop by when I get back from the funeral. We are going to bury Jack in Arlington, so I won't be home until next Tuesday, but I need to talk to you about something. Something I don't understand."

"Of course I'll be here, and if you need anything before then, just ask. If I'm not home, leave a message with one of my boys. I'll get it. I'm truly sorry I won't be able to make the funeral, but I have to keep on this thing."

"I know, and thanks," Sally said and turned back into the kitchen, hiding the tears beginning to run in tiny rivulets down her cheeks. She knew Dan would do everything he possibly could, and of all the men she and her husband had known over the years, he could be counted on to do as he said.

Breakheart stepped into the sunshine, a heavy sigh escaping from his lips as he jammed his piss cutter back on his head. "Shit," he said aloud, addressing the pines and oaks, "shit, shit, shit!" He took long strides to his car, yanked the door open hard, and climbed in. I'll solve this thing if it is the last thing I do, he thought as he raced much too fast down Jefferson Street.

SEVEN

Breakheart pulled the black Firebird to the road's shoulder, near where the pavement ended. A Marine corporal stood in front of him not more than twenty feet ahead, a night stick in hand. The young man was dressed in camouflage utilities, the standard work day uniform…guarding the entrance into the crash site. Getting out of his car, Breakheart walked briskly toward the man.

"Good afternoon, sir," the corporal saluted crisply.

"Corporal," Breakheart replied politely, returning the salute. "Hotter'n than the hinges of hell out here, isn't it?"

"That's for sure, sir," the young man said, glad to have a chance to talk to someone. He'd been standing in the burning afternoon sun for almost two hours, and was bored beyond tears.

"Has everything been okay?" Breakheart asked. "The chow been eatable?"

"Yes, sir, everything has been fine. I've even won a few dollars at the nightly poker game. How much longer do you think we'll be here?"

"I'm not sure. We'll know more by this evening. Keep up the good work." Breakheart broke off the conversation and began walking toward Major Dyke, who was approaching at a near trot.

"Welcome back to hell's furnace," Major Dyke grinned, a bit out of breath, and wiped the sweat from his brow. "Glad you could make it out this afternoon. We have something rather interesting. Private Timms reported he'd found a good size hunk of the engine in the ditch the second day out. He plotted it and moved on, but when he heard we were really scouting for engine parts he thought I might want to examine it personally this morning. I had Sergeant Reddock examine it as well, and he tells me it comes from the right side of the engine, and includes the fuel control."

"Fan-fucking-tastic," Breakheart could not hide his elation. "Where is it located?"

"In the ditch, not far from where we found Colonel Adams. There is something interesting about the location. It looks like someone was digging around and under the engine after it was located by the private, and there are brown stains on the soil under it. Timms swears he didn't disturb anything while he took his plot. Of course, the stains could be hydraulic fluid, but there are no apparent drips of red fluid from the engine. One of the troops suggested it looked like blood. I think you should have a look."

Breakheart thought for a moment, digesting what he had just been told. "Have you removed the fuel control from the engine section yet?"

"No, I thought I had better wait until you had a chance to have a look. I figured you would be out here this afternoon."

"Right. Let's have a look."

The two men started moving for the ditch. As they stepped off the road, Breakheart noticed a Marine kicking the left front tire of a HUM-V, a vehicle much like an over grown Chevy Blazer. He touched Major Dyke's arm and paused in mid step, then walked up to the brown and grey vehicle.

The private who had been kicking the tire was now opening the hood. "What seems to be the problem, Marine?" Breakheart asked.

The surprised man wheeled on his heel and saluted at the same time, almost gouging his eye out in the process. Breakheart found it difficult repressing a grin, but maintained a stoic posture.

"Sir, "the fuck'n fucker's fucked," the private blurted out.

"Say again," Breakheart asked, and this time could not repress the smile.

"Sir, I say again, the fuck'n fucker's fucked." The young Marine stood at ridged attention.

"Can you unfuck it?" Breakheart was finding it very difficult not laughing out loud.

"Yes, sir, I think so."

"Well then, carry on," Breakheart said, turning so the Marine would not see him laughing.

He rejoined Major Dyke and told him what had just transpired. "Only in the Marine Corps could someone develop an entire sentence using the word 'fuck'," Breakheart said as he chuckled. "A very descriptive sentence at that."

They continued across the field and entered the ditch. Walking was not as laborious as it had been the last time Breakheart had been in the bean field. The sun, though roasting the Marines working in the field, had sucked the wetness from the ground like a sponge. The earth was not yet dry, but at least you didn't sink to your knees with each step. Breakheart surveyed the far reaches of the plowed course and nodded approvingly. Marines were moving with determination, gathering bits and pieces of metal and hunks of airplane. Two flatbed trucks stood near the dark hole, one partially loaded. He saw the cherry picker looming over the burnt gash of the hole, its operator lifting what appeared to be a large portion of the aft fuselage. The brown and grey paint of the Harrier was covered with black, oozing mud which dripped in globs back into the crater. Far across the field's expanse, a group of six Marines were struggling with the first stage fan section of the engine. They had rigged a skid, looking very much like a sled used by children after a big snow fall, and were breaking their backs pulling it across the muddy earth.

"You've been busy, Bill," Breakheart complimented Major Dyke. "Have you got any idea how soon you'll have everything out of the field?"

"I think we'll have all the important parts back at the Point by tomorrow afternoon. It will take a week to clean up the smaller pieces, maybe longer."

"Good work. My God, it is hot out here. Have the troops got plenty of water?"

"Yes, sir. I had Gunny Hicks place five, twenty gallon water igloos around the field so the troops have ready access to water all day. We are refilling them three times a day."

As Major Dyke finished speaking, they arrived at the broken engine. Two Marines stood near by, watching over the find.

"I thought it best to have it guarded," Major Dyke answered the questioning look on Breakheart's face. "If someone did tamper with it earlier, I didn't want to give him another chance."

Breakheart nodded his approval, and squatted before the engine. He carefully examined the entire section, careful not to disturb any of the moving parts. When satisfied with the exterior exam, he motioned for the two Marines to help him turn it on its side.

"Holy shit, you weren't kidding, it does look as if someone has been digging. This indentation wasn't caused by the engine, that's for sure."

"Yes, sir, and do you see the dark stains?" the Major asked, kneeling down beside the colonel.

"Yeah. That's damned peculiar. I don't understand. What could have cause them? Certainly not JP-5, and you're right, there is no hydraulic fluid dripping from the engine. I don't think there are any hydraulic lines near this section of the engine anyway. So what could it be."

"Like I said, sir, one of the troops suggested it might be blood. But that doesn't make any sense at all."

Breakheart stood and stared into the distance. He said nothing for several moments, then abruptly made up his mind. "Bill, get on the horn and radio back to the squadron. Have the Duty Officer get in touch with Major Collins at NIS and tell him to get his agents out here ASAP, like before dark. I don't give a damn if they have to use a Military Police escort, I want them here and I want them now! Also, have them tell Collins I want a forensic specialist from NIS or the hospital."

Major Dyke stepped back a pace at the flurry of orders his boss was giving. "Jumping Jesus Christ, Colonel, you think this might suggest foul play, or something?"

"I'm not suggesting anything," Breakheart answered in a voice wrapped in iron. "I just don't want to pass up any evidence involving this accident. Now, please, get the message out."

Major Dyke took off at a high port, jogging through the ditch for the base camp. Breakheart turned his attention back to the engine. His mind was spinning. From the beginning, he had suppressed the inauspicious feeling rumbling like a dark gargoyle through his mind. Now the hair on the back of his neck prickled with foreboding. This was not right, something did not register correctly. The ejection seat was bad enough, but if this was blood, human blood…?

Two hours slowly sweltered by before Breakheart heard the wailing of sirens. He'd bent over the engine section for thirty minutes, just staring at the unless hunk of metal, hoping it would speak to him subliminally. He could find no answers either rational or irrational to explain his anxiety. In fact, he decided, he wasn't even sure what he feared. Disappointed in his ability to find a solution to the disturbed engine or the dark stains, he returned to the base camp.

The wailing of the sirens found him sitting under the shade of a tarpaulin the troops had stretched between a truck and three spare tent poles. No one had bothered him, for his expression said clearly to leave well enough alone. Now two Military Police cars slid to a stop at the entrance to the camp, and Breakheart rose to meet them. He noticed Major Collins had joined his enlisted agents, as four car doors opened simultaneously.

"Thanks for responding," Breakheart called to Collins.

"No sweat, Colonel. What have you got for us?" Major Collins said, cutting his salute sharply.

"I'm not sure, but I want you to have a look at it before we move anything. It's a section of the engine located over there." Breakheart pointed down the ditch. "We think it was tampered with before any of the accident board had a chance to view the area. It looks to me as if someone moved it to dig a shallow hole, and in the hole are some stains which should not be there. I wanted your people to have a look before we haul the engine segment out of the field and back to the Point."

Breakheart spoke as he walked, now passing the men beside the police vehicles, and the group stepped off with him for the ditch.

"Did you bring someone from forensic?" Breakheart asked.

"No, sir. We don't have forensic capability at Cherry Point. I did call the hospital before we left. The pathology lab assured me they could analyze soil samples for us, and explained to the Gunny how to go about collecting them. I'll send samples to Washington for a more detailed examination, if it becomes necessary."

Clearly disappointed, Breakheart said, "Yeah, okay. Shit! I was hoping to have someone here to tell me what the stain is right now. No matter, do your best."

They arrived at the site, and the team began filling small plastic bags with the soil surrounding the engine. The sun was fast dipping for the horizon, and the entire group standing grimly around the chunk of Harrier engine knew there was little time to waste.

"Sir?" the gunnery sergeant from NIS asked? "Can we move the debris and get samples from underneath the engine now?"

"Sure, go ahead," Breakheart answered. "Be careful though. I still have some investigative work to accomplish on it."

"Yes, sir, we'll be careful," the gunny said, and turned back to his task.

It took an hour for the NIS team to collect soil and comparative fluid samples from the engine. They were thorough; Breakheart would give them that. They had dusted the entire engine section, raising a variety of finger prints. These could be checked easily enough with military records. Hopefully, a set would be found which should not be there. When they finished, the group retired to the base camp. Marines were drifting in from the field, and some were even heading for the make shift shower set up in the rear of the camp. Gunny Hicks was one of the men heading for the shade of the camp.

"Gunny Hicks," Breakheart yelled. He had caught a glimpse of the approaching figure as he had stepped out of the muddy field. "Can you get the engine section out of the ditch and loaded for a trip to the Point tonight?"

"Yes, sir. I'll take care of it personally. Anything else the Colonel need?"

"No, not tonight. And, Gunny, thanks. I appreciate your help."

Gunny Hicks turned and retraced his steps back down the dirt road. He stopped the flatbed driver just as he was starting his big diesel for the trip back to the base. He yelled at the driver to move his rig down to the ditch and wait for another load. The driver nodded, and slipped the big truck into gear.

Breakheart watched the gunny for a moment then turned to face the two majors by his side. "Bill, we'll hold the board's evening meeting at my quarters tonight. Same time, twenty-one hundred. Major Collins, I would very much like it if you would join us."

"Why your quarters?" Major Dyke asked with a perplexed look.

"Because I don't want the off chance of anyone hearing our conversation. I know my house is secure from eavesdropping. Is there a problem?"

"No, sir. I just wondered. I'll pass the word to the team. Anything else?"

"No, that will be all. What about you Major Collins, can you make it?"

"No problem. I'll be there. You live on base, don't you?"

"Yeah. Here, I'll give you the address." Breakheart took a notebook from his breast pocket and scribbled down the address and passed it to Major Collins. "I'll see you at twenty-one hundred."

"Yes, sir," Collins said, and returned to his waiting car.

Left alone, Breakheart looked westward into the setting sun. Carolina sunsets are some of the most spectacular in the world, he thought. Colors blazed the horizon. Purple, pale oranges, reds, and lavenders ran like wheel spokes from the crescent top of the sun, which now looked so close he could reach out and touch its fire. I've got to get home, he thought. I haven't seen the boys for so long I can't remember what they look like.

As the sun disappeared into its void, Breakheart's Firebird hummed deeply, its engine a well-tuned mastery of today's technology. Breakheart was not driving fast; he held the speed limit of fifty-five. As he approached the town of Maribel, he slowed. There were three Highway Patrol cars sitting on the embankment just short of a bridge. As he accelerated on the other side of the overpass, he wondered what the problem might have been, then promptly forgot all about it, as his mind drifted to more pleasant thoughts…Sena Zaffke.

It was well past 1900 when the Firebird pulled into his driveway. Turning off the engine, his face twisted into dismay. From his house, a stereo blasted hard rock music loud enough to wake the dead. How many times do I have to tell them, he thought, as he walked to the front door. As he entered, the blast of noise damn near took his ears off his head. He removed his cover, threw it on the foyer table, then strode for the den.

"Turn that damned thing down," Breakheart screamed above the din. "You'll blow the speakers out. Besides, I'm sure the neighbors are not enjoying your choice of music as much as you seem to."

Three boys moved at once. They had been sprawled in various positions throughout the den, and now each tried to reach the stereo's controls at once.

"Hey, Dad," Bill yelled. "We didn't think you were going to be home tonight."

"Obviously!" Breakheart yelled, just as the music volume reached a whisper. His voice echoed through the entire house. "That's better. How many times have I got to tell you not to play that crap you call music so loud? You would think you were all deaf, or at least that's what you are going to be if you don't turn it down."

"Oh, Dad," Rod Breakheart pretended to whine. The youngest of Dan's sons, having just turned fourteen, was grinning at his father. "We didn't think you were coming home again tonight."

"Well, I'm home," Breakheart said, feigning anger. "Have you all had supper?" It was always hard to stay mad at his boys, but they sometimes exasperated him beyond tolerance. "If not, let's see what we can whip up." He started for the kitchen.

"Pops, we have had our supper already…macaroni and cheese," Steve Breakheart said. Tall for his age, standing five foot eleven and only fifteen, he was the cut up of the crew…always joking and teasing his father. He knew his dad hated it, but he knew he could get away with calling Breakheart, Pops. "But I'll give you hand making yours," he offered.

"Thanks. I'll just make a sandwich," Breakheart answered, continuing to the kitchen. As he disappeared, the stereo was turned off and the TV on.

Breakheart made himself a ham sandwich, popped a beer and rejoined the young men watching a movie which appeared to have at least thirty shooting deaths every five minutes.

"Guys, I've got a meeting here at nine o'clock. Do you mind making yourselves scarce for about thirty minutes when they arrive?" Breakheart asked, during a commercial break.

"What's up, Dad?" Bill asked. "You don't ever have meetings here." Bill ran his fingers through his longish hair. He would have liked it longer, but Breakheart would have none of it. 'You can have it down to your toes as far as I'm concerned, but not until you're out of this house,' his father had told him a thousand times.

"It has to do with the accident investigation. I'm sorry, but I'll need the den for just awhile. By the way, would you like to attend Colonel Adams' memorial service tomorrow?"

The boys glanced at each other, seeking approval from each another. They had known Jack Adams most of their lives, and gone to school with his children.

"Yes, sir," Bill answered, seriously. "I think we would all like to attend. Right?" He looked at the other two youngsters and received affirmative nods. "Will you pick us up, or should I take the 'Yellow Terror'."

"You had better plan on driving yourselves," Breakheart said, as he stood to answer the knock on the front door. "Now, disappear for a little while."

The boys groaned, but left the room, turning the TV off behind them. As they retired to their rooms, Breakheart opened the door for Major Collins.

The rest of the board arrived shortly after Collins, and Breakheart offered beers around. They sat in the darkly paneled den, which was Breakheart's 'I love me' room. The far wall was covered with plaques and awards Dan had received over the years since being awarded his wings. The wall looked like it belonged in a museum.

"All right, Major Dyke, where in hell is Hamilton?" Breakheart asked after everyone was settled.

"I don't know. In fact, no one has seen him since yesterday afternoon. I've tried his BOQ room a half a dozen times since we returned from the crash site tonight…no luck."

"None of us have seen him, sir," Captain Borgerding stated. "It isn't like him not to show up. He's always very dependable."

"Shit!" Breakheart said aloud. "What else can go wrong?" He paused briefly, then asked Collins, "Have you got anything yet from the hospital?"

"Yes, sir, I have. It seems the stain under the engine is blood… human blood. The odd thing is, it is not Colonel Adams' blood. The Colonel's blood type is O-negative, what we found was A-positive." There was an audible sucking of breath throughout the room, as Collins paused to let his words sink home. "We've sent the prints we lifted off the engine to Washington, but we probably won't have information back on them until sometime next week."

"Bull shit! I want them by close of business Friday. I'll talk to General Geise about it, if you can't convince them in the almighty Washington arena. Get back with their Duty Officer tonight."

"Yes, sir," Collins answered, not at all sure he could force Washington to do anything, or could Geise for that matter. Washington worked at its own pace…slowly!

"All right, I'm going to bring all of you up to date with what I know. Again, I remind you, nothing leaves this room. As far as I am concerned, what you hear tonight is classified top secret. If there is a leak, I'm going to hang the son of a bitch from the highest rafter in 203's hanger. Understood?" If the press got a hold on this information the shit would hit the fan for the big time. If that happens, we'll never get to the bottom of this thing. Every Tom, Dick, and Harry would be screaming for somebody's blood." He paused, letting the words register his concerns. "Okay then."

Breakheart spent the next half hour bringing the board members up to speed on the ejection seat. How it had definitely been sabotaged, and the method by which it was accomplished. Giving the rational he and the NIS agents had discussed earlier, he suggested the saboteur was more than likely attached to VMAT-203. He finished by telling them about the findings under the engine section.

"There you have it. We have more than just an accident, but we won't be able to pin point the reason someone tampered with the seat until we find the reason the bird went down. If we discover the accident was caused by additional sabotage, then we may have a murder on our hands as well. He paused, lost in thought for a moment. "Major Dyke, I want you to assign someone from VMA-542's maintenance department to lay out the remains of Double Nuts in the hanger. I'll talk to both your CO and Lieutenant Colonel Jones over at 542, so they will be expecting your call."

Bill Dyke nodded his understanding. If someone had tampered with the engine in the field, Breakheart didn't want to provide him another opportunity in the hangar.

"Finally, I want Hamilton found, or I'll declare him AWOL, and put up on charges. So I suggest one of you guys," he glared at the three captains seating straight backed before him, "find him tonight."

A chorus of "yes, sirs" followed.

"Okay, then! At fifteen hundred tomorrow there will be the memorial service for Colonel Adams. Any one of you who wish to attend, feel free to do so. But, remember, I want the bulk of the crash sitting in the hangar by tomorrow night. Is there anything else?"

"Yes, sir." It was Major Dyke. "What about this weekend. Are we going to work through Saturday and Sunday?"

"No! Not if we can get most of the major hunks of bird in the hanger by tomorrow night, we won't. If not…we'll see. For sure I want to get as many of the troops out of the field as possible. They rate a few hours of liberty. However, we'll still have to maintain a security watch at the site until we have every scrap of airplane out of the field and into the hangar. Have Gunny Hicks decide who he wants to send home on Friday night, and arrange for their transportation."

"Yes, sir, I'll do that," Dykes replied.

"Another thing. I would prefer to have the same men back in the field on Monday. They are all familiar with what is going on, and it will make it easier to finish the cleanup."

"Got it," Major Dyke said, as he scribbled in a small notebook.

Breakheart rummaged through a drawer in the den's coffee table, pulling out a pack of cigarettes. The pack, half empty, looked like as if it had been around for several weeks. He took a Doral Light 100 from the battered pack and placed it in the corner of his mouth. "Been trying to quit," he said to the men in front of him. "Hardest thing I've ever done, and after today I don't know if I want to stop." He took a deep drag and exhaled slowly. "God that tastes good!"

"Dad, are you smoking?" A yell from Bill's room reverberated through the large house. "I can smell it clear back here."

Major Dyke laughed, along with the others. "With that statement, sir, I think we'll take our leave. Will you be at the site in the morning?"

"Not right away. I want to review the recording Twilight made of Colonel Adams' last few transmissions, and I will want to supervise the layout of the bird in the hangar. We'll see, but don't expect me. If I don't show, I'm sure you'll handle everything fine. Check with the Squadron Duty Officer about tomorrow night's meeting. If we don't meet in the evening, then expect to get together at oh-dark-sparrow-fart Monday morning."

The men were standing and on the way out as Breakheart gave his last directive for the night. He said his goodbyes and yelled to the boys the all clear. It took them about three seconds to reenter the den and turn on the TV. By the time Breakheart had cleaned the empty Bud's from the tables, they were already deeply engrossed in the remainder of their shoot'em up movie.

Breakheart retired to his bedroom. The queen sized bed with its maroon bedspread looked inviting, but lonely. Tara, his wife had been gone a couple of years, and though there had been plenty of women in his life since her departure, this room still had an empty air about it. He sat on the bed and removed his grimy, accident investigating boots, and stripped the sweaty flight suit from his tired body. He emptied the multiple flight suit pockets and threw the contents on a night stand. Gathering his dirty clothes, he padded into the bathroom and threw flight suit, skivvies, dirty socks, and T-shirt into the hamper next to the shower stall, then reached through the open door and turned the water on. As he slipped under the fine, hot spray of the shower, his mind drifted to Tara.

They had been married eighteen years, and during the union, produced the best things in his life…the boys. However, the last five or six years together had been like living in a private hell. In the end, they had run out of compromises regarding almost everything involving their lives together. When the final confrontation came, in a drunken stupor, she slapped him and told him she was leaving.

He had helped her pack! She did not want custody of their sons, and told him so. That had been just fine. Her not wanting their boys relieved him of a legal battle. Still, she had wiped him out financially. Something for which he would never forgive her, nor the court judges who allow such lopsided, illogical allotments. He was lonely for a meaningful and lasting relationship, but was not ready to leap at just any woman. In fact, if the truth be known, he didn't trust them, nor their motives for wanting a husband.

He finished his shower, dried and grabbed a clean pair of skivvies from the dresser. Putting on his bulky and comfortable old cotton bathrobe, he retrieved Sena's business card from the small notebook he always carried in his flight suit. The notebook, with its contents lay on the night stand along with a small pocket knife, change, and billfold. He had started for the kitchen when the phone rang.

"Colonel Breakheart's quarters," his son Steve answered…"Yes, sir, I'll get him. Dad! It's for you," he screamed down the hall.

"Thanks, I'll get it in the kitchen," Breakheart yelled back, and barefooted off to pick the phone off its wall hook. "Colonel Breakheart, can I help you?"

"Hey, Cuda. This is General Blake. Just thought I would call and see if you've got anything new to report."

"I'm briefing General Geise in the morning," Dan answered flatly, recognizing the voice immediately.

"Yeah, yeah. I know, but I thought I would call. I've been very curious about this whole affair," Blake said lightly.

"Yes, sir, I understand, but I would prefer not to discuss the accident over the phone. I'm sure you understand." Breakheart was perplexed. Blake had never called his home…ever. Why now?

"Sure, I understand. I'll see you in the morning. Have a good evening," Blake said, and hung up before Breakheart could reply.

"Stupid bastard," Breakheart said aloud. "Why would the good Lord put such a stupid son-of-a-bitch on earth?" He shook his head and dialed 203's CO.

After talking to both 542 and 203's CO's, explaining what he needed in manpower, but not revealing the full details of why, Breakheart went to the cabinet above the sink and retrieved a bottle of Bacardi. He poured himself a stiff drink, mixed the dark rum with diet Coke, and sat down next to the phone. He sat silently for several minutes, sipping the rum drink, then picked up the phone for the fourth time and dialed Sena Zaffky's home number. She answered immediately.

"Hi, it's Dan Breakheart," he answered her hello. "Thought I'd better call before I crash for the evening. I'm sorry it is so late," he said looking at his watch for the first time since he arrived home.

"That's okay. I just got out of the shower. Have you got any more information on who might have sabotaged the seat?"

"No. Not yet, I haven't. I wish I did. But that isn't the reason I called. I wanted to confirm Saturday. Do you still want to race with me and the boys?"

"Sure. I'm looking forward to it. You realize, I've never been on a sailboat before don't you?"

"Not to worry," Breakheart laughed. "The boys and I will do all the hard work. If you want to learn, you'll have some very willing teachers aboard. If not, well, you can just sit back and enjoy the sun and water."

"Sounds fantastic. Should I meet you at your boat or will you pick me up?"

"If you don't mind, could you meet us at the boat? We'll have to get her ready, the boys and I. It would make it easier," Breakheart asked tentatively.

"That's fine. What time and where?" Sena said cheerfully.

"Do you know where the Hancock Boat Docks are?" Breakheart asked.

"Yes, I think so. It is near officers country isn't it?"

"That's right. Just drive from the Main Gate down Roosevelt until you see the sign for the Yacht Club on your right. Then follow the road to the docks. Meet us there around nine-thirty. *Dreamer*, that's the boat's name, is on B-dock. You can't miss it."

"I'll be there, and thanks for the invitation. I'm really looking forward to my first experience at sailing."

"I'm looking forward to it as well," a short pause "having you there, that is," Breakheart said.

"Great. Then I'll see you on Saturday. Good night, and thanks again," Sena answered.

"Good night. Sleep well," Breakheart replied. He heard a soft laugh and the phone went dead. He leaned back on his chair's legs, took a sip from his glass, smiled inwardly, and lit another Doral.

EIGHT

Colonel Breakheart sat quietly in General Geise's office. He'd arrived ten minutes earlier and been escorted directly into the richly paneled room by Staff Sergeant Gilbert. It was 0600, early for morning business to start, even for the Wing Staff. However, General Geise, Breakheart knew, made a habit of arriving in his office sharply at 0530 every morning. The general felt he could accomplish more between 0530 and 0700 than any other time of day, clearing his desk of the mountain of paperwork which gathered daily. Plus, it gave him time to read the morning message board. At 0530, few callers or staff members would interrupt his concentration. Of course, his office staff had to arrive at least an hour before the general. The message board needed to be cleared and updated, the coffee made, and the Wing's Duty Officer debriefed from the prior evening's activities. General Geise commanded over twenty thousand men and women, and he took his responsibilities with serious pride.

Breakheart had purposely picked the early hour to confer with Geise, not so much out of a need to do so as to exclude General Blake. Blake rarely arrived in his office before 0730. By talking with General Geise one on one, Blake would have to be updated secondhand by Geise. It was petty, Breakheart knew, but it gave him a rush of pleasure to rub a bit of salt into Blake's day.

Rolling his overstuffed chair away from the desk, and throwing a pen down on top of the stack of papers covering his desk, General Geise made his acknowledgement of Breakheart's presence. "Sorry to keep you waiting, Cuda. What's up? It must be something important for you to be here this early."

"Yes, sir, I'm afraid it is, and I may need some help from you."

The big general stood, grabbed his coffee cup and silver decanter in both hands and moved to sit across from Breakheart. "Want some coffee?" he asked.

"Yes, thank you," Breakheart answered.

"Staff Sergeant Gilbert," Geise bellowed. "Bring a cup in here for Colonel Breakheart."

The heavy oak door muted Gilbert's "Yes, sir," but it was only seconds before it opened and the good-looking sergeant handed Breakheart a heavy mug. He smiled his thanks, as she backed out of the room, closing the door behind her.

General Geise reached across the table separating them and poured Breakheart a cup of steaming black coffee. "This stuff is thick enough to cut with a knife, but that's the way I like it this early. Makes my heart get going," the general said, in a quieter voice. Now, what have you got?"

Breakheart spent the next fifteen minutes bringing his boss up to date on the events of the day before...leaving nothing out, including the apparent disappearance of Captain Hamilton. Geise listened closely, gathering the information like a sponge.

"Shit, Dan! What have we gotten into here?" General Geise asked when Breakheart had finished. "Sure sounds to me that you have one hell of a lot more on your hands than an accident investigation. Do you need more help?"

"Not yet, but I may in the next couple of days. I don't want to jump to any dire conclusions, and we have Major Collins and his

NIS team working as well. No, let me keep digging. Believe me, if I get over my head, I'll be begging for help."

"Good. Now what's your plan of action. Where do we go from here?" General Geise asked. He wrinkled his forehead in concern, and poured himself another cup of coffee.

"I'm going to review the transmission tape for the morning of Jack's crash at Twilight's radar room this morning. I should have listened to the tape earlier, but I've been so damned busy with the ejection seat, I haven't had a chance. When I'm done there, I hope to start laying out what we have retrieved of the bird on 203's hanger deck."

"All right, Dan, but if anything important turns up, let me know immediately."

"Yes, sir. No problem. However, there is a favor I would ask."

"Ask then. If it is something I can do, then consider it done."

"Major Collins does not think Washington will put any great priority on returning their findings on the fingerprints we sent them. Would you mind throwing your weight behind him to see if they could expedite their findings?"

"I'll give a try. Tell Sergeant Gilbert to get the number from Major Collins on your way out. Anything else?"

"No, I don't think so. At least not now, and thanks for your help. I'm sorry I interrupted your morning routine, but I wanted to bring you up to speed," Breakheart said as he stood to leave.

"You interrupt me any damned time you want too on this matter," General Geise bellowed in a more characteristic manner.

Breakheart took his leave, stopping in the outer office to relay General Geise's message to Staff Sergeant Gilbert. He started for his car, then stopped abruptly when his stomach gave a growl of hunger. Maybe the snack bar is open, he thought, and headed down the long passageway to the small gedunk located at the far end of the building.

"Hey, Cuda," it was Colonel Blain yelling from a flight of stairs leading to the second deck of the headquarters building. He had been recently assigned as the new G-3, replacing Jack Adams.

"Morning, Jim," Breakheart greeted the caller. "What's up?"

"Nothing much, just trying to get settled into my new job. I understand you're doing the investigation on Jack's accident. Anything you can tell me?"

"Not really. I haven't gotten that far into it yet. We are just now getting part of the bird back to the Point."

"Scuttlebutt has it there is something queer going on. Something to do with the ejection seat," Blain pressed.

A cloud passed over Breakheart face. He was thinking someone had leaked information, and he'd kill the bastard. Aloud he said, "Well, we know the seat didn't fire, but we are still trying to find out why." He paused long enough to study Colonel Blain's face. "What have you heard?"

"Like I said, the scuttlebutt around the building is that the seat was meddled with in someway."

"May I ask where you heard the rumor?"

"I'm not really sure," Blain said, pausing to think about the question. He was a tall man, over six feet, and he looked back down on Breakheart. "Why? Is it some big secret, or something?"

"Listen, Jim. Try and squelch rumor control on the seat issue. I don't need a bunch of illogical questions coming from every direction right now. Can you do that for me?"

"Sure, I guess so, but why?"

"Let's just say I have my reasons and leave it at that. I'll fill you in on the details when necessary, but not right now. Okay?"

"Fine with me. It's been good talking with you," Colonel Blain said and started walking for Geise's office.

"Jim," Breakheart stopped him in mid stride, "I'll be up in your office in the next couple of days to rummage through Jack's papers. It's just a routine procedure. You know, I have to be able and discount any work or family problems he might have had. Just part of the accident report."

"I'm sorry, Dan, but all of Jack's things were gone when I took over the office. Everything was cleared out down to the last pencil."

Breakheart's jaw went slack. "Why would anyone do that?" He asked in confusion.

"Hell, how should I know. Is it important?" Blain asked.

"Probably not," Breakheart regained his composure. "Still, would you ask around and find out who stripped the office for me. I'd appreciate it."

"Sure thing. I'll be in touch. Listen I've got to go. The Chief is waiting for me. See you later," Blain said, as he walked off.

"Yeah, later," Breakheart whispered, his mind trying to assimilate yet another anomaly involving Jack's accident.

Breakheart pulled into the parking space reserved for Colonels in front of Base Operations. Under normal circumstances he would have used his own, but Lieutenant Colonel Barry, his replacement as Wing Safety, had a Chevy Van in its place. The gut bomb of an egg and sausage sandwich he'd purchased at the gedunk felt like a lead weight in his stomach. It had been lukewarm and greasy, but he had gobbled it down in just a couple of bites. Now he was paying the price.

Getting out of his car, he straightened his piss cutter and stretched, taking in a deep breath. He could smell the pungent odor of burnt jet fuel. To many it might have been repugnant, but to Dan Breakheart, the raw fragrance was like Carolina low country magnolias. He loved everything about flying, the smells, the noise, and the exhilaration. He walked to the corner of the whitewashed Base Ops for a better view of the airfield.

The first flights of the day were stacking up in the warmup areas, waiting for clearance to take the duty runway. Marine pilots from every squadron had been briefing the early morning launch, and now, like ants encased in camouflaged metal casings, were scurrying for the center mat. Jet engines filled the morning quiet with sound so tangible it could be felt and touched. Breakheart surveyed the huge expanse of concrete and tarmac before him. Harriers were lined up in Warm Up Area One, waiting their turn for the takeoff position, while two A-6s' slammed their throttles to full and began rolling on a section takeoff. At the South Pad, an AV-8 shook the ground beneath it while it hovered motionless at fifty feet…engine roaring. To his left, a C-130 taxied into view, its shear size dwarfing the other aircraft it passed. Just watching the field come alive made the knot in his stomach seem small in comparison to the raw power being displayed all around him. MCAS Cherry Point was open for business for yet another day.

Breakheart stood watching the choreographic wonder of the busy airfield for fifteen minutes. He was caught up in the magnificence and splendor of it all. He thought of the thousands of men it required to run an air station the size of Cherry Point, and the amount of training each man must have to ensure it all functioned smoothly. The sole product was the launching and recovering of jet aircraft, but to fly even one aircraft required men in the tower and radar rooms. Pilots had to be briefed on weather conditions and updated on area restrictions. Maintenance men by the hundreds worked on broken jets, and they needed parts from supply. Every man and woman had to be fed and housed, requiring the base to be a small city with all the necessary utilities any town might have. In the end, all of this was for one reason…to put an aviator in the seat of a fighter and send him into the air. God, I ought to pay the government to fly their airplanes, not the other way around, he thought, and turned back to Base Operations entrance.

He stepped off briskly. The time spent drinking in the sights had cleared his head. He was ready now to listen to Twilight's tape. He passed two captains as he mounted the stairs into Base Ops, returning their salutes. The young pilots, dressed in clean green NOMEX flight suits, were likely filing flight plans for a weekend cross country, he thought to himself. Removing his cover as he entered the building, Breakheart turned left for the stairs leading to the basement and the radar rooms.

The transmission tape of Colonel Adams' ill-fated flight had been pulled from the commercial size tape recorder as soon as the aircraft had gone down. The tapes used by Twilight recorded every word spoken between the radar operators and the pilots airborne, turning on spindles at less than an inch a minute. The machines were loaded each day with fresh tape, and at the end of field flight operations removed, labeled, and filed for thirty days. However, technicians had carefully dubbed Colonel Adams' last few minutes of conversation onto a cassette for use by the Accident Board. Breakheart was escorted by a Master Sergeant to a small office away from the darkened radar room. With a portable cassette player, he listened to the tape several times. The sound of his friend's voice saddened him, but he remained professional and listened with intensity.

The key transmission had been Colonel Adams' first call to Twilight that he was experiencing problems. "Twilight, I've got an emergency up here. The engine won't accelerate above idle." The first night's meeting with his board, Breakheart had said to eliminate everything that could not have caused the accident, and then they would know what had. Colonel Adams' one sentence narrowed the requirement of sorting through the wreckage to four major items: fuel, fuel control, engine, and throttle. It was time to head for VMAT-203's hanger and supervise the layout of the wreck. He thanked the Master Sergeant for his help, and requested Twilight make three more copies of the tape for the final accident report.

The hangar deck was alive with activity when Breakheart stepped out of the sunlight into the dim coolness of the gymnasium-sized bay. Nine of 203's AV-8Ts, the two seat model of the Harrier, were in various states of repair, with wings, engines and tail sections removed. Marines in green coveralls busied themselves with the work of fixing or inspecting everything from fuel tanks to radios. At the west end of the hangar's expanse, a section had been roped off for the layout of the wreckage of Zero Zero.

As Breakheart approached the secured area, he caught the unmistakable smell of "crashed jet." An odor permeated by the pungent aroma of burnt electrical wiring, melted plastic, and metal which had been overheated. Every accident I've investigated smells the same, he thought, as he stepped over the rope barrier.

"Good morning, sir," a Staff Sergeant said, walking up to greet Breakheart. "I'm Staff Sergeant Howard from 542."

"Sergeant Howard," Breakheart acknowledged, taking the man's extended hand. "How is it going?"

"Well sir, we have been sorting the bigger pieces out and laying them in the general area where they were located on the aircraft. You can see, we have what's left of the tail plane and fuselage organized into a semblance of a Harrier, and we'll just keep building from there."

"That's fine. What about the engine and its components? Are you keeping those separate?"

"Yes, sir. Everything to do with the engine is being laid out on the other side," he walked a short distance to the rear of the hanger and pointed to a mass of twisted metal and wires, "over here. I think we have most of the fan section, though the individual fans aren't attached to each other anymore. From the looks of it, I think the engine must have split down the center, dividing it in half longitudinally. The fans and turbine spools broke out intact, and were scattered as individual segments. Sir, this bird must have hit the ground and exploded from the looks of it."

"You're right about that. You should see the hole it made in the bean field." Breakheart paused and thought for a second. "Have you seen anything of the cockpit yet?"

"No, sir, I haven't. There is supposed to be another truck load arriving soon. Maybe it will have the cockpit."

"I hope so. Regardless, when you find anything that might resemble a black box, gauge, or switch that might belong in the cockpit, set it to one side, and make absolutely sure none of your people change any settings on dials, gauges, or switches."

"I understand, Colonel. This is my fourth accident layout. I'll keep a sharp eye on everything."

Breakheart excused himself and went straight to the area the engine pieces were haphazardly spread on the hangar floor. He found the large right-hand side of the engine that had been located in the ditch and began examining it closely. Standing before the remains of the big F402, he closed his eyes and tried to visualize how the fuel metering system operated. Because the Harrier's engine was required to accelerate so rapidly, from idle to 100 percent in less than three seconds, it demanded a technological nightmare of a fuel control. The AV-8A's had used an antiquated hydro-mechanical fuel control, which had been extremely complicated. But with the introduction of the AV-8B, it was even worse. The AV-8B had transported the V/STOL era into the "digital" age, where computers accomplished tasks done in earlier times by mechanical means or pilot manipulations.

The AV-8B fuel control system's heart and brain is the DECS, Digital Engine Control System, Breakheart catalogued. The DECS, actually two mini computers, has complete authority over the engine's control systems throughout the range of engine operation. Detecting all items affecting the employment of the engine such as throttle position, altitude, airspeed, angle of attack, inlet air temperature, and aircraft configuration (landing or up and away), the DECS keeps the engine performing at optimum performance.

Breakheart opened his eyes. He knew he was getting over his head trying to remember everything there was to know about the DECS and its three main components: Two identical Digital Electronic Control Units and a Fuel Metering Unit. Still, he knew each of the identical Digital Electronic Control Units could, if need be, operate independently with no degradation to flight operation of the engine or aircraft. That meant, both units would have had to fail simultaneously for Zero Zero's engine to suddenly go to idle and stay there. No! Breakheart didn't believe it possible. The odds were too great. Still, he jotted a note on his pad he'd retrieved from his breast pocket.

Okay, he thought, if it isn't the DECS then what about the Fuel Metering Unit? The DECS electronically controls the single Fuel Metering Unit, which is nothing more than a mechanical device metering the proper amount of fuel to the engine. The DECS is the brain and the Fuel Metering Unit the heart. It contains the hydro-mechanical controls required to pump, filter, and meter the fuel to the engine. He scribbled more notes; *Could the Fuel Metering Unit have gotten plugged, not allowing fuel to the engine?*

Remembering his emergency procedures for a failed DECS, Breakheart knew Adams would have switched to Manual Fuel

Control if indeed both DECS units failed. "My God, his warning light panel would have lit up like a Christmas tree and the warning tone would have blasted his ears off if that had happened," he spoke aloud to no one. Another note was added to the fast filling page: *Find manual fuel control switch, note position.* Still, Breakheart continued running possibilities through his mind. If he did have double DECS failure and didn't switch to Manual Fuel, or was unable to, then the engine might drop to idle and stay there. Maybe? Another note: *Check with NARF engineers on possibility of engine going to idle if both DECS s fail.*

The noise of a diesel engine brought Breakheart back into the reality of what was transpiring around him. A flatbed was pulling along side the open hangar door, and Marines were preparing to unload more of the broken remains of Zero Zero. Sitting in the center of the big truck was the torn and battered cockpit. It was still dripping black mud from its sides, even after the long drive from the crash site. Breakheart realized correctly, it must have been dug out of the pit.

"Sergeant Howard," Breakheart yelled.

"Yes, sir," Howard answered, walking to join the colonel.

"Sergeant, I want the cockpit cleaned up first thing. Have your men do the job very carefully. Don't use water or solvents, just wipe as much of the mud away as you can. I'm going to make a couple of phone calls. If I don't return before quitting time, arrange for security to watch this mess over the weekend."

"I'll take care of it, sir," Howard answered, and strode off to direct the unloading efforts.

Breakheart climbed the stairs to the second level and walked directly to Major Dyke's office. Above the door a sign read Squadron Safety. The office was small, but neat. NATOPS manuals, safety literature, and a variety of naval safety publications were stacked on Dyke's desk and in corners of the room. On the desk were two pictures, one of Dyke and his wife with a baby in her arms, and the other of a Harrier in a hover. Over the desk was taped a paper placard with the words *SAFETY IS NOT A CLUB, IT'S A TOOL* inscribed in bold black and red letters. Breakheart smiled at the inscription and gave it his full endorsement.

Picking up the phone, he dialed Sena's work number. She answered on the second ring.

"NADEP Engineering, Ms. Zaffky speaking. May I help you?"

"Hi, Sena. Dan here. How are you this morning?"

"I'm fine, Colonel," Sena answered formally. "What may I do for you?"

Breakheart grinned, realizing there must be others in the office with her, or she would not have been so starched in her greeting. "I need to make arrangements to have Zero Zero's DECS and Fuel Metering Control Unit scrutinized by your people. I'm about ninety-nine percent sure the crash was caused by something involving the fuel system. The DECS and metering unit are probably the best place to start. Can you arrange for a speedy breakdown and examination?"

"Sure, I can handle it. No problem. How soon do you think you'll have it here?"

"Probably later this afternoon. Say around fourteen hundred. It will be delivered by a Staff Sergeant Howard."

"That will be fine. Tell him to take it directly to the engine shop, and I'll notify the appropriate people. He will have to get a NADEP pass from the front desk. I'll have it waiting for him. Anything else?"

"Will your people work on it over the weekend?"

"Probably not. It would mean overtime pay, and like everyone else, we are short of fiscal funding. If you really want them to work over the weekend, you'll have to have General Geise call the NADEP CO."

"Okay! Thanks for the help. See you tomorrow."

"That you will," Sena's voice softened. "Until then, bye for now."

Breakheart hung the phone back on its hook and headed for the Readyroom. He spoke briefly with the duty officer, asking him to relay a message to Major Dyke. The board meeting would be at 0600 Monday morning in one of 203's briefing rooms. As he was leaving, Major Beasly, the squadron's operations officer, hailed him from behind.

"Colonel Breakheart, how goes the investigation?"

"It's going," Breakheart responded to the tall, slender major. "Nothing firm, but we'll sort it out one way or the other."

"I boxed and sealed all of Colonel Adams' flight logs and training records. I've got them in my office when you need them. They are locked in my safe."

"Thanks. I'll have Major Dyke retrieve them from you on Monday after our meeting."

"Right! If there is anything my office can do for you, don't hesitate to ask," Beasly smiled. "We're here to please."

Breakheart checked his watch. "Thanks, I'll remember that. It's pushing on to 1330. I've got to run and change into my "alphas" if I'm going to make the memorial service," he paused, "and I have to give some instructions to Sergeant Howard on the way. Are you going to the service?"

"Yes. Most of the squadron is. I'll be changing here, though. See you later, Colonel."

The shower felt good. He'd left 203's spaces after briefing Staff Sergeant Howard on the removal of the DECS and Fuel Metering Unit and its subsequent delivery to NADEP. Driving home, Breakheart's mind raced with information and questions surrounding the accident. Now, the hot water streaming over his tanned body washed the morning away in spiraling cascades down the chrome shower drain. He stood with his back to the plummeting spray, letting it hit him on the back of his head and neck. The pounding drops relaxed him, and the disquieting thoughts washed down the drain pipe with the water. Then, shutting off the shower, he stepped from the stall to start getting ready for his friend's memorial service.

The boys were laughing in their rooms, and Breakheart could hear them chattering and teasing each other. They didn't dress up in their Sunday best very often, and Bill was trying to teach Steve how to tie a Windsor knot in his necktie.

On his bed, Breakheart laid out his "Greens." The Summer Service "A" uniform which included a blouse. The Marine green uniform, its color patented so no other clothing could be produced in the same shade, lay naked on the bed. In his skivvies, Breakheart began putting it together. First, he fastened the two shooting badges an eighth of an inch above the left breast pocket. One badge displayed crossed rifles the other crossed pistols, signifying he was an expert shot with both weapons. Above the shooting badges, he attached his four rows of ribbons. These included a range of achievement on his part from "Alive in '65" to the Distinguished Flying Cross. There were sixteen ribbons in all. Breakheart gave little thought to their meaning, but was secretly proud of his medals, as most Marines were.

Ensuring the ribbons and badges were straight, he attached the gold wings of a Naval Aviator above them both. On the epaulets, big silver eagles were pinned on either side. He checked the entire uniform for Irish pennants, and when satisfied it was as sharp and neat as it could be, hung the blouse on a hanger behind the door. Next came the shoes. Corfam leather maintained a shine of its own, but Breakheart took a spray can of Pledge Furniture Polish from his night stand and squirted a small amount on each shoe. With a clean, white cloth, he wiped the polish into each shoe's surface. When he could see himself smile in the black toe of each, he set them aside and grabbed a can of Brasso. For several minutes, he polished the buckle on his belt, until it sparkled gold in the light. Satisfied his uniform looked like a Marine's should, he began dressing.

Breakheart pulled the Firebird into the old PX's parking lot which now served the Base Chapel. PX was really a misnomer, as what the Marine Corps actually possess are MXs, Marine Exchange, not the Army's Post Exchange. However, trying to convince most Marines they were going to the MX was a useless endeavor, much like teaching a pig to sing. Since World War II, it had been known as the PX and the PX it would be called.

Getting out of his vehicle, he was hit by a blast of furnace like air, and he immediately began to perspire in the long-sleeved shirt he was wearing. *I should have worn "Charlie's,"* Breakheart grumbled to himself. Reaching behind the driver's seat, he retrieved his blouse and slipped it on, buttoning it carefully from the top down so the cloth would hang correctly. As he buckled the belt, he appraised his surroundings.

The Base Chapel was a large structure, made of red brick and trimmed in white. A front veranda boasted beautifully sculptured columns supporting a low overhanging roof. A sky piercing spire rose from the main structure's roof, offsetting the stained glass windows lining the walls. There was no doubt it was a church, yet in this case, nondenominational. The chapel served every faith… Protestant, Catholic, even Buddhist if need be. This afternoon, cars filled the parking lot and men and women congested the chapel's grassy side yards. Breakheart was caught by the contrast of colors. The stark white of the building's trim against the red brick, green and brown uniforms, and the muted colorless attire worn by the women foretold of the somber occasion about to transpire. Men spoke to men in whispers with no hint of laughter. He joined the procession on the front lawn, acknowledging greetings as they came from those he knew, and making quiet salutations himself. The boys arrived to join him in muted respect. The four Breakhearts entered the chapel together and with Dan in the lead, strode purposefully to the third pew on the right. On the podium, sat six men; three on each side facing one another. Five were Marines dressed in Dress Blues, a uniform for formal occasions, and if you were a participant in a ceremony such as this. The midnight blue blouses, sporting their gold buttons and complemented by the lighter blue trousers with a blood red strip running the length of each leg, was the uniform most remembered by civilians. Breakheart tried to remember the last time he'd worn his "Blues." Over two years ago, he remembered, at a wedding. Dress Blues came out of the closet for occasions such as weddings, the Marine Corps Ball, and funerals.

The sixth man, seated in front of the congregation, was a Navy Captain…the Protestant Chaplin. He wore the cloth of a minister, its pure white cape trimmed in gold. Breakheart looked around, noting it would be standing room only by the time everyone settled into the church. Jack Adams had made a wealth of friends during his twenty-six years of service.

The hushed hum of voices suddenly fell silent as Sally and her children were escorted to the front pew by two majors in Dress Blues. Once settled, the escorts did a smartly executed facing movement and took their place on either side of the podium and came to rigid attention. The memorial service began.

The pomp and ceremony of a military memorial service, Breakheart drifted in reflection, was set in as much tradition as were other uniformed rituals. The very formality and familiarity of the act helped sooth open wounds of loss. It was here, in the confines of a chapel, that the amenities of service etiquette and protocol served the needs of family and friends. It was here, in Cherry Point's chapel, the men Jack had flown, worked, and played with for so many years could say goodbye. They would salute him later, but here, conventional decorum gave each a chance to reflect upon their own vulnerability. "There, but for the grace of God, go I," Breakheart whispered silently to himself.

The red, white, and blue of the Flag marched forward with an honor guard. The Chaplin opened the spoken service with a prayer. Then a colonel stepped to the podium to read a passage from the Bible. The difference between one memorial and another was imperceptible, except for the eulogy.

When it came time for Major General Geise to speak, he rose slowly from his chair. His Dress Blues fit perfectly, yet as he reached his full height, he pulled his blouse straight with determination. Walking to the podium, his shoulders ram rod straight, one would think he was preparing to address his command of a forth coming operation, save for the damp wetness evident on his cheeks. Reaching the podium, he began in a soft, but fully audible voice.

"I knew Colonel Jack Adams throughout my entire career as a Marine. He was not just an officer in my command, he was a friend. A very cherished friend, for he was a man I could trust. Today, we come together to wish our comrade fair weather as he makes his last flight into God's own hands. We will miss him, but we will also remember."

"His accomplishments in the Corps were many, as all of you know. He flew A-6s most of his career, serving two tours in Viet Nam. He was awarded the Distinguished Flying Cross and the Silver Star for his heroic actions during that war. But that is of little importance compared to the intangible achievements he afforded the men and women who served under him. No greater compliment can be given a Marine Officer than to label him a leader among leaders. Yet, Colonel Adams was just that, a superb leader in a Corps of leaders. He stood above the pack, his gentle determination ingratiating him to all with whom he came in contact. I, no all of us here, will miss his counsel, and quick wit. There will be an emptiness in our daily lives, for we will no longer have Colonel Adams with whom to associate. The legacy he leaves us is one of example. A standard of excellence to be imitated by all, each and every one of us."

The big man paused to regain his self-control, as tears were openly flowing down his face. He took a handkerchief from his rear pocket and roughly wiped the salty drops from his chin and cheeks.

"Jack Adams left something else. A wonderful family. Sally," he looked directly at the crying woman in the front pew, "I, better than anyone here, know how much Jack loved you and his children. He talked of you every chance provided him. I know too, how much you loved him. There are no words to console the loss you are now feeling, but we, the extended Marine family, feel your loss with you, and we wish we could bear a small part of the pain for you. Farewell, Jack. You may be gone in flesh, but you'll live in our hearts forever." The big man made an about face and returned to his chair.

Breakheart sat staring after the general, tears of loss streaming unashamedly down his face. His was not the only damp face in the room. More than a number of hard-boiled Marines were reaching for something to wipe away the emotion showing clearly in their eyes.

The service came to an end with the Flag retracing its path from the chapel. Sally's escorts stepped forward to walk silently beside her as she left the congregation seated quietly in their seats. As she came abeam the pew Breakheart was seated she paused for a second and looked at Breakheart, giving him a brief smile.

Behind Sally and her children, the assembly stood and walked slowly from the air-conditioned coolness of the chapel into the oppressive heat of a late Carolina summer afternoon. Little was said, as men and women drifted to the waiting automobiles. Breakheart walked with his sons to the "Terror" and told them he would be home around seven p.m.. He was going to Happy Hour at the officer's club, and he instructed them to fix their own supper. The boys nodded knowingly. Their father rarely got drunk, but Friday's Happy Hour was something he rarely missed, and they knew this particular bout at the club would be for Colonel Adams. They had grown up in the Marine Corps, not unlike their father. They knew the drill.

Breakheart stripped off his blouse, and hung it on a hanger behind the driver's seat. That done, he walked with purpose into the Officers Club. It was approaching 1700, and the liquor had been flowing for an hour. As soon as he opened the door to the club, the noises of men and women in full party swing invaded his ears. They were happy sounds of Marines having fun…a far cry from the chapel's somber atmosphere. Happy Hour was a time to let the pressures of the week dissolve into back slapping nonsense.

There were few rules surrounding a Marine Happy Hour, but those that had been established were closely kept. In the bar, located at the far end of the sprawling club, overlooking the Neuse River, one did not talk of politics or religion. Nor did an officer enter the bar covered. If he should happen to make the mistake of leaving his piss cutter or utility cap on his head, and walked through the bar's portals, he bought the house a round. A costly deed at best, and a credit card buster at worst depending on the strength of numbers in the bar. Breakheart was ready to let his hair down just a little.

At the bar, ordering a rum and diet Coke, Breakheart spotted General Geise sitting at a table near the patio door with several other senior officers. Actually, there were three tables, but they had been pushed together making room for the group to sit and drink.

"Hey, Cuda," Geise's voice blared above the noisy den. "Get your ass over here and join us."

Breakheart waved acknowledgement and walked to the table dragging a chair behind him. "Thanks, don't mind if I do."

"We're saluting Jacks departure," the general said, gravely…then burst into a smile. "Here's to Jack Adams, one hell of a Marine and a great jet jock."

"Hear, hear," the men came back in a single voice.

"May his rotten heart make way for mine when the time comes," Breakheart interjected.

Laughter.

Breakheart spent his allotted time at the bar reminiscing about his fallen friend. The group talked of adventures in foreign ports of call, of flying with Jack, and the troubles they had all seemed to get into as junior officers. Talk was light, however, the feelings were real and went deep into each man's soul. Always, they knew, death stood on their shoulders just waiting to reap yet another aviator who made a critical mistake. Or, as in Jack's case, an airplane whose systems failed at the wrong time. Dying in an airplane was something they joked about outwardly; inwardly fearing the fire which could and might envelop them at anytime. So, they drank, laughed, and made light of the grim reaper as if he were a false bogey man only children feared on a dark night.

By the time Breakheart said his goodbyes, the ship's clock behind the bar had rung eight bells. He headed home to fall into bed thinking about Sena, why Jack's desk had been emptied, fuel controls, and what his dead comrade might have been thinking when he bought the farm.

NINE

BREAKHEART WOKE WITH a snap, his eyes springing open to the sun's rays streaming through his bedroom windows. An early riser every day, Saturday was no different. He rolled out of bed and made for the bathroom. When finished, he slipped on blue cargo shorts, a light blue polo shirt with the inscription *Dreamer* printed above the left breast pocket, and deck shoes. The cargo shorts were held up by a wide leather belt, and a rigging knife hung from his hip. It was a sailing day!

He started down the hall, banging on the boys' doors as he passed. "Up and at 'em," he yelled at each door. "Time's a wasting, and we're burning daylight."

The loud call was a familiar morning cry for the Breakheart teenagers. Their father was a morning person, and because of this peculiar personality trait, a bane to their existence every time the sun elected to rise. They each groaned as their individual door accepted the pounding Breakheart tattooed on the wood.

By the time Bill entered the kitchen, the coffee had been made and the skillet was sputtering bacon grease over its low sides onto the stove. Breakheart stood beside an island chopping block in the center of the kitchen peeling a mound of potatoes.

"Good morning, son. Sleep well?" Breakheart asked in a lighthearted voice.

He felt great. Though he had imbibed more rum than was his normal happy hour intake, he had no hangover, and rarely did. He felt fresh…clean. The memorial service and the time spent at the club had rinsed the raw wound of hurt away. Now he could begin the healing process from the loss of a friend.

"Dad, why do you always have to be so darned cheerful in the morning?" Bill's greeting was less than chipper.

"Have some coffee and you'll feel better," his father grinned, and began chopping the potatoes into thin slices. Several minutes earlier, he'd emptied a full pound of bacon into a hot skillet, and scrambled fifteen eggs in a bowl. The toaster was already popping crispy browned bread…the start of the entire loaf which would be toasted and set in a warming oven. "We're having a Breakheart breakfast, so I hope you're hungry."

"I'm always hungry, Dad. You know that." Bill grinned. "Need some help?"

"Yeah, you can watch the bacon for me," Breakheart said, as he heaped the sliced potatoes on a plate.

"You're fixing breakfast!" Rod said, padding his way into the cheery warmth of the kitchen. He hadn't dressed yet, and standing in his underpants, grabbed a slice of toast as it jumped from the toaster. Slathering a huge hunk of butter over the hot bread, he asked, "Are we going racing?"

"Indeed we are, lad. So, my son, you had better get your young rump in gear and get dressed."

Rod's face burst into a smile. "Cool!" He exclaimed, and trotted off to his room, eating the toast in three bites.

The Breakhearts sat in shorts around the dinette table. Breakfast was a hit, as it always was in their house, and the conversation light. Breakheart tried to make a big breakfast at least one morning out of the week. Normally, he would have prepared their morning feast on Sunday, but today was different. He had not been home for supper all week, and this small time gave him a chance to catch up on his youngster's activities.

With the dishes washed, dried, and put away and the kitchen put back into a semblance of order, it was time to head for the boat. The boys took the "Terror" to the marina and Breakheart followed in his own car. A short five minute drive through officer country and off an oak and pine lined asphalt road, Hancock Boat Docks lay on the creek from which the facility took its name. The Club's meeting house sat perched on a hill overlooking the three major docks which were filled with boats of various sizes. Masts of the sailing vessels far outnumbered the more cumbersome looking power rigs. The marina, though not fancy nor heaped with the amenities a sailor might expect at a commercial facility, was adequate. Breakheart considered the area to be beautiful, particularly on an early summer morning with the sun struggling above the far shore's pines. Hancock Creek emptied into the Neuse River, which Breakheart knew to be the second largest river on the east coast. At the entrance to the creek, stood the Navy Boat Dock where a detachment of sailors lived and worked. The Naval detail was equipped to recover aircraft downed in the river, and viewing it as he parked the Firebird reminded him of the investigation he was conducting.

Dreamer, Breakheart's Hunter 37 rested quietly in her slip on B-dock. By the time he'd opened his car door, the boys were already clamoring aboard. Bill had been entrusted with a key to the companionway hatch when he had turned sixteen, and he was now brandishing his authority over his brothers. Breakheart retrieved a cooler filled with food and drink he'd prepared while the boys cleaned the kitchen of the remains of breakfast, and moved after his sons.

The three docks were awake with activity. Men and women busying themselves with the activities required before leaving their berth to race. Main sail covers were being removed and folded, halyards attached to the head of the main, and cushions snapped into place in cockpits. Breakheart answered the hello calls from several boats as he walked slowly, struggling with the weight of the cooler, to *Dreamer's* finger pier.

"Bill, give me a hand with this thing," Breakheart called to his son.

Both Bill and Steve came to his rescue. "What's the matter, Pops? Getting too old to carry a little cooler?" Steve gibed his father.

"You're cute," his father retorted, noting that Bob Burns was as good as his word. On *Rainbow*, lying two slips from his own, four ladies dressed in the tiniest of bikinis, were laughing while they helped ready the boat. "Hey, Snake, do you need some help?" He asked, hailing his best friend.

"You have got to be kidding," Burns answered good naturedly. "Does it look like I need help?" Stripped to the waist and in canvas sailing shorts, he was supervising the ladies, and enjoying every minute of it. "I've got the best crew around."

"Well, it certainly is the best looking crew I've seen in sometime," Breakheart said. He knew most of the women aboard *Rainbow*, and they waved their collective greetings, acknowledging his compliment. He waved back and ducked below into the cabin.

Dreamer was Breakheart's pride and joy. Except for his son's, who he loved more than life itself, the boat was most cherished. Sailing, he often thought, was much like flying. When you strapped on a jet and soared in the clouds, there was no one but you, the airplane, and the sky. When the sails were full, and the breeze lively, it was no one but you, the boat, and the water. The analogy had its merits.

The main saloon was neat as a pin, Breakheart noted, just as it should be. The boys had stowed the few bits of gear they had brought, knowing their father would raise hell if they forgot to do so. He stepped to the navigation table, and reached over its teak surface to turn on the master circuit breaker. Then, in a set routine, not unlike the prestart check list he used in the Harrier, he turned on the remaining electrical equipment. Satisfied everything was in working order, he returned to the cockpit, stepping behind the wheel. In a moment, the deep chug of *Dreamer's* three cylinder diesel vibrated the air around the boat.

The boys were busily removing sail covers and attaching halyards to main and staysail. *Dreamer*, a cutter rigged sloop, had two headsails and running back stays. The Breakheart's had more work to accomplish before leaving the dock than did those crews now readying smaller, single headsail sloops.

"Hi! May I come aboard?" Sena asked, surprising Breakheart who had his back turned toward her.

"Please," he stammered when he caught his first glimpse of the vision standing on the finger pier, "certainly, do," he managed to sputter. Sena stood in white shorts, and a pale pink well-filled halter. The sun behind her, created a blond halo of finely luscious hair, which hung loosely on her tanned shoulders. She was smiling down on Breakheart, and he felt himself melt under its radiance. "*Dreamer* awaits her lady," he said gaining self confidence.

"She's beautiful," Sena exclaimed, stepping lightly aboard as if she had been raised on the water. "I had no idea what to expect, but certainly nothing as extravagant as this."

"She's my second love, next to the kids," Breakheart said, taking a small cloth overnight bag from her hand. She's absolutely astonishing, he thought, taking her hand as she stepped into the cockpit next to him. "You look radiant."

"Why, thank you. I wasn't sure what to wear, but I thought shorts would be best, and I brought a bathing suit as well."

"Perfect," Breakheart said. "A bikini, I hope."

Sena gave him a hard look of reproachfulness, and then smiled. "Yes, I'm afraid that it is."

Seventeen year old Bill Breakheart, stood staring in utter wonder, then stepped forward. "Hey, Dad, aren't you going to introduce us?"

Breakheart made the introductions, and cuffed Bill lightly on the head for what he knew his son was thinking. "Get your mind out the gutter," he said to the boy in a whisper. Bill just grinned and punched his father in the shoulder.

On the river, the breeze freshened to a steady twelve knots. *Dreamer,* heeled, close reached on a port tack. The sky was a true Carolina blue, the color produced in State literature touting the glory of the South. On the bow, Sena stood holding the headstay, listening to the sigh whispering from the bow as it split the surface. Gulls cried and circled overhead, hoping to reap bounty from the intruder in their world. Sitting behind the wheel, feeling its gentle pressure, Breakheart thought he'd just died and gone to heaven. What could be more perfect, he mused, than to have my sons sailing with me on a clear day, and a beautiful woman standing on the bow?

The men aboard watched as Sena started to move aft. She had changed into her bikini shortly after they had left the creek. Now, easing her way along the deck, she looked as if she had stepped from the pages of a *Vogue* magazine. Her legs were perfectly proportioned to her five feet eight inches, and the skin taut under a golden tan. When Breakheart had first met her at the NADEP, he knew she would be pretty when dressed in something other than work clothes, but he had never imagined just how stunning she truly was.

"What do you think of sailing so far?" he asked lightly.

"It's fantastic. I wish I'd taken up the sport earlier," she smiled. "When do we start racing?"

"Soon," Bill answered. "Look!"

They all scanned the river near the entrance to Hancock Creek. White sails darted everywhere. Over fifty boats were tacking and jibing their way to the center of the river where the race would begin.

"Are all those boats from your yacht club?" Sena asked, surprised to see so many boats.

"No. They're from other clubs up and down the river," Steve answered for his father. "Cool, huh?"

Sena smiled at the teenager. "Yeah, cool."

Dreamer didn't make a very good start. Breakheart mistimed his outbound leg at the ten minute warning horn, and was thirty seconds behind the lead boat…*Rainbow*. He knew he'd be hearing more about his mistake from Snake when the race was over. The first leg of the triangular course was up wind, not the best point of sail for *Dreamer*. They started tacking for the mark. The boys, with years of experience under their belts, took positions assigned them for the race. Bill held the main sheet, trimming the big sail to every whim of the wind, while Steve tended to the bow. The cutter's big Genoa, without help, would hang up in the slot between the forestay and headstay every time the boat tacked, and Steve would pull the sail roughly between the heavy wires each time Breakheart brought the boat about. Rod, though the youngest, had a knack for trimming headsails manned the jib and staysail sheets. He was a natural sailor, which was perfectly understandable. He had still been in a bassinet when he'd gone for his first sail.

Sena watched father and sons work the thirty-seven footer, and was amazed at the lack of communication required among the four. She thought he must be a good father to have raised three boys on his own. Plus, she realized how much fun she was having. She did not date much, though the young bachelor aviators on base certainly gave her every chance to enjoy an evening with them. She found most of their antics immature and a bit too wild for her personal comfort. Working her own way through college required her to mature earlier than most of her friends, particularly as an Aeronautical Engineering major. Fighting battles had become a way of life for her. Battles against men's prejudice, against her being an engineer, and against their bold sexual advances. Now, sailing the Neuse with Dan Breakheart, she felt comfortable. Safe.

Dreamer rounded the first mark more than a hundred yards behind the lead boats. Though they had crossed the starting line second, the sluggishness of the boat, tacking to windward, had lost them their initial advantage. As the orange anchored ball slipped behind in the wake, Breakheart smiled. Now we'll start moving, he mused to himself, as the boys trimmed the sails for the reaching leg of the race.

The boat accelerated to a fast six and a half knots. "Now we'll show them a thing or two," Breakheart said. *"Dreamer* loves a close or beam reach," he explained to Sena. "See," he pointed ahead, "we're already starting to gain on the boats up there."

Sure enough, Sena realized, the distance was rapidly evaporating between them and the boats in the lead. "Why are we going faster than before?" She asked, puzzled. "It felt like we were really moving on the first leg."

"Because we've broken off the wind. *Dreamer* isn't very fast close hauled, but break her on to a reach, and watch out."

"Dan, you're speaking another language. I've got no idea what you are saying. Close hauled? Reaching?"

Breakheart, paying close attention to the wind, sails, and feel of the helm began explaining the various points of sail to Sena. She asked several questions, and he did his best to clear up her need for information. He was hoping she was enjoying herself. Looking at her sitting on the cockpit seat stirred something inside him he had not felt for a very long time. He recognized the sexual urge, but it was far more than just a wanton need. Deep inside, he felt this woman before him could fill a void long since sealed and forgotten.

By the time the second mark was left astern, *Dreamer* held a respectable fourth place position. They had passed two boats before the mark, and a third at the mark, forcing the other boat to the outside of their jibe. Even downwind on the final leg, their boat was inching forward on the remaining boats before them.

"Dad, we can cover the yellow boat with just a small turn to starboard," Bill edged in a stage whisper.

"Right," Breakheart acknowledged, moving the wheel to the right. "If we can get around her, we'll have a real shot of beating *Rainbow*."

"Maybe we'll win," Rod grinned. "But if we don't, let's at least beat Snake."

Aboard the yellow sloop in front of Breakheart, there was little they could do to protect themselves other than tack off in another direction. They elected to hold course, and it was to their detriment. In less than ten minutes, Breakheart called "mast abeam," and they were sucked up in *Dreamer's* wake. The lead boat, a slim hulled racing sloop, sped for the finish line too far ahead for Breakheart to catch, but Snake's *Rainbow* was another matter. With each passing minute, *Dreamer* crept for her stern.

"Come on, Dan, you can do it," Sena was caught up in the struggle with Breakheart's sons. "I'll blow in the sails, if that will help?" She laughed.

The bone in *Dreamer's* teeth hissed with the speed she fought to maintain for her crew. The big Genoa was poled out wing and wing, with the main on a starboard tack. Steve had doused the staysail when they had jibed at the mark. It was less than useless running down wind. Now, fifty feet directly astern the blue of *Rainbow's* stern, Breakheart created a huge hole for Snake. *Dreamer's* sails were stealing his friend's wind, and she began to slow.

"Come on, Dad," the boys were yelling over and over. "We can do it. Just a little more."

Dreamer's bow veered to port slightly, clearing *Rainbow's* stern by mere feet. As Breakheart's mast slipped along side Snake's cockpit, he started to give the "mast abeam" hail.

Bob and his bikini clad crew sat quietly in the expansive cockpit. Snake knew that *Dreamer* was a faster boat down wind, and had, in the last half hour or so, been preparing for this moment.

"Mast abeam," Breakheart yelled, smiling broadly at Snake. "I'm going to beat you, you miserable no count. I told you I would."

Snake, smiled good naturedly, and nodded to the women aboard.

Suddenly the air was filled with water balloons. As fast as the ladies could fling the missiles at *Dreamer*, the red, blue, and purple projectiles arched from one boat to the other. Breakheart was caught off guard, and let the bow swing to port slightly, giving up a few feet to Snake. Balloons struck everywhere, raining cold water on Sena, Breakheart, and the boys. The cries of foul, you son of a bitch, and other niceties filled the air, and the balloons still came.

Not every balloon broke, and the boys started catching what they could and returned fire. Sena joined in, retrieving a well-filled balloon from the cockpit, and heaving it at their enemy. The balloon struck Burns full in the face, and *Rainbow* wavered to starboard. Now the boats were neck and neck and the ladies racing with Breakheart's nemesis had depleted their ammunition supply. They laughed, they insulted each other, and they tried to force each other off the rhumb line to no avail. *Dreamer* and *Rainbow* sailed across the finish line in a dead heat.

At the dock, sails flaked and covered and *Dreamer's* decks washed free of salt, Breakheart sat quietly under the cockpit's Bimini top talking to Sena. The Bimini's canvas shaded the two from the Carolina sun. The boys were helping set up tables for the Bar-B-Que the yacht club was throwing for the racers.

"It's been a perfect day, Dan," Sena sighed. "I can't remember when I have had so much fun."

Breakheart smiled, and took a sip on his rum. "It was fun, wasn't it? I might add, your being here made it all the more so. I hope you'll sail with me again."

"All you have to do is ask." Sena smiled gently at the older man next to her. "Would you care to join me for dinner tomorrow night? I'm not a great cook, but I can burn a steak with the best of them."

"Yes, I would like that very much," Breakheart replied, somewhat surprised he'd been asked. "You are going to stay for the party, aren't you?"

"Heck, yes. I figure you and your sailing friends will throw a great party, if what goes on the water is any indication," she laughed, thinking about the balloon fight. "How long have you known Snake?"

"Forever, I think. We've burned a lot of shoe leather off over the years, and I guess if I had a brother it would be him. He's a piece of work, no doubt about that, but we have fun together, and he'd do anything in the world for me, and I him."

"It must be wonderful having such a close friend. I don't think I've ever had such a relationship."

"It is, and I cherish his being there when I need him," Breakheart answered honestly. He thought this woman had much the same qualities he recognized in Burns, honesty, courage, and the strength to stand against odds. "

Sena's face darkened, "I can't stop thinking about the ejection seat. There is much more to your investigation than meets the eye. Am I right?"

The change of subject caught Breakheart off guard. He studied her soft features for a moment, debating his answer. "Yes, I'm afraid there is. Every time I turn over something new in the investigation I find another mystery. I've had a bad feeling about this accident from the moment I first set eyes on that damned bean field, and it gets worse daily. I don't like it."

"Can you talk about it with me?" Sena asked. She could see the worried expression her question had tacked on Breakheart's face. She wished she hadn't brought the subject up in the first place. Her remark wiped away the mood they had been enjoying.

"Sena, if there were anyone I would discuss the accident with it would be Snake. But, no, I can't. At least not right now."

"Hey you two love birds, get your butts up here and join the party." It was Bob Burns yelling at them from the dock. "We've got rum aplenty, chicken hot from the grill and some of the best darn hush puppies you've ever put in your mouth."

"I suppose you made the hush puppies?" Breakheart grinned up at his friend standing on the dock. Snake Burns was a gourmet cook, and anything his hands touched in a kitchen or galley was well worth the effort to hasten to the invitation.

"Damned straight I did, and they are the best you'll likely eat during the rest of your miserable life. Now, come on up and join the fun."

Sena and Breakheart left *Dreamer* to fend for herself and followed Snake along B-Dock to the shade of several huge oaks covering picnic tables and charcoal pits. Fifty or so sailors milled about talking and drinking. The dress was casual and colorful. T-shirts, the standard dress, announced everything from boat names to past regattas. One, worn by a bearded man weighing over two hundred and fifty pounds, his belly hanging a foot below his belt, read: Sailors do it on the heel! Bill and Steve joined Sena and Breakheart at a table, their paper plates overflowing with golden browned chicken, potato salad, baked beans, and hush puppies.

"Pops, we've got to do this more often," Steve smiled, his mouth full of chicken. "Are we going to get the second place silver for the race?"

"Yes," Breakheart answered his son. "Snake told the race committee he'd cheated just a little with the water balloons. So we get second, and *Rainbow* takes third."

"Yes!" Both Bill and Steve exclaimed together, slapping a high hand, while Sena laughed.

Much later, over a cup of steaming coffee, Breakheart and Sena sat alone on *Dreamer*. The boys had left for home over an hour before, and the docks had slowly been vacated. Snake and his ladies went to the O-club for an evening's dancing, which they had encouraged Breakheart to do as well. However, as the sun slid behind the oaks, and the sounds of evening began breaking the stillness of the creek, the two had elected to remain. Breakheart had boiled a pot of thick black coffee and laced it with Jamaican rum for them to enjoy as night fell slowly.

Sena leaned back, snuggling into the softness of an overstuffed cushion Breakheart had thrown her from below. Her brown eyes reflected dots of silver moonlight as her gaze followed a school of jumping mullet on the water's black surface.

"Have you ever thought of saying to heck with it all and just sailing away?" She asked pensively.

"Oh, not very often, just every day," Breakheart laughed. "Sailing this boat to far off places has been a dream of mine for as long as I can remember. Someday I'll do it, but not until the boys are out of high school."

"Well, when you do, give me a call," she said half seriously. "I can't think of a better way of spending time than drifting about in the sun."

"I couldn't agree more." He sat down next to her and leaned back against the cabin's bulkhead. "I think I would like to start with the Bahamas and then explore further south."

Sena shifted slightly and let her back rest on Breakheart's shoulder. They sat, not speaking for a long while. It was enough to be together, with the night songs of buzzing insects and the rippling of the water against *Dreamer's* hull. A grey gull, resting on a piling, shifted and squawked a harsh warning to an imaginary adversary, while stars winked in and out of sight as wisps of clouds drifted across the ink well sky.

"You're a very special man, Dan Breakheart," Sena unpresumptuously whispered, turning to face Breakheart.

He looked deeply into her eyes and leaned forward. Taking her face in his hands, he touched his lips to hers. She did not resist, but strained upward to meet him with heated desire.

They kissed for several minutes, finally coming up for air after a prolonged meeting of the souls. "I think we had better go," Breakheart said. "I'm not sure I can restrain myself from having this go too far for our first date."

Sena hugged him closely. She had wondered if he would try and take her. The events of the day, and the evening's magic would have given her little to resist with, for she wanted him as she knew he needed her. "I suppose you are right, but I hate to leave. It is beautiful here, and all of life's cares seem to melt away."

They cleaned the mess made by the coffee and Breakheart closed *Dreamer's* companionway. He walked Sena to her car and kissed her once more before she drove away. He was suddenly tired. Very tired! It had been a long week, too filled with worry and questions. He drove home, said good night to the boys and fell into bed, asleep before his head met the pillow.

TEN
★ ★ ★

THE PHONE RANG for the second time, its bell cutting through the silence like a knife. Breakheart rolled over under the sheet covering him and opened his eyes. Reaching for the phone on the night stand, he glanced at the clock. "Jesus H. Christ, its five in the morning," he cried to himself. I know this is going to be bad news. No one calls this early unless something's gone haywire.

"Hello, Colonel Breakheart here," he said gruffly.

"Sorry to wake you so early, Colonel," Major Collins greeted. "I thought you would want to know we've located Hamilton."

"Couldn't that bit of information wait till a more reasonable hour?" Breakheart said with an edge in his voice.

"No, sir, it can't. The Highway Patrol found him Friday afternoon, but didn't bother notifying military authorities until late last night. I just got the word not more than five minutes ago. Hamilton was murdered." Collins spoke in a flat monotone. "His head was bashed in with something heavy, and then his car was driven into a tidal creek east of Oriental."

Breakheart set upright on the edge of his bed, stunned. He gazed out of the window at the Neuse. Dawn was struggling to open the day. Foretelling of a brewing storm, heavy black clouds with wart-like blisters bubbling from their bases raced across a yet sunless sky. The word "murder" rolled through the corners of his mind like the clouds swirling in the darkened sky.

"Do they know where and how it happened?" Breakheart asked, gathering his thoughts around him like a worn security blanket.

"No, sir! The police wouldn't talk details over the phone. I'm going to get dressed and head to the hospital morgue in New Bern. That's where the autopsy is going to take place, and I want to be there. The Highway Patrol doesn't want our help, but they're going to have it whether they want it or not. I've already called NIS headquarters in Washington, D.C., and I have their full support. We'll be deeply involved in the investigation."

"You know what I need don't you, Major? I want information, like yesterday, if this has anything to do with my accident investigation. I have a sick feeling it does, but I don't want to jump to any conclusions."

"Yes, sir, I understand. The fact that the car, with Hamilton's body in it, was found so close to the accident site gives me the feeling the two are connected somehow. Hamilton's car was obviously dumped into the creek by someone who didn't think about the tide. Apparently, the Corvette was out of sight under the muddy waters until the tide went out. At low tide, the top of the car was totally exposed."

"Okay, Major, I'll leave this up to you. I want you to call me the minute you have anything. Here is my car phone number, 466-2341. Keep trying until you get a hold of me." It was an order, and Breakheart knew Collins would realize how important any information might be. "I'll notify General Geise, if he hasn't already been told. Regardless of what you find out, call me sometime today, or stop by the house later this evening."

"Yes, sir, you can count on it. I'll talk to you later, Colonel." Collins broke the connection.

Breakheart moved zombie like into the kitchen. He didn't beat on his sons' doors, as he normally would, but went straight to the Mr. Coffee and poured a large scoop of Butternut into the paper strainer. He'd need to get a jump start on life today, he realized. While he waited for the water to heat and drip, he walked to the screened porch attached to the rear of his quarters. In his robe, a thick white cotton garment worn and slightly tattered with the age of many years of use, he sat on a lawn chair and waited for the sun.

A ragged crack split the eastern horizon, angry clouds galloping on either side of the cavern. The sun grew, like a field weed, through the fracture in the churning, water laden clouds. A fiery orange spread through the opening, accented by the reflection of billions of liquid drops which would soon be rain. Breakheart huddled in the nylon chair, his mind blank. He watched Nature gather Her forces for a general onslaught on Carolina's seaboard. He was totally absorbed by heavens fury.

The first streak of lightning struck the center of the river directly in front of him. He started at the sight and the thunder's roar which were simultaneous. As if the lightning were a signal for Nature's army, the trench closed, quenching the fire where the sun had been but a moment before. More silver orange lightning smudged the grey of the morning. Breakheart lit a Doral and watched the storm.

It was six o'clock before Breakheart moved from his personal grandstand. He let the storm cascade around him like a water fall… the downpour cleansing his mind. Rain fell in buckets, splashing him through the porch screen. On a morning he was feeling very old, the coolness of the water on his face felt refreshing. Finally, as the squall began abating, he stood and stretched like a cat after a long nap, and went back to the kitchen and poured a cup of coffee. He squirted a shot of "Sweet-10 "into the steaming cup and picked up the phone.

"General Geise speaking." The phone had rung only once before the big general reached for the receiver.

"Good morning, sir. This is Colonel Breakheart."

"Hey, Cuda, what's up? It is still pretty early on a Sunday morning to be calling," Geise boomed into the phone.

Breakheart grimaced, holding the receiver away from his ear. "Sir, remember I mentioned Captain Hamilton hadn't shown up for work on Thursday or Friday? Well, he has been found."

"That's fine, Dan, but not important enough to be calling so early on a Sunday morning," Geise interrupted.

"I know, sir, but there is more. Major Collins called about an hour ago. It seems Captain Hamilton is dead. They found his Corvette in a creek east of Oriental. Sir, he was murdered. At least that's what the Highway Patrol is saying."

There was a pause on both ends of the line.

"Dan, are you suggesting this has something to do with Jack's accident?" Geise spoke in a low voice of concern.

"General, I don't want to believe it either, but I can't help feeling that way, and so does Major Collins. He is on his way to New Bern as we speak, and will let me know if he gets any more information, but damn it General, if we find out Hamilton was murdered…"

"Yeah, yeah! I know. Well, where do we go from here?" the sizable man asked, his voice roaring once more. "Do we call in the Fed's in Washington or something?"

"No, I don't think so. But I need you to do me a favor. Would you call the CO of NADEP and ask him to have his AV-8 engine experts work on Double Nut's fuel control for me today? Sena, er, Ms. Zaffky informed me on Friday it would take a call from you to disburse the funds necessary for the overtime required."

"Sure, I can do that. I'll phone him the moment we finish here. What time do you want them there?"

"Say around zero nine hundred. I've got a few things I want to do before I leave here. One more thing. I would like to replace Hamilton with Lieutenant Colonel Burns. I know it's a bit unusual, but, as I've said before, there is no one who has more knowledge about the Harrier than Snake."

"I don't have a problem with your selection, but does his being on your team jeopardize the status of the final report with higher headquarters? Will there be questions about your choice? He's on the Group staff and not in 203," General Geise inquired.

"I shouldn't think so. Regardless, I want him working on this with me. If there are any questions, we can use his expertise as a reason. No, I don't think there will be any problem."

"Consider it done then. I'll call Colonel Heib, Snake's boss, and let him know my decision personally. Anything else?"

Breakheart thought quietly for a moment. "No thanks, General. It is times like these when I really appreciate your being the Commanding General. I'll let you know if I learn anything more, and, again, I'm sorry to ruin your Sunday," Breakheart said. He sounded tired, even to himself.

"No sweat, Cuda. You just keep hanging in there."

"I will, you can count on it. Talk to later, sir," Breakheart ended the conversation and carefully replaced the phone. He was pouring another cup of coffee, when his youngest walked into the room.

"Dad, it's Sunday. Why are you up so early?" Rod asked.

"I've got a problem brewing. I'll be leaving soon. Sorry, we won't be able to race today. The regatta will probably be canceled anyway. Have you had a look outside?" Breakheart studied his son.

"Nasty, huh?" Rod agreed with his father. "Well, I'm going back to bed. Will you be home for supper?"

"I don't know for sure. It depends." Breakheart paused, remembering his dinner invitation. "In fact, I will be having dinner with Sena. She invited me yesterday afternoon. I almost forgot about it."

Rod showed a perfect set of even teeth, and his eyes lit up mischievously. "Going to her house huh? That's great. I like her. She was fun on the boat yesterday. So you're going to have supper with her… cool!" He patted Breakheart's shoulder and headed back to his room.

Breakheart took a sip from his mug, and smiled. His offspring were growing up too fast, he thought to himself. Then he dialed Snake.

"Sure, I'll meet you there," Burns said. Breakheart had just finished explaining the situation and asked his friend to meet him at the NADEP. "I don't know if I can help you much or not. Damn it, Dan, you know as much about the Harrier as I do, but if you think I can be of help, I'm your man."

"Thanks, pally. I knew I could count on you. Just having you around will help. We can bounce things off each other better than

I could alone or with the members of the Board. I'll see you in a couple of hours."

"Right," Lieutenant Colonel Bob Burns promised, "see you then."

The line hummed with a dial tone, and Breakheart immediately phoned Sena. He went through the entire morning's events with her, and explained about having the engineers work on the engine. She listened carefully, and when he finished, immediately told him she would be at the NADEP as well. He agreed her presence might be helpful, though thinking to himself, he didn't know how. Yet, it would be nice having her nearby.

With the phone calls made, Breakheart returned to his bedroom and stripped the robe from his shoulders. After a familiar stint in the bathroom, he grabbed a clean flight suit from the top drawer of his bureau. He laid it out on the unmade bed and stuck a Velcro backed AV-8B patch on his left breast pocket and a name tag under the sewn cartoon picture of a Harrier. He retrieved the set of government pens he'd placed on his night stand and stuffed them in the left arm pocket. Finally, he filled two additional pockets with his wallet, knife, and a pack of Dorals. When he was finished, he slipped into the NOMEX suit and stepped into his boots.

The illuminated clock on the Firebird's dash radio read nine o'clock as Breakheart parked across the street from the main door at the NADEP. Lieutenant Colonel Burns was waiting for him, standing in front of the double glass doors. As he stepped out of his car, he jumped at the sound of a horn. It was Sena. She parked behind the Firebird, and joined Breakheart on the street. The two crossed to where Burns stood patiently.

"Good morning, you two," Burns said pleasantly. "You may be wondering why I've called you together today to stand in the rain."

"Right! You called us together. Nice try Snake. You remember Ms. Zaffky?" Breakheart asked.

"No, as a matter of fact, I don't. I do recall a Sena, but she was much better looking and wore a bikini. Any relationship?" Burns teased.

"Don't pay any attention to him, Sena. He thinks he's a comedian, but as you can tell he falls short of breathing, much less being funny on a Sunday morning," Breakheart remarked.

Sena smiled at both men. "Do you two go on like this all the time, or is it just for my benefit?"

"Only when we are together," Burns voiced with a sly twinkle in his eyes. "Wait until you really get to know us. You'll probably wish you had never run across this useless excuse for a human being." He slapped Breakheart on the shoulder. "I'm stuck with him because he's my senior officer, but you don't have that problem. Run now! Get away from him while you still have the chance."

"Thanks a lot, Snake. You can be so damned charming. If you are quite through, do you suppose we could get out of the rain?" Breakheart said, holding the door open for Sena.

Sena, removing her raincoat, wondered about these two men. To hear them talk, one would think they hated each other, but she instinctively knew it was the other way around. They were brothers in the heart, and could say whatever they damn well pleased to each other. She walked to the enclosed guard post and retrieved their badges. "Here, you jerks, pin these on and follow me," she declared, thinking she would not be out done. She could play verbal games with the best of them.

Breakheart looked at Burns with mild astonishment. "I think we might create a monster here. Do you think she'll be able to keep up?"

"I think you may have your hands full," Burns retorted. "She's got more brains than you." He smiled.

Located two blocks from the main entrance, it took ten minutes for the three to walk to the F402 engine shop. Several engineers, dressed in white coveralls, were already hovering over the blackened, twisted mess which had been the right side of Zero Zero's engine. Looking up from their work, greetings and names were exchanged.

"I'm sorry to have you come in on your day off, but there are some answers I need today, if that is possible. I'll tell you what I know for a fact, and I hope you can start looking for the cause." Breakheart opened the session. "We know from the transmission tapes held by Twilight, that the engine was at idle when Colonel Adams made his initial call for help. We also know the engine would not accelerate and throttle position had no effect."

"Sounds like a throttle disconnect," a young engineer said immediately.

"No, I don't think so," Breakheart stated firmly. "If it was as simple as a throttle disconnect, I don't believe the engine would have immediately gone to idle. In fact, if it was a manual disconnect, the engine could just as likely overspeed, or, according to the NATOPS manual, if it had decelerated, it would have gone to a sub idle condition, not just altitude idle."

"That's correct," an older man spoke. "I've been working on the Rolls Royce, Harrier engine since nineteen seventy three, and I have never encountered a situation which held the motor at idle. As I recall, I have never heard of an actual throttle disconnect. Here look at this diagram."

Spread out on a large work bench nearby, a technical blue print of the entire fuel control system had been laid for reference. The group leaned over the table, studying the maze of nearly unintelligible lines and boxes.

"See, look here," the grey haired engineer pointed. "The actual mechanical linkage of the throttle is relatively short. The throttle is attached to a rod, mechanically, and the rod extends to the Dual Wound Resolver, which is nothing more than an electrical device. The mechanical throttle setting is converted into an electrical potential, and sent to the Fuel Metering Unit."

"Yes, I understand," Breakheart spoke, shaking his head. "If that's the case, and there was a throttle disconnect between the throttle and the Resolver, what would the chances be of the engine going to idle?"

"Oh, there is a very good possibility. The question is, why would it stay at idle. With nothing controlling the Resolver, the engine would, in all likelihood, continue to search for a RPM. In other words, if the throttle had no control through the Resolver, the engine would change RPM up and down again and again."

"That is not what Colonel Adams reported to Twilight. He said the engine had gone to idle, period. What about the Fuel Metering Unit, could its filter clog to such an extent that not enough fuel could get to the engine?"

"I can answer that question," Burns announced. "If the filter had clogged with bad fuel, or for any other reason for that matter, the pressure differential across the filter would have been sensed electronically. If that happened, a bypass valve opens automatically. The pilot would not even know it occurred, except for the caution indicator on his refueling panel. It most certainly would not cause the engine to go to idle."

"He is absolutely correct," the older engineer nodded. "No, it has got to be something introduced into the system. The DECS and FMU are about as fool proof as a system can be. There are back ups to the back ups."

"What if," Breakheart began, "the Dual Wound Resolver got fooled somehow? I mean, no matter where the throttle was placed, it kept sending the signal to the FMU for idle RPM."

"Highly unlikely, but something we'll have to check on," another of the engineers said quietly. "In fact, tearing down the Resolver is as good a place to start as any. Was there any mention of Colonel Adams switching to Manual Fuel Control?"

"Not on the tape," Breakheart replied. "However, I knew Jack Adams, and he was a damned fine aviator. He was well versed on his emergency procedures, and I'm sure he tried Manual Fuel. Still, we will check it out. They brought the remains of the cockpit in on Friday. Hopefully, we'll be able to discover what actions he took to try and solve his problem."

"That's good. Maybe you could provide us with that information while we start tearing down the Resolver." It was the older engineer speaking. "It could help us narrow down the areas we need to look at in detail."

"Right, Breakheart exclaimed, "We'll head that way now. Sena, would you mind staying here? If they come up with anything, you could act as a messenger."

"Sure, I was planning to do just that. Besides, working with these gentlemen will provide a perfect opportunity for me to learn more about the Harrier's engine. You go on, and I'll get up with you later."

"Thanks. You have been a big help already," Breakheart smiled. "Come on, Snake, let's you and I see what information we can rummage out of the cockpit."

VMAT-203's hangar was as quiet as a tomb. Cross country flights had not begun to return from their Friday launch, and the night crew would not be due for another six hours. Burns and Breakheart entered the immense hanger bay through the back door, and were immediately challenged by a corporal guarding the wreckage of Zero Zero. They explained who they were and flipped their wallets open to show identification cards. The Marine waved them on, and they went straight to the cockpit.

"Christ, you weren't kidding about being muddy in that field of yours," Burns proclaimed in awe. "I thought you said you told 542's sergeant to clean this thing up?" He ran his hand down the side of the cockpit and then wiped the mud covering his hand on a rag draped on the first stage fan. "If this is clean, I can't imagine what it must have looked like before."

"Yeah, it's a mess all right. I think we had better find some gloves before we start digging around. We don't want carbon fibers in our hands, and it appears the cockpit's skin was burned by the explosion."

Breakheart began searching for gloves, while Burns wandered around the scattered remains of the crashed aircraft. Most of the AV-8B's skin and internal frames were made of a carbon fiber material much like those found in today's fishing rods. Smooth and strong, the fibers, under normal conditions, presented no problem, but when burned or fractured, the tiny hair like fibers could puncture skin easily. Once the small fiber got under the skin, it was virtually impossible to locate, and could enter the blood stream to travel throughout the body. Gloves were certainly in order, and Breakheart located a neatly piled stack of heavy gloves laying on one of the stanchions used to rope the area off from unwanted guests.

"Here you go," Breakheart yelled at Burns, and threw him a pair. "Put these on before you hurt yourself," he grinned at his friend.

The cockpit, though mostly intact, was an accumulation of confused tangles…wires, ripped and torn metal, dangling avionics "black boxes," and broken glass. The stick was bent almost in half, more than likely from the force of Jack being thrown through the windscreen, seat and all, Breakheart thought. The DDI control panel and its associated TV monitor were missing altogether. Gauges, with their glass face plates broken, covered the cockpit floor, and what few remained attached to the panel, were suspended by wiring, no longer recessed into their proper ports. To make matters worse, if that were possible, the cockpit was inundated with oozing mud. Though the men from 542 had tried to clean the mess as best they could, there remained globs of still wet slime clinging to everything, inside the cockpit and out.

"Let's start cataloguing everything," Burns said. I'll record, you sift. Is that okay with you?" He stripped off the gloves Breakheart had handed him earlier.

"Sure. I wouldn't want you to get your hands dirty," Breakheart smiled at his friend. "I gather you have a notebook and pen with you?"

"Never leave home without them. You never can tell when I might need to copy down a lady's phone number. Now get on with it, will you. I have a date tonight."

"Well, will wonders never cease? As it so happens, so do I," Breakheart retorted. "Sena is having me for dinner."

"Lucky you! Seriously, she seems to be a great gal. You might want to give her consideration for a long term relationship."

"Right, and you're telling me about long term relationships. Hell, you haven't kept a woman around longer than it took you to get her in the rack. You're a fine one to advise me on anything to do with the ladies."

Burns smiled at Breakheart, "Someone has to. Now, are you ready?"

Carefully, Breakheart began sorting his way through the ruined cockpit. The first switch he searched for was the Manual Fuel Control. Normally located on the left console panel just aft of the throttle quadrant, he found both the switch and quadrant ripped free of their tie downs, and laying on the cockpit floor.

"Snake, the Manual Fuel Control switch was switched to Manual Fuel. The entire throttle control box is intact with about eleven inches of the rod still attached to the throttle itself. So, Jack did try manual fuel, and he still couldn't get the engine to accelerate. The damn thing is burned all to hell, but you can still make out the switch position. It's definitely over centered into the manual side."

Breakheart sat the throttle quadrant aside and continued to explore through the rubble. He found the RPM gauge, the dial stuck at 25 percent. The Jet Pipe Temperature indicator was destroyed, but he set it aside with the throttle. Perhaps the engineers at NADEP could detect the final reading by breaking it down and probing the internal workings of the gauge, he thought to himself. As he sorted through the disordered mess that had once been Double Nuts' instrument panel, he gave the final readings and positions of gauges and switches to Burns, who wrote the findings down in his notebook. They worked steadily for two hours, going over the entire cockpit in detail, leaving nothing unturned.

Immersed in their work, they had not noticed the activity which was beginning to take place around them. Marines dressed in utilities were meandering their way through the hangar, stopping to look questioningly at the two officers grubbing in the piled wreckage covering the deck. These were plane captains, part of the night crew, arriving early to receive the cross country birds. It was mid afternoon, and the roar of a Harrier could be heard executing a vertical landing on the South Pad, directly across from where Burns and Breakheart worked.

"Damn it, where did the time go?" Breakheart said. "We had better get the throttle quadrant down to the NADEP before those engineers decide it is time to head to the family trough."

The rain had stopped about the time Breakheart and Burns had entered 203's spaces, and now the sun was trying to poke its way through the remaining clouds. A section of A-6's entered the break, as the two left the hangar. Both men looked up to watch the bulbous nosed aircraft peel hard for the downwind leg of their landing pattern. Pilots could never stop watching formations in the break; they had to critique such actions.

"Lousy, pussy break," Burns commented. "A-6 drivers have no class."

"Boy, aren't you a hard bastard. Not everyone flies with your manic tendencies. Thank God!" Breakheart chided his friend. "Besides, an A-6 is nothing but an inverted bathtub with a long spout. What do you expect, the Blue Angels?"

"Just making a comment on their pussy break. I'll bet they didn't pull more than a G and a half. Hell, a good break requires at least four or five G's to make it something worthwhile."

"Snake. Don't ever change," Breakheart laughed, and carefully placed the cockpit pieces in the trunk of the Firebird.

Sena and the engineers were just getting ready to close up shop for the day when Breakheart and Burns stepped into their work spaces. Both men had their arms filled with charred remains of cockpit gauges and the throttle quadrant.

"Think we forgot about you?" Breakheart asked. "We have a pile of gear here, and hope you can come up with something. Any luck with the Fuel Metering Unit, or the Resolver?"

"Yes and no," the elder engineer replied. "We stripped the Resolver, and found it working properly. It is our assumption, not only was it working correctly, it was telling the FMU to maintain the engine at idle. We can't figure it out. If the throttle did disconnect, then it would not have been stuck in the idle detent, but that's what it looks like."

"Yes, and the FMU was one hundred percent okay," a younger man interrupted. "I dismantled it myself, and you can be rest assured, nothing was wrong with the Fuel Metering Unit. In fact, the filter looked brand new. There wasn't enough material in the filter housing to cover the head of a pin. It wasn't the FMU, that's for sure."

Breakheart took in the information he was being provided, and sorted it with what he already surmised. "Okay then, where do we go from here?" He asked. "I've got the throttle quadrant here," he handed the quadrant to the grey haired engineer, "and, as you can see, Colonel Adams did switch to Manual Fuel. He did everything right, yet the engine still went to idle. I'm going to tell all of you something, but it is not to be told to anyone else. I mean, gentleman, and lady," nodding to Sena, "I don't want a word to be passed to anyone. Is that clearly understood?"

The faces looking at Breakheart accepted his statement without comment, but still had questions. Even Burns appeared confused.

"I'm about ninety percent sure we are going to find out the aircraft was sabotaged. If it was, then how, and why? I don't expect you to help me with the why, but I do need to know how. We know the ejection seat was tampered with prior to Colonel Adams' flight. Up until now, I have been thinking it was done randomly. Now, with what you are telling me, I think we have much more. I want you to brainstorm a method of causing the engine to go to idle and staying there no matter what a pilot might do to correct the situation."

The shop was silent after Breakheart finished. No one moved or spoke. The smell of JP-5 permeated the surroundings, and in the background the dripping of engine cleaning fluid could clearly be heard above the plant's emptiness.

"You're talking murder," one of the engineers mumbled. "Are you kidding?"

"No, I'm not kidding," Breakheart said seriously. "There have been two deaths since Double Nuts took off on its last sortie, and I think they are related somehow. Do any of you," he looked at each man before him, "have any idea how someone could cause such an accident?"

Again, a long silence. "It could be done, I suppose." It was the older engineer who spoke. "But he would have to have a detailed knowledge of the F402, and unquestionable access to the airplane."

"But how?" Burns asked, and then turned to Breakheart. "More importantly, why?"

"I'm not sure yet, but I'll be damned if I won't find out," Breakheart said flatly, and with a touch of anger in his voice. "Look, I want everybody to go home. Think about what I've said, and if anyone comes up with an idea, call me." He reached for his wallet and passed out calling cards with his name and phone number. "I don't care what time it is, call. If I'm not at home, leave a message with one of my boys. They will pass it on to me. And, thanks for all your help today. I'll be in touch tomorrow. Remember, not a word to anyone…please!"

Sena, Breakheart and Burns took leave of the engineers, walking out to their automobiles. They walked in silence, each cloaked in his or her own thoughts. As they left the drab greyness of the brick building housing the Harrier engine shop, they were met by the steamy remains of the afternoon. The sun was shining in full force, and puddles were evaporating into the air causing the humidity to reach uncomfortable levels.

Sena broke the lack of conversation, "Dan, are you still planning to come for dinner?" she asked softly.

Pushed from his thoughts, Breakheart stopped and looked at the woman beside him. "Yes. I would very much like to come. If you still want me to?"

"Please do," Sena answered sincerely. Her face was flushed from the sudden onslaught of August heat. "Here, let me give you directions." She asked for a piece of paper, and Bob Burns handed her a sheet from his notebook. She lived in Newport, a small town east of Cherry Point, and the subdivision where her house was located was known to Breakheart. "I don't think you'll have any trouble finding it," she continued, while sketching Breakheart a map. "It's a light blue, two story on Turner Street."

"Don't worry, I'll find it. What time do you want me there?"

"Make it around six or six thirty. If that's okay with you?"

"Six thirty is fine with me. I'll be there with a bottle of red wine," Breakheart answered.

The three got in separate cars and drove away. Breakheart accelerated for his quarters, and thought how much he was looking forward to seeing Sena for dinner. He felt a little discomfited about leaving the boys yet another night, but knew they would understand. He was beginning to realize just how special Sena was, and he was thinking about her more than he should. Mix within all of his thoughts were the chunks of information surrounding Jack's accident. More and more he was becoming convinced his friend had been set up.

Later, after showering and changing into slacks and a sports shirt, Breakheart drove east on NC Highway 70 to the turn off leading to Newport. He was feeling much as a school boy might when, to his surprise, the head cheerleader accepted an invitation to attend a dance after the homecoming game. Nestled beside him was a bottle of red wine he thought might go well with steak, though he was no wine connoisseur by any stretch of the imagination. The boys had understood completely, and had almost kicked him from the house when he asked for the tenth time if it was all right with them.

"For God's sake, go!" Bill had finally howled in exasperation. "We'll be fine. Have fun. Just get out of here before you drive us all nutso!"

Breakheart smiled, thinking about his eldest's remarks. They were great guys, and they took care of him as well as themselves, he thought. Finding Sena's house was not difficult, and he drove into her driveway shortly after six. Gathering the wine, he walked to the front door and knocked.

"Come on in." Sena yelled from her kitchen.

Entering the foyer, Breakheart was immediately struck by the homeyness of Sena's living room. Not feminine, as he expected, rather it was comfortable…not reflecting a totally woman's view, but a mixture of deep, rich earth colors mingled with soft pastels. There were no "period" items or antiques cluttering the decor, only familial articles giving the place a lived-in appeal. He felt at home instantly.

"I'm in the kitchen. Like I said, I can burn steaks with the best of them, and I think that is exactly what I'm doing…burning them."

Breakheart peered around the corner into the brightly lit kitchen. The walls were a pale yellow trimmed in a soft red. Again, it reflected the down to earth personality Sena had exhibited since he first met her at the NADEP. The room was large for a kitchen, and was filled with hanging pots, and utensils of every sort.

"I don't believe you for a minute," Breakheart said. "Your kitchen looks as if it is used often and with a purpose. Don't try and kid a kidder. I love to cook as well, but I've got nothing like this." He waved his hand suggesting the efficiency exuded by the kitchen's atmosphere.

"Thanks. I do love to cook, but it isn't much fun preparing large meals for just me. I'm glad you came. It gives me a chance to grub around in here." As she spoke, her hands were busily stirring a white sauce to be used on the fresh asparagus spears cooking in a Chinese bamboo steamer.

Breakheart poured the last of the vino into the tall wine glasses Sena had set earlier as part of the formal dinner setting she had carefully laid as they talked. "Your dinner was delicious. I can't remember when I've eaten so much at one sitting," he complimented Sena, rubbing his stomach. "This has been a very nice evening."

While the steaks broiled, they had sipped a cocktail on Sena's patio, watching the sunset. Clouds, remnants of the day's storm, still pranced through the sky like colts chasing butterflies. If the sunrise had been spectacular by its absence, Breakheart thought, the setting sun was its antithesis. The array of colors crowding the western horizon was truly awe-inspiring…a perfect ending to the perfect meal.

"Let's finish our wine on the patio," Breakheart suggested. He rose from his chair and helped Sena from hers. "We'll do the dishes later."

Sena smiled her acceptance of his offer, and they slid the glass door open to the warm night. The evening air hung heavy, even steamy, but the sweet smell of summer flowers drifted with the coming night. They sat on a patio sofa admiring the view across the yard which edged a large man made lake. A single boat glided silently across the smooth dark water with a lone man casting the shore for an unsuspecting bass.

"You have a lovely spot here, Sena. You have done well with your life. Are you happy at the NADEP?"

Sena thought a moment before answering. "Yes, I enjoy my work, and the NADEP provides me with unending challenges. Yes, I guess I'm happy."

Breakheart looked long into the dark brown eyes of the woman sitting close to him. Without warning, he leaned forward, and took her face in his hands. He kissed her lightly, with a tentativeness approaching timorous. Sena responded, sliding her arms around his neck, and drawing him closer.

Later, the dishes long since forgotten, Breakheart drew Sena close, her sheet covered nakedness reacting to his gentle touch. "I've got to get home sometime tonight," he voiced without strength. "My sons will be wondering if I've fallen off the edge of the earth."

Sena snuggled closer, "I would rather you stayed here." She was completely unpretentious in her request. "It has been a perfect evening. I don't want it to end. Not now, not ever!"

Breakheart smiled, his eyes turning to meet hers. "I know. I feel the same way. Somehow, I don't think either of us is going to let what we might have together slip through our fingers. Do you?"

"I hope not," Sena returned his smile, and stretched to brush his lips with her own. "You may find me hanging around more than you want."

"I doubt it," Breakheart laughed. "But I really have to go."

An hour later, his hands on the wheel of the Firebird, Breakheart let his mind wander aimlessly. He could not believe the magic the evening produced. It was as if a void had suddenly been filled. A dark hole in his heart opened and the flood of life ran into the vacant spot with the force of a rolling tide. It felt good. No, he thought, it felt wonderful, as he pulled into his drive.

Getting out of the car, he could hear the phone ringing inside. He hurried to the front door, but the ringing stopped.

"Dad, is that you?" Steve yelled sleepily.

"Yeah, what's up?"

"The phone's for you," his son said from the kitchen. "I'm going back to bed. This guy has been calling about every half hour since six. I'm glad you're finally home."

"Thanks, son. Good night. See you in the morning," Breakheart said, and rumpled his son's hair as he passed on his way to the bedroom.

Breakheart picked up the phone where Steve had left it on the counter. "Colonel Breakheart here."

"Evening, Colonel," Major Collins spoke. "Seems I'm always reaching you at the damnedest times. Sorry!"

"No sweat. What do you have?"

"Well, Hamilton was definitely murdered. There is absolutely no doubt about it. But here is the real kicker. During the autopsy, traces of mud were found on his face and hands, and completely covering his flight suit. Of course, the creek washed most of it clear, but enough was still evident to cause me to ask some hard questions."

"The bean field, right?" Breakheart interrupted.

"Right, the bean field. I sent my team along with the Highway Patrol detectives to the accident site earlier this afternoon. They gathered mud samples from where we found the engine part Friday afternoon. Plus, I got the results back from the Point's hospital.

The blood type from the engine and mud we collected earlier is a match. I don't think there is any doubt about it. Hamilton was killed near the engine, and was probably buried under it for a time."

"I wish I could be as excited about this news as you appear to be," Breakheart said without emotion. "Unfortunately, it doesn't surprise me, particularly with the information I got from NADEP's engineers this afternoon. Can you be at my team meeting tomorrow morning?"

"Sure, Yes, sir. Where is it going to be, your house?"

"No. Meet me in VMAT-203's readyroom at zero six hundred. I'm going to be addressing the team in one the briefing rooms."

"Okay! I'll be there. Will there be anything else?" Collins asked respectfully.

"No. I'll see you in the morning. And, thanks for calling. I'm sorry it took you so long to get in touch with me. Bye!" Breakheart hung the phone up, and sat quietly in the dark, thinking.

ELEVEN

SERGEANT REDDOCK PACED his small room. He had been walking back and forth for over an hour, wearing a hole in the drab rug. It was late now, on a Sunday night, but the worry he was feeling had plagued him since he had passed the several police cars lining the bridge where he had dumped Hamilton's Corvette.

Christ, how could I have been so damned stupid, he kept thinking to himself. The tide, he'd forgotten about the fucking tide. Now what was he going to do? Panic sometimes ripped through him like a searing hot knife, and the fear would well up inside like a living entity. He stopped his relentless treading, and sat heavily on his bunk. Normally, his roommate, another sergeant from 203's Hydraulic Shop, would have been sharing the small quarters, but he was on leave. He'd gone to visit his family in New Hampshire. Left alone, Reddock could only think of what might happen to him if he got caught. That God-damned, self-righteous colonel had been too interested in the engine section he'd hidden Hamilton under to be coincidence, he thought.

He studied the wall over his bed. Covered with Playmates in various states of disrobe, they would have, under different circumstances, aroused his interest. Not tonight! His mind kept drifting to thoughts of a gas chamber, with him sitting in its single chair, strapped down and gasping for breath. He could be executed if caught.

Suddenly, Reddock made a decision. He got to his feet and walked with purpose to the door. Several minutes later, he was dialing a number in a pay phone located a block away from his barracks. The night air, though warm, smelled fresh and clean from the day's rain, and he sucked it into his lungs with a gusto he did not feel. On the other end of the line a man answered.

"This is Reddock," the sergeant said before the other could say anything more than, 'Good…' "I've got a problem and you have got to help me."

"What the fuck are you calling me at home for, you idiot?" the man raged. "This had better be good."

"Listen, you pompous son of a bitch, I've got to get out of here… like now. Do you understand? I've done your dirty work, and more. Now it's over. I want to leave Cherry Point tonight."

"What do you think I can do for you? What's your problem?"

"Never mind my problem. I set the accident up, but things are getting out of hand. I might get caught, and if I do, I'm not going down alone. I'll squeal like a stuck pig, you can bet on that," Reddock said, anger seething in his words.

"Are you threatening me? Do you think you can blackmail me with veiled innuendoes? Forget it. You got paid, and that's that."

"You don't understand, do you? There are two men dead now, and I did them both to save your stinking hide. Now I've got to get clear, and I need money, twenty-five thousand."

A burst of humorless laughter crackled across the line. "Fuck you! I don't have that kind of money laying around, and even if I did, I certainly wouldn't be passing it on to you."

"Well, then get it from your boss, or I'll blow the whistle on the whole damned thing." Reddock was getting madder by the minute. There was a long pause, the phone humming quietly in his ear. "Well, what's it going to be?"

"Okay, I'll tell you what. I'll get in touch with my partner and if he agrees, I'll pay you. But, and I want to make this perfectly clear, if I give you twenty-five grand, that's the end of it."

"I'll agree to those conditions. I don't want any of your friends breathing down my neck for the rest of my life. I'll take the money and disappear, that's a promise."

"Fine! Meet me on the west side of the Emerald Isle bridge tomorrow night at ten o'clock. Do you know where the bridge is?"

"Yeah, I can find the fucking bridge. I'll be there and you had better have my money." Reddock slammed the phone back on its hook, and smiled for the first time in two days. "Whew," he whistled aloud, "that was easier than I thought it would be."

Sergeant Reddock walked back to his room, already counting the money he would shortly have in his possession.

TWELVE

BREAKHEART SHIFTED DOWN from fourth to second as he pulled into 203's parking lot. It was a little before six in the morning, yet the sun was already a hot oak coal in the sky. He thought he could see wisps of steam rising from the puddles remaining from the rain the day before. Of course, imagining the vapor rising off the water was ridiculous, Breakheart acknowledged to himself, but the sweat pouring from his forehead made him feel that way. To his right, as he walked for the hangar, a Harrier was winding up through its start cycle, and another was taxiing from VMT-231's flight line. Cars began filling the parking lot, lieutenants and captains coming to work. Marines scurried around the hangar, busily preparing for the day's maintenance on AV-8's downed for repairs.

Colonel Breakheart walked swiftly to the hangar and took the stairs two at a time. He wanted to prepare the briefing room prior to the arrival of the other members of his team. As he entered the readyroom, he was surprised to see Snake at the Acey Duecy table.

"Morning, Cuda," Burns smiled up from his chair. "You're here bright and early."

"Not as early as you it appears," Breakheart greeted his friend. He walked to the coffee pot, and poured himself a Styrofoam cup full of what looked like black mud, adding a touch of sugar to soften the blow of the strong brew. "I want to write some things on the blackboard before everyone arrives. When you're done with your game, come join me," he said to Burns.

"I'll be done in a minute. I'm beating this young captain so thoroughly, he will probably wish to leave the Corps and seek an occupation elsewhere," Burns gloated.

Breakheart ignored the insult to the young man and turned to the Duty Officer. "Which briefing room should I use for the Accident Board meeting?"

The First Lieutenant behind the raised desk greeted the colonel and shrugged, "Just pick one sir, it doesn't make any difference to me."

"Right," Breakheart acknowledged, and strode off to the briefing rooms located at the far end of the large readyroom.

It wasn't long before Major Dyke and the rest of his team arrived and took seats around the small briefing table. Breakheart greeted each member as they came through the door. The last to take his seat was Burns, who came aboard with Major Collins.

"Gentlemen, I'm sure you have noticed we have two additional members on our team this morning. Well, they are here for a very good reason. I need their help." Breakheart opened the conference. "You all know Major Collins, he was with us at my quarters the other night. As you are aware there is an NIS investigation taking place concurrently with ours, and for good reason. I'll go into more detail later. Lieutenant Colonel Burns is a familiar figure to all of you I am sure, and he is now part of our team."

Questioning looks spread across the table.

"Captain Borgerding, will you please shut the door," Breakheart said to the man closest to the small room's entry. "What I have to say this morning, like in our past few get togethers, is for your ears only. We don't need a passerby thinking he has the general scoop on the accident. Now, as for Lieutenant Burns, I asked General Geise to allow me to have Snake join us because of Captain Hamilton's absence. What you probably haven't heard is Captain Hamilton will not be coming back. He is dead."

Breakheart's hard, cold statement had its immediate effect. Hamilton was a friend of all the VMAT- 203 officers, and to be told he was no longer among the living was a shock. Their faces contorted at the revelation.

"To make matters worse, we know he was murdered. Major Collins, will you please fill us in on the details?"

Collins nodded and began relating the facts about Hamilton's death. He spoke quietly, and with a touch of reverence, but he did not leave out the gory details.

Major Collins told it like it was, in full, leaving nothing to the imagination. The wound to the side of the dead captain's head, he explained, was caused by a blunt instrument, perhaps a wrench. He continued with the information about the body being buried under the engine located in the ditch. Stunned silence shook the small room forcefully. When Collins told of the car being found in the tidal creek, at least one of the board was crying openly.

"Reggie was my best friend," Captain Tom Hicks mumbled. "He can't be dead. What's happening here, Colonel?" He asked, trying to control the shake in his voice. "This is a whole lot more than just an accident investigation."

"You're correct, Captain," Breakheart consoled. "Much more, and the very reason we are sitting in this room right now. We have to find out what caused the accident. Once we find the reason why, we might be able to narrow suspects down to a workable number. Right now, every one of us in the bean field could have been the murderer. I'm going to count on each of you to give me your undivided attention. We have to solve the mystery surrounding the accident, and we have to do it quickly. I can't expect to keep the events of the past week under wraps much longer."

Not a sound was uttered from the men around the table, just a nod or two.

"Okay then, let's get on with it. I've written a few things on the board. Remember, the first night we got together I said we needed to find out what did not cause the accident and then we would know what did. Well, at least we're ahead of the game in that regard. I listened to the Twilight tape on Friday and from the recording we can discount aircraft problems dealing with hydraulic, flight control, electrical supply, and general avionics. Colonel Adams stated clearly his engine went to idle, and nothing he could do would accelerate the engine's RPM. Yesterday afternoon, Lieutenant Colonel Burns and I began sorting through the cockpit. What we found confirms the Manual Fuel system had been selected by Colonel Adams. So, we are reasonably sure he followed his emergency procedures correctly. From the NADEP we learned that the FMU and Dual Wound Resolver were working properly. What we don't understand, and neither do the NADEP engineers, is why. If the Resolver was working properly then it should not have been sending a signal to the FMU to remain at idle."

"It couldn't be a throttle disconnect then." Captain Borgerding interrupted.

"You're absolutely correct," Breakheart took charge once more. "At least, it appears that way on the surface. But, we can't rule completely out the possibility of a disconnect. At least not yet. Nor can we rule out an engine electrical or computer problem, including the DECS."

"What are you looking for from us?" Major Dyke asked. "We still have to get the remaining parts of the aircraft out of the field. That is going to take at least another six or seven days."

"I know," Breakheart replied. "I want you to select one of our team to lead the removal, the rest will stay here and sift through Double Nuts one burnt part by burnt part."

"Do you want the same enlisted men in the field? I did as you said and kept the same Marines under Gunny Hicks. They are on their way to the field right now."

Breakheart thought for a moment, wondering if he should recall the bus loaded with 203's enlisted men. "I think we can keep the same group working in the field. Besides, it would create too much of a delay to recall them and gather another detail. Yes, let's leave well enough alone on that manner."

"I'll want to interview the guards who were on duty the night of Hamilton's murder, Major Collins interjected. "Plus, I'll want to talk to every man who was in the field last week."

"Where do you want to conduct your interviews?" Major Dyke asked.

"I'll set up an interrogation tent using my men, and we can start at the accident site this afternoon. If that's okay with you, Colonel?" Collins asked.

"If NIS starts nosing around the accident site," Burns broke in, "we are going to raise a lot of eyebrows. The scuttlebutt will be buzzing around the Point faster than at an old ladies sewing circle."

"Yes, sir, I know, but I have to start questioning those men. Besides, I can guarantee the Highway Patrol and local authorities are going to start busting in on your investigation. After all, the murder occurred off base on civilian property. I'm not going to be able to stall them for more than a few hours."

"The local newspapers and TV stations are going to jump on this like stink on shit. Whoever killed Hamilton probably had something to do with the crash, but I don't want the media to get wind of that until later. Of course, they will probably put two and two together and come up with six, but, in this case their guessing might help rather than hinder us."

"Why do you think that?" Snaked asked.

"The longer we can make the saboteur feel he is relatively safe the better. If the newspapers and TV do their usual style of reporting, then we'll have more time. Those stupid SOBs couldn't report a story correctly if I wrote the details down for them."

Burns nodded, though thought Breakheart was being over optimistic.

"Sir, you want us to concentrate on the engine and fuel control systems, right?" Major Dyke asked, already knowing the answer.

"Yes, that's correct. Major Dyke, you take charge here in the hangar, Lieutenant Colonel Burns and I will be at the NADEP."

"If I'm going to get my interrogations started, I had better be on my way," Major Collins stated, rising from his chair. The rough scraping of the chair's legs on the linoleum floor grated like chalk on a blackboard. "I'll try and get in touch with you," he gestured to Breakheart, "sometime this afternoon or sooner if I come up with anything important."

Silently, the remaining men watched the tall major leave. Their friend, wingman and section leader was dead, and they each hoped this man, now on their team, would find the son of a bitch who killed him.

"Okay then, you all know what we are looking for, let's get on it." Breakheart shook a Doral from the pack he'd retrieved from his flight suit and touched a Zippo to its end, sucking deeply. "Snake, you go on down to the NADEP. I'll meet you at the engine shop later. I've got a session with General Geise."

Burns signaled his understanding as the group rose and filed from the small room. Breakheart erased the few points he had written on the blackboard, and followed. His pace through the readyroom and out of the hangar was slow. He was deep in thought, still trying to understand why the engine would not accelerate. Clouds were gathering over the Neuse, preparing a thunder storm for later in the day, but he did not notice.

"God damn it, your order for me to kill Adams has touched off a shit load of problems for me."

Raoul Bolivar poked tentatively at the freshly halved and sectioned grapefruit surrounded by a china bowl setting before him. "Look, you honky bastard, I don't care about your problems. I am only concerned with results, and I'm not getting any from your end. I told you, if you can't handle the situation, I've got men here who will be glad to visit North Carolina. I've even got volunteers."

"No! No, that won't be necessary," his voice was slightly contrite and condescension. "I'll find some way of taking care of everything, but your demands are putting me in a tight situation."

"Tough, compadre. Now what's this about needing twenty-five grand for some blackmailer? You don't really believe I'm going to send you that kind of money do you? If so, you're a bigger jerk than I could have believed possible," Bolivar uttered in a tight voice.

"I guess not, but I wanted you to know what was going on up here. I'll take care of this latest development myself, but if things keep going as they are, we may have to shut down operations for a while."

"Look, you pissant, nobody's shutting down anything," Bolivar's anger was rising with each word. "You came to me, remember. This entire operation was your doing, and by God you'll live up to the bargain or you're going to be floating head down in your own shit. Do you understand me?"

"Yes, sir, I do," the voice shook with a trace of fear. "I'll see to everything. You can count on me." He hung the phone up, not waiting to be insulted or threatened further.

Bolivar, his face red with fury, looked across the expanse of his desk. His office, decorated in a Spanish motif, exuded opulence. Overstuffed, leather chairs sat on either side of a matching sofa facing the desk. On every wall, save one, hung antique weapons of every sort, including two complete sets of fifteenth century armor which had been carefully restored and cut in half to allow them to be hung on the wall. The effect was startling, with knights of old walking straight out of the well-oiled wood. On the far wall, facing Bolivar, a huge coat of arms, one he would have liked to believe was his own, overlooked the angered man. Suddenly, the outrage overwhelming him, Bolivar picked up the grapefruit and threw it against the rich mahogany wall paneling. "God damn that cock sucker. If he doesn't take care of things, I'll eat his liver for lunch," he screamed aloud.

"You look worn out," General Geise said with a trace of sympathy. "This investigation is a rough one, huh?"

"Yes, sir, it is," Breakheart acknowledged. "But we're zeroing in on the bastard." He went on to explain the latest developments involving Adams' crash, including Hamilton's death and his suspicions of a link between the two.

"Bullshit," General Blake said acidly. He had joined Breakheart and Geise as Breakheart was ushered into the Commanding General's office. "You don't even know if someone caused the plane to crash, only that the seat was tampered with prior to his flight. You don't seriously believe someone could have sabotaged both the aircraft and the seat, do you?"

Breakheart's eyes blazed momentarily with indignation. God I hate this stupid SOB, he thought to himself. "Yes, sir, I do believe it is all connected and I intend to prove just that. If it is quite all right with you, that is?" The ice in Breakheart's voice betrayed his feelings directed at his superior officer.

"Enough," General Geise spoke uncharacteristically subdued. "It won't help this investigation for the two of you to be at each others' throat. I must agree with Cuda on this issue, Gene," he spoke directly to General Blake.

Blake sat back in his chair and glared at Breakheart. He was not used to having colonels speak to him in the manner Breakheart had just spoken. He was a "general" and that gave him rights, one of which was respect from junior officers. Just because he and Breakheart had been colonels together until a year past, didn't give the man a right to speak in such a manner. To make matters worse, Geise had sided with Breakheart.

"When do you think you'll have more about the cause?" Geise continued.

"With luck, this afternoon. Snake is with the F402 engineers right now, and I hope we'll find more about the fuel control system." Breakheart paused to take a sip of coffee from the mug he held in his left hand. "I've got some other areas to pursue."

"What areas?" General Blake asked, his tone mellowed. "I thought you were concentrating on the fuel control system?"

Breakheart eyed the brigadier with a cautious look, not wishing to cause more trouble with his answer. "Nothing of real importance. It really is little more than finding out Jack's state of mind prior to his flight. It is all part of the final accident investigation report. I want to get it done before folks start forgetting what he might have been doing for the last couple of days or weeks prior to his crash."

Breakheart's comment seemed to satisfy any misgivings Blake might have had earlier. General Geise nodded his approval.

"Sir, if there are no more questions, I would like to get busy. I've got people spread from the bean field to Cherry Point and back again."

"Of course, I understand. General Blake, do you have any further questions for Colonel Breakheart?" Geise asked as he stood to return to his desk.

"No, sir, I don't believe so," Blake answered. He started walking for his own office when Breakheart stopped him.

"Sir, if I might have a word with you?"

Blake looked questioningly at Breakheart. "Sure, I suppose so. What have you got?"

The two men stepped through the side entrance into Blake's office. It was much like General Geise's, only slightly smaller. Where Geise had pictures of F-18's hanging on his wall, Blake's displayed Cobras and AV-8s. Blake indicated a chair to Breakheart, and sat behind his desk.

Breakheart remained standing, not quite at attention, but stiffly. "Sir, you have been wanting to try your hand at out flying me ever since you took over as the Assistant Wing Commander. Well, I need a break from this mess, and a good hop would clear my head. What do you think, you want to give me a try?" Breakheart issued the challenge. He felt a tad childish, for he knew he could fly circles around Blake, but he felt it was time to shut the man's arrogance up for good.

General Blake smiled with mirth. "Sure! Let's do it. It will give me great pleasure whipping up on you. What say we make it a bombing hop on BT-3, and use the remaining fuel for a couple head-on-head dogfights?"

"Sir, your recommendation sounds perfect. I'll arrange it with one of the Harrier squadrons for later this week. Will that be okay with you?"

"Fine! Fine! I'll be available, but let me know at least a day in advance. I'll have to arrange my schedule," General Blake declared.

"I'll take care of it, sir," Breakheart said without humor. "I'll be in touch."

He left Blake's office, passing through the swinging doors, not unlike a tavern, straight out of the old west, without further comment. The hinged doors led to the Chief of Staff's office, which was vacant, from there he walked swiftly down the hall to the stairs leading to the second deck.

"Hey, Colonel," a massive Master Sergeant boomed, as Breakheart entered the main offices of the Wing's Operations division, G-3. Master Sergeant Bloom was dressed in his Summer Service Charlie's, Marine green trousers and a tan shirt. Above his left breast pocket six rows of brightly colored ribbons adorned his powerful chest, evidence of his involvement in practically every significant Marine Corps operation since Viet Nam.

"Morning, Top, how goes it?" Breakheart greeted the big man. He'd known the Top for several years, and respected him as an outstanding enlisted leader.

"Well howdy, colonel. How is the investigation going?" He asked with interest and a Texas drawl.

"It's still a touch rough around the edges, but we're narrowing it down."

"Colonel, you always do. You're the best damned accident investigator around, and everybody knows it. Do you want to see Colonel Blain?"

"That's why I'm here," Breakheart smiled. "And thanks for the compliment. I'm not sure it's deserved, but thanks anyway. Frankly, I would rather be a captain again, flying two or three missions a day, like in the good old times."

"Yeah, I know what you mean. This desk work gets on my nerves too," the mountain of Marine said, walking to the G-3's door. He knocked twice and announced Breakheart, "Sir, sorry to interrupt, but Colonel Breakheart is here to see you."

Breakheart did not wait for an answer. He slipped by the giant standing in the door and waved off handily, "Hey, Jim, told you I would be by. Can I ask you a few questions?"

"Sure, come on in," Colonel Jim Blain greeted him cheerfully. "Sit down. Do you want a cup of coffee?"

"No, thanks. I just came from the General's office. His coffee is enough to last a person for a week. One cup has enough caffeine to jump start a horse."

Both men laughed, as Breakheart looked about the office. Two desks stood side by side. One for the G-3 and the other for his assistant, who was absent. Four telephones were stationed strategically around the desks, allowing easy access for either officer. The desks were positioned in front of three sets of windows. Blain now sat with his back to them all, while Breakheart squinted against the sun's reflection radiating through the glass. The spacious office had the feeling of frenzied accomplishment. Papers were stacked haphazardly on both desks, and boxes of operation plans lined a side wall.

"You know why I'm here. Did you find out who directed the removal of all Jack's effects? I still don't understand why," Breakheart inquired.

"Yeah, I remember your asking. The Top here cleaned everything out. He boxed it up and gave it to the Chief."

Breakheart looked inquiringly at the big Master Sergeant, who had remained standing in the door. "Who gave you the order, Top?"

"The Chief called up about an hour after the crash and asked me to clear Colonel Adams' desk and bring it down to him. I did as he directed. That's all I know. Why? Is it important?"

Breakheart sat studying the deck. The rug, he noticed, was a dirty maroon color, worn thin by constant use and there was little Wing money to replace it. "I don't know. But it is an unusual order, don't you think? Did the Chief say why he wanted everything so soon after the crash?"

"No, sir, and I didn't ask. Didn't think it was my place. After all, my boss had just bought the farm."

Breakheart turned back to Colonel Blain. "You didn't happen to find anything since we talked the other day, have you?"

"No, I'm afraid not. Sorry. I wish I could help, but that's about it," Blain answered. "I guess you had better talk with the Chief."

"I'll do that, and thanks for your help." He looked back to the Top. "Do you recall if Colonel Adams was working on anything special before the crash?"

The Master Sergeant thought for a moment. "Just a minute sir, I'll be right back." He left, disappearing into one of the four side offices adjoining the G-3's.

The phone rang, and Colonel Blain picked it up. It was General Geise's private line to the '3. Blain mumbled a few words and hung up. "That was General Geise, he wants me in his office, like yesterday. I've got to go. The Top will take care of you. You can use my office if you like," he said gathering a raft of papers from his desk and hurried out of the room.

Breakheart yelled his thanks to a disappearing back, as the Master Sergeant returned with a young captain in tow.

"Sir, this is Captain Dunn." The Top made the introduction. "He was working on something special for Colonel Adams regarding Cross Country flights. That's about the only thing out of the ordinary the Colonel was working on before he died."

"Thanks Top," Breakheart said, sticking his hand out to the captain. "Nice meeting you, Captain Dunn."

"Nice meeting you too, sir," Dunn answered. "What can I do for you?"

Breakheart led the captain to a chair, and they both sat. "What were you doing special for Colonel Adams?"

"Well, there wasn't anything really special about it. He just wanted me to compile a list of cross country flights scheduled for the past three months, where they were going, and who the pilots were requesting flights. You are aware, sir, all cross country flights have to be approved by the Wing, so it wasn't all that difficult to assimilate the information for Colonel Adams."

"So you had finished gathering the information for Colonel Adams and given it to him before he had his accident?" Breakheart pressed.

"Yes, sir. In fact, I gave him the report at least a week before his accident. Why, is it important?"

"I don't know," Breakheart whispered more to himself than to the other two men. "I just don't know. Top, did you ever see the report?"

"No, sir. I just knew Colonel Adams was anxious to have it in his hands. I don't know what he did with it, and it wasn't in the effects I gathered from his desk." The big man paused for a second. "I wonder what he did with it."

"Did he often take work home with him?" Breakheart asked.

"Rarely, if ever. Colonel Adams worked hard, but when he left the office, he left the office. If you know what I mean." The big Top's blue eyes studied Colonel Breakheart with renewed interest.

"Captain, do you have a copy of your report?" Breakheart asked perplexedly.

"No, sir, I don't. I only made the one copy and it was handwritten. Colonel Adams asked for it before I had a chance to have it typed."

"Could you do it again for me? It may mean nothing at all, but I would like to see what Colonel Adams was so interested in."

"I would be happy to, sir, but I can't. When the Top was clearing out Colonel Adams' desk, the Chief asked me to bring all the Cross Country requests for the past six months to him. I explained we only kept them on file for three months, and he told me to bring them to him ASAP."

Breakheart shook his head in confusion and lit a Doral. "I just don't understand," he muttered.

"I'm sorry, sir, say again," the captain asked.

"Never mind. Thanks, Captain, for your help," Breakheart let the young officer go. "Top, I may need more information from you later, but frankly, I don't know what it might be right now. Thanks, you have been a big help."

"No thanks necessary, sir. I hope you figure out what happened to the plane. I really liked Colonel Adams. He was a fine officer."

"He was at that," Breakheart said, waving goodbye to the Top and hurrying for the stairs. Retracing his steps down the long hall, lined with pictures of Marine Aviators who achieved the distinction of being called Aces during World War II, Breakheart stepped into the Chief's office. A First Lieutenant behind the Adjutant's desk was on the phone. Breakheart took a seat next to the coffee pot and waited.

"Yes, sir, Colonel, what can I do for you?" The lieutenant asked, hanging up the phone.

"Where is Colonel Keller?" Breakheart inquired casually.

The lieutenant smiled, showing even teeth, "Oh he's on leave. Left this morning with his whole family. He's on a three-week sabbatical in the Bahamas. The Chief has done nothing but talk about it for the past month. He and his family are staying at a place called The Other Shore Club on Green Turtle Cay. There is supposed to be great fishing and diving there, and they have a cottage overlooking the marina. He showed me pictures of the place, and it really looked wonderful."

Breakheart's face betrayed his disappointment. "He'll be gone for three weeks, huh?"

"Yes, I'm afraid so, but I have a number for him if it is really important. Of course, he won't even arrive there until late tonight. They fly into Miami this afternoon, and then board one of those island hoppers to Treasure Cay. From there they have to take a boat to Green Turtle. It's an all-day trip."

"Well, if he calls in, tell him I need to speak to him." The disappointment was evident in Breakheart's voice. "Thanks! By the way, the Bahamians pronounce the word 'key' and not the way it is spelled 'c-a-y'. See you later, Lieutenant."

Breakheart stepped out into the midday heat. The day felt like soggy Corn Flakes soaking in brown milk. A coppery haze bore down on every horizon, cutting visibility to a few miles at best. It was typical weather for a Carolina summer, thought Breakheart as he climbed into his car.

While Breakheart spent his time at the Wing Headquarters, Lieutenant Colonel Burns and Sena were busy at the NADEP's engine shop. The morning's efforts had produced nothing in the way of solving the mystery of why the engine would not accelerate. Importantly, they, along with the five engineers working with them, had determined the DECS was operational at the time of the crash, as were the Step Motors and Resolvers. Engineers were now in the process of interrogating every computer board associated with the fuel management system. So far, all of the boards that did not sustain crash or burn damage showed the computers and microprocessors appeared to be in working properly prior to impact. Every stone rolled suggested the engine was at idle at the request of the pilot.

"It just doesn't make any sense," Burns said to no one. "If everything was working properly, the engine couldn't have been at idle. If I didn't know better I would think Adams committed suicide."

"What did you say?" Sena, forced her way into Snake's thought. "You think it was suicide."

Brought back sharply from his vocal day dreaming, Burns turned to face Sena. "I said, if I didn't know better. Something has to have gone haywire. The F402 just doesn't decide on its own to fly around at 28 percent. No way, there has to be a reason for it. Have they," he indicated the engineers busily working nearby, "had a look at the throttle quadrant yet?"

"No. I think they believe it has something to do with the computers and are saving the throttle until last. Why? Do you think we should start with it now?"

"Yeah, I do. Like Dan says, 'Find out what didn't happen and you'll find out what did ' or words to that effect. We have gone over every molecule of the fuel management system and everything works fine. Soooo! Lets have a look at the throttle."

Sena nodded her agreement, leaving him staring at the cement deck, and walked to the same elderly engineer who had been with them on Sunday. The two exchanged words, and she returned to Burns. "He thinks it is a waste of time, but if it is what you want, they'll start breaking the throttle down."

Burns smiled his best "lady's man" grin, and thanked her.

When Breakheart entered the shop, Sena, Burns and two engineers were closely studying the field stripped throttle quadrant. It had been carefully brushed clean of dirt and burnt residue, then laid out in pieces on the work bench.

"I don't understand," the greying engineer shook his head. "This break on the push rod leading to the Dual Wound Resolver doesn't appear to be crash damage. It's shattered, not broken or cracked as you would expect." He paused and looked around. "Hey, Glen," he yelled at a young engineer working on a computer board, "come over here a minute."

"Well, hi to you all too," Breakheart broke everyone's concentration. "What have you found?"

Sena smiled up at Breakheart, obviously happy to see him. "Good morning, Dan. Er...I mean Colonel Breakheart."

Burns caught the slip of tongue and smiled inwardly. "Sly old devil" was the phrase rumbling through his mind. "Hey, yourself, Colonel," he voiced. "We haven't found anything helpful from the computers, microprocessors, or Resolvers so I had them start on the throttle. Mr. Lucus here thinks something is out of whack with the throttle push rod."

Breakheart sidled up to the work bench, brushing Sena lightly. "What is it Mr. Lucus?" he asked. Peering at the broken down throttle didn't reveal anything unusual at first glance.

"It's this break on the push rod. See, look here," he rolled the rod back and forth under a magnifying glass held on a work stand. "If this rod, which is made of solid stainless steel, was broken during the crash, it would be slightly elongated and smooth, not shattered. These jagged edges would suggest it was instantaneously separated by something akin to an explosion. I suppose it could have happened when the aircraft hit the ground. You did say the plane exploded on impact, didn't you?"

"Yes, that's right. It was one hell of a bang, but the cockpit remained mostly intact. The explosion occurred around the engine and fuel cells. The cockpit was more than likely deep in the mud when it blew."

"If your reasoning is correct, that the cockpit didn't sustain major damage due to the explosion, then something doesn't make sense. The throttle is connected by this rod to the Dual Wound Resolver which is located just aft of the cockpit bulkhead. The rod is only about three and half feet long. With what you brought me, it separated right at the bulkhead or inches behind it. If the cockpit was buried in the mud when the plane blew, then we would not see this sort of break."

"Can you determine what caused it?" Breakheart asked hopefully. "I have a feeling you may be onto something."

"Well, we can spectra analyze it fairly easily, and I'll arrange for some time on the electron microscope. Between the two we might be able to find out what caused it to break. Maybe!"

"Let's do it then," Breakheart commanded. "And while you're at it, why don't you do the same to the Resolver. At least where the rod enters it mechanically."

"Sure, we can do that," Lucus nodded his affirmation. "I'll get right on it." He turned to the engineer he called to earlier. "Glen, get in touch with the folks over in the metal lab. We'll need some microscope time along with the spectra."

The young man acknowledged the request and headed for the phone.

"How long do you think it will take before you have some answers?" Lieutenant Colonel Burns asked.

"Probably late this afternoon or tomorrow morning. That's the best I can do. We'll spend a couple hours on set up before we can even start looking."

Breakheart let out a long sigh. Answers, I need answers he thought. "Okay! Sena would you stick with them this…" He was broken off in mid sentence by a page on an over head speaker system.

"Colonel Breakheart, you have a call on line four. Colonel Breakheart, line four." The call was insistent.

Sena pointed to a phone on a corner desk, reading the questioning look on Breakheart's face.

"Thanks," he said walking for the desk. "Colonel Breakheart here," he spoke into the mouthpiece.

"Sir, this is Major Collins. I'm at a pay phone not too far from the accident site. I've been trying to reach you on the field phone to 203, but they said you had not been back since early this morning."

"I've been busy. What's up?"

"Well, sir, I've been here for a little over four hours. My men and I have been questioning your field team, as you are aware. Nobody knows anything. It's like the day Hamilton was murdered didn't exist. Anyway, the entire crew is here except for one sergeant."

"Well, who is he?" Breakheart was irritable and wanted Collins to get on with it. "Cut to the chase, will you?"

"Yes, sir, sorry. It's a Sergeant Reddock. He has been here every day, but didn't show up this morning. He's one of 203's best engine mechs."

An engine mechanic, Breakheart thought. "What does Gunny Hicks think about Reddock?"

"Hicks suggested Reddock was a good man, always dependable. He figures he just overslept and missed the bus. I took him at his word earlier, but after lunch I called 203's readyroom and had them check if he'd shown up at work this morning. No one has seen him since Saturday."

"Okay! Keep looking for him."

"Sir, do you think Reddock's absence means anything? It certainly does to me. Why does he suddenly become undependable? I don't like it. I'm going to put the Military Police in action and see if we can't pick him up this afternoon."

"Shit, at this point I don't know what to believe, but I think you're right. I'd bet next month's pay he is involved somehow. Good work, Major, and thanks for calling me."

He hung the phone up and sat heavily in a swivel chair next to the desk. For the first time he looked around the engine shop. He counted seven F402s in various states of repair on engine stands. There were at least twenty men and women working at workbenches that surrounded the area where his small band of his people hovered. He hadn't even noticed the others until now. He was getting too wrapped up in this accident, he thought. Too many questions and not enough answers.

Sena joined him at the desk. "Is everything all right? You look like poop warmed over."

"Not quite the way I would put it," he smiled, "but yes, I'm fine. Thanks for asking."

The lady smiled down at Breakheart. "Dan, you'll figure it out. Plus, you've got a lot of help."

"I know." He paused, then smiled. "How are you and Snake getting along? He can be a pain in the ass sometimes."

Her laugh was like a crystal bell, filled with warmth and merriment. "He's great. I can understand why the ladies go for him, but he isn't my type." She reached with her hand, touching his arm lightly. "Well, I'm off to the science fiction room. The big microscope awaits for no man…or woman, for that matter." She started to leave.

"Sena, if I get off early enough tonight I would like to call. Maybe you could join the boys and me for a late dinner?"

"I'd like that," she smiled. "Just let me know." She strode off at a rapid pace, trying, without luck, to catch Mr. Lucus.

"You getting serious on me, pally?" It was Snake. He'd slid up behind Breakheart while he was asking Sena to dinner. "Better watch out, she'll have you building a nest soon."

"Snake, you are the most repulsive son of a bitch I have ever known. Mind your own damn business."

"Yeah, right!" Burns grinned. "Where to now, boss?"

"Christ, I don't know. What time is it, anyhow?"

"Pushing fifteen thirty. What say we go get drunk somewhere? Couldn't hurt, and it might clear our heads."

Breakheart laughed. "Not a bad idea. But, no, not this afternoon. Maybe when we figure out what happened, but not today. I've got to make a run by VMA-542. I did something really stupid this morning and challenged General Blake. I want to set the hop up."

"You challenged Blake? Shit he couldn't find his ass with both hands. Why did you do a dumb thing like that? If you win, he'll make your life miserable."

"I know! But the bastard pissed me off one too many times when I was with Geise. He is such a worthless piece of shit. Oh well, it's done now and I don't dare back down. If I did, he'd be blabbing it all over the base."

"Better you than me. I still would like to pin eagles on someday," Burns said seriously.

"You will, Snake, you will. And if you don't, we'll just sail off to the Caribbean together."

"I'm for that. See you later." The two had been walking as they talked. Burns crossed the street to his car, and waved farewell to his friend.

Breakheart pulled a Doral from its pack in his arm pocket and lit it with a click of his lighter. The sky had clouded over. Dark shadows crossed the tall buildings and shaded the sun. A drop of rain fell on his piss cutter, so heavily it almost knocked it from his head. He took off on a run, reaching the Firebird just as the sky opened for one of old man Noah's downpours.

Sitting in the den, Bill, Steve and Rod sat watching TV. They looked up in surprise when the front door opened and Breakheart entered, throwing his cover on the small table next to the door.

"Hey guys, thought I would try and get home in time for supper. What are you cooking?" Breakheart smiled.

"Nothing yet. Why are you home so early, Pops?" Steve asked. "Are you done with the accident?"

"I wish," Breakheart smiled back. And it isn't all that early. It's after five. If its all right with you guys, I'd like to ask Sena for dinner. If she comes, I'll whip up some fried fish for us."

"Sure, that's fine," Bill answered for them all. "What kind of fish?"

"We've got a package of trout left from our last cruise. Remember, the night we spent on the South River?"

"That sounds great, Pops," Steve slapped his father on the back. "So you want Sena to come over here now. What's going on anyway?"

"None of your business, and stop calling me Pops. You know how much I hate it."

"Yep, I know 'Pops'." He ducked as Breakheart took a mock swing at his head. "Your getting slow in your old age, Pops," Steve teased, easily dodging the cuff.

"I give up," Breakheart threw his arms in the air and laughed. How could he be mad at the blond bundle of energy, he thought?

Later, Sena sat with the Breakhearts at their oval dinning table. Breakheart had prepared his house specialty…fried fish. The delicate fillets had been prepared in a batter of egg and milk, and rolled in Corn Flakes seasoned with over a dozen herbs. Flash fried in a skillet heated to over four hundred degrees, the trout on the table were golden brown, and when touched with a fork, broke with a crispness few thought possible of a fried fish.

"Dan, this is delicious. Where did you learn how to cook?" Sena asked, through a mouthful of fried delicacy.

"He had to out of necessity," Rod smirked. "We all would have starved to death if he hadn't."

Sena caught the youngsters meaning and let the question drop. "Well, it is the best fish I've ever eaten, I can tell you that."

"Thank you. I must admit, there are people who say they don't like to eat fish then I have them taste a mouthful of mine and, suddenly, there is another seafood lover in the world. Of course the recipe is an old family secret. One which I give freely to anyone who wants it."

It was a pleasant meal for them all, especially Breakheart. There was no talk of AV-8 crashes, or of the ongoing investigation. Conversation was lively, with the boys injecting their witticism and teenage humor. The table erupted in laughter more than once, and by the time Breakheart served coffee to himself and Sena, the boys felt as easy around the lovely woman as he did himself.

Sergeant Reddock spent the day at a motel on Atlantic Beach. When he had returned to his room the night before, he gathered a few of his belongings together, packing them in his B-4 bag, and drove to the beach via Highway 70. He checked into the Ramada Inn, located several miles south of the carnival atmosphere of Atlantic Beach proper. He didn't need the Ferris Wheel music interrupting his thoughts of financial freedom. His bank account, filled with over one hundred thousand dollars, was safe in an account he had opened six months earlier, when he'd first been approached to help smuggle drugs into Cherry Point. Now, he thought, with another twenty-five thousand, he could do just about anything he wanted for a long time.

Raised on a tobacco farm in Alabama, Reddock was having trouble believing his good fortune. Never in his wildest dreams had he imagined so much money in his pocket at one time. He sipped a Bud, and turned off the TV he'd been watching since noon. I'm smart enough to keep a low profile until I'm well clear of North Carolina, he thought smugly. As far as the Ramada was concerned, his name was Jones, a Marine on a ninety-six-hour pass. The room he'd rented was for two nights, though he had no intention of spending another evening staring at his room's four walls. Once he got his dough, he was long gone. He was still trying to decide where he would like to go, but for sure it would be far away, and nowhere near Alabama.

The hot shower felt good. It cleared his mind of the cobwebs caused by the six pack of Bud he'd downed since noon. Reddock let the hot stream pound his back like a petite Japanese massage girl walking on his shoulders. He thought of when he'd been stationed in Okinawa, and the girls he had bedded there. Of course he'd had to pay through the nose, but they'd been worth it. At eight, he began dressing…slacks and a sport shirt made up his ensemble, set off by a pair of brown loafers.

By eight thirty he was behind the wheel of his car, heading south on NC 58, the narrow tarred road extending the length of this segment of the Outer Banks' islands. Reddock noted the many miniature golf courses, with their gaudy flamboyant lights and tiny putting greens. One had the dumbest looking pirate he'd ever seen standing over twenty feet high in front of a throng of screaming children wielding putters. The giant sculpture looked more like a sea sick fisherman than an ancient rouge from the sea. Reddock laughed silently.

He drove slowly, not wanting to draw attention to himself. Stop lights were scattered along the twenty-mile stretch to Emerald Isle, slowing summer traffic to a crawl. Young girls, clothed in nothing but the skimpiest of bikinis, walked along the highway; one or two even waved at him as he drove by. Reddock, under different conditions might have considered stopping to see if he could talk one of the young ladies into his car, but not tonight. The only thing on his mind was the twenty-five thousand dollars he was about to pocket, and where he would end his night of driving. He thought he'd head west, at least for a while, but he was thinking more and more of the Florida Keys as being a great place to spend a few months. Reaching the small town of Emerald Isle, he felt an emptiness growling in his gut, and stopped at a corner Burger King for a charcoal broiled hamburger, wolfing it down in four or five bites, followed by a Mountain Dew. It was nine thirty. He had time to kill for the next half hour.

At nine twenty, Reddock parked his '93 Mazda off the road on the west side of the Emerald Isle Bridge. The high-peaked structure crossed over the Intra Coastal Waterway, a stretch of natural and man made channels extending from Norfolk, Virginia to Miami, Florida. Reddock did not notice the forty-one foot sloop passing southward under the bridge as he drove over the rounded crest.

The Mazda chugged and coughed when he turned the key off, and Reddock cussed the day he'd bought the blue hunk of junk. I'm going to buy a decent car when I get out of here, he thought. Maybe a Firebird like that miserable, God damned colonel who'd been investigating the accident. Yeah, a Firebird would be nice.

He waited for less than five minutes when headlights glared in his eyes, as a shadow of an automobile pulled in front of him. Reddock covered his eyes against the brightness of the lights. "Is that you?" His voice echoed in the surrounding darkness.

"Yeah, it's me, and I got what you asked for," a disembodied voice resounded from the darkness behind the lights. "Come and get it."

Reddock took three steps toward the blinding lights, then his face contorted in pain and understanding.

The man behind the lights pumped five forty-four slugs from the silenced automatic he held in his hand. He grinned at his own joke, "come and get it."

Reddock was dead before he hit the ground. His body had been thrown five feet by the impact of the powerful hand gun. Two rounds had struck his heart, and the blood fountained from his chest like a fire hose.

After their fish dinner, followed by a cup of strongly brewed coffee, Breakheart poured Sena a small glass of sherry, while the boys laughed and finished the dishes.

"You have a wonderful bunch of sons, Dan," Sena commented honestly.

"Yeah, I know, but please don't let them know I said so," he grinned. "How would you like to go down to *Dreamer* and look at the stars? This afternoon's rain cleared the haze, and the stars are out in the millions."

"That sounds wonderful," Sena answered.

Later, as the two lay in the V-berth aboard *Dreamer*, Breakheart drew Sena close. "You know this thing could get serious, don't you?"

"Is that bad?" She asked, gently running her hand across his forehead. "Worse things have happened, you know."

THIRTEEN

BREAKHEART STARED AT himself in the steamy mirror. It had been a fantastic evening with Sena. Their lovemaking had been natural and giving, neither asking the other more than could be given. Unpretentious and easy, they clung to each other late into the night, finally sleeping in each others arms to the tune of water dropping softly from *Dreamers* running rigging.

As the sun rose over the marina's tree tops, it streamed through the forward hatch, awakening them together. It was seven o'clock, and both laughed like guilty school kids, as they hurriedly dressed and headed for their individual homes to change clothes for the work day.

Now, scraping the stubble from his chin, Breakheart smiled inwardly, thinking he had found someone special…finally!

Rod yelled from the kitchen that the coffee was ready, along with toasted English Muffins. Breakheart acknowledged his son's commands and told him he'd be out in a minute. He slipped on his flight suit, the same one he'd worn the day before. It hung on a hook behind the bedroom door, and had dried from the rain it had soaked up during Monday's afternoon thunder bumper. He silently hoped Sena had made it home safely and in time to change and arrive at work on time. He would see her later, he was sure, and he could ask her then if she had made it without too much notice from other NADEP employees.

Joining his sons gathered around the kitchen table, Breakheart greeted the boys. "What's on your agendas today?" He asked.

"We've got a job," Steve answered. "Mr. Thomas hired us to clean the bottom of his boat *Silver Sides*. He wants it scrubbed for a race this weekend up at Oriental."

"Yeah, and we talked him into letting us clean the topsides and the cabin as well. He is going to pay us fifteen dollars each for the job," Steve said excitedly.

"Hey, that's great," Breakheart complimented them, taking a bite from his lightly buttered English Muffin. "I should be home for dinner tonight, but if I'm not here by six, round up some left over fish and rice for yourselves."

"Speaking of fish and supper, I noticed you didn't get in till early this morning," Bill said, smiling the wicked grin of a seventeen-year old. "Where were you, searching for accident clues?"

"Never mind where I was." Breakheart feigned anger at his son's enquiry.

"Yeah, right! I bet you and Sena were down on the boat." Again the grin. "Seriously, Dad, we all like Sena."

"Thanks! I like her too. And, it still isn't any business of yours where I was." Breakheart spoke lightheartedly, without any real intent of chastising.

"Pops, why is it you have to know where we are every night, but you don't have to tell us where you go?"

"I hadn't planned on being out so late, or I would have told you. And, my son, you are absolutely correct. I should tell you where I will be, and most times I do, don't I?"

Steve nodded his agreement, but couldn't help throwing another jab. "What could you have been doing on the boat all night?" He asked, scratching his blond head in simulated confusion.

"You're a smart ass, do you know that? I may decide to get rid of you early, say when you turn fifteen. Lets see, that's next week isn't it? Yeah, maybe I'll put an ad in the paper and see if I could sell you off to some Arab as his personal slave. And stop calling me Pops!"

The table erupted in laughter. For all the time I have to spend away from home, I still have a fine bunch of lads, Breakheart thought. I could do a whole lot worse.

The Breakhearts were still eating and poking fun at each other when the phone rang. Breakheart grated his chair on the floor and went to answer the persistent ring.

"Good morning, Colonel Breakheart speaking."

"Good morning, Dan. This is Sally."

"Sally!" Breakheart exclaimed, surprised to hear her voice. "I was going to call on you later today. How are you doing?"

"I'm fine, or as good as one could expect to be after her husband dies. The funeral was beautiful. General Anderson, the Commandant, even attended. It was really wonderfully done, and I'm sure Jack would have appreciated all the help the Corps provided me."

"I'm glad it went so well. Sometimes, just sometimes, the Corps does something right, and very special. It sounds like you had one of those times."

"Yes, I think we did. I just wanted to remind you to stop by today. I need to talk to someone I can trust."

"Of course! I was planning on it. When would be a good time for you?"

"Right now, or anytime this morning would be best."

"Sure! Now works for me. I'll be over in a few minutes. I've got to clean up the breakfast dishes, since I notice the boys have just disappeared out the door."

"Thank you, Dan. I really appreciate your coming. See you in a little while." She hung the phone up, leaving Breakheart wondering what was so urgent.

It took fifteen minutes to clean up the kitchen, and put the dishes back in their proper place in the cabinets. When he finished in the culinary department, Breakheart returned to the bathroom to brush his teeth.

Straightening his piss cutter, Breakheart decided to walk to the Adams' home. It was not more than five minutes away, and the morning was comfortable with the humidity down for the first time in weeks. As he stepped out of the front door, he again straightened his cover unconsciously. From out of now where a terrified scream cut the air, causing goose bumps to raise on his arms. It sounded as if a child was being strangled in its crib. Startled, Breakheart searched frantically for the cause of the commotion. Stunned, he saw a large grey squirrel under attack by a hawk not more than ten yards away. The two were fighting, causing fur and feathers to fly in several directions. The small rodent had the large bird by the leg and was trying to eat his way through the tough hide and bone. The hawk was terrified. His easy meal was causing great pain, and he couldn't get into the air. It was the squirrel screaming, but it was also getting the best of the fight. Suddenly, the hawk broke free, and the two separated as rapidly as they must have come together. The Hawk, squawking his amazement, took to the sky, and the rodent disappeared up an oak.

Breakheart, his jaw agape, shook his head in awe. Nature, he thought, is a wonderment. We are so small in the giant scheme of things, and yet we think we are so damn important. He shook his head, and started walking to the Adams'.

Sally opened her door before Breakheart could knock twice. She looked tired and drawn, her face showing lines of a much older woman. She wore light blue slacks with a soft pink blouse. She brushed a wisp of blonde hair from her face and smiled. "Come in Dan. It is really good to see you." Barefoot, she stood on tip toe to give Breakheart a peck on the cheek.

"It's good to see you too," Breakheart whispered, hugging her close.

"Come on in. I've got a pot of hot coffee brewing and some fresh pastries Mrs. Geise brought over last night. Everyone keeps feeding me. If it doesn't stop soon, I'll weigh two hundred pounds by the end of the week," she tried to sound flippant, but the inflection bore sadness.

Sally lead Breakheart into the kitchen, which the architect had seen fit to lay out identically to his own. "Sit down, please, and I'll pour us a cup." She silently busied herself, gathering two cups and saucers, and filling them to the brim with black coffee. Setting a steaming cup in front of Breakheart, she returned to the oven where she produced a platter of homemade pastries. Setting the plate on the table, she took a seat across from her guest.

Breakheart took a sip from his cup…burning his upper lip slightly. "Boy, you weren't kidding," he exclaimed, "this is hot."

She nodded, taking a small sip from her own cup. The silence stood for a full minute, neither speaking. Breakheart was not sure what to say. No matter how many of his friends died over the years, he was never quite sure what to say to the newly widowed wife. He, over the years, had to make the first calls to the wife of a pilot who had found his own patch of North Carolina soil. It was never easy. As the Commanding Officer of VMA-542 he'd lost a pilot shortly after taking the helm. It had been one of the hardest things for him to fully accept during his entire career.

Sally finally broke the silence. "Dan, have you found out anything more about the cause of the accident? I would really like to know what happened, and no one will bring me up to date."

Breakheart looked out the window, not answering immediately. A mocking bird was busily feeding her brood of small fledglings who stretched their necks from the top of their nest. The nest, carefully built in the branches of an Azalea bush, swayed gently under a building breeze. New life always appears regardless of how we try to kill it off, he thought to himself. He turned to face Sally. "I'll tell you as much as I can, but I want you to realize I haven't come up with a final answer. I do have some ideas, but that is about all they are at this point."

"Anything, Dan. Right now I just want to try and begin to understand the reason I had to lose Jack. I'm not going to moan and cry out to the world, 'why me,' or 'it isn't fair,' but I do want to know what caused the accident."

"Sally, let me first of all tell you, it was not anything Jack did. He was a good aviator, one of the best, and he did everything possible to alleviate his situation in the bird."

A tiny smile crooked the corners of Sally's mouth. "I knew it. I just knew Jack didn't do anything wrong," she nodded.

"What I'm about to tell you isn't going to be pretty. More importantly, you can't tell anyone else. Not even your children."

Shock registered on Sally's face. "What do you mean?" She asked, brushing the hair from her face once more.

"I think, and all the evidence we have been able to gather suggests, there was sabotage involved. Somehow, the plane was disabled in flight, but we just don't know how yet."

"You mean Jack was murdered by some son-of-a-bitch," Sally almost screamed. She immediately regained her composure, and tears suddenly began running down her cheeks. "Why would any one want to hurt Jack?" she asked in a controlled voice.

"I don't have a clue," Breakheart said, his voice not reflecting the emotion he was feeling inside. "I was hoping you could help me with that question. You said the other day you had to talk to me, and I presumed it had something to do with Jack's accident."

"Dan, I've been a Marine aviator's wife for most of my adult life. You know that? I knew Jack better than any person alive." She stopped speaking, looking hard into Breakheart's eyes, and then got up from the table to retrieve the coffee pot. Silently, she refilled both their cups and placed the pot on the table between them. "Jack," she began after sitting back down, "was working on something for about three weeks before the crash. Whatever it was, it had him really upset. Jack rarely brought work home with him, but for several days he would sit here," she indicated the table, "and study a ream of papers he'd bring home."

"Did he ever say what the papers were?" Breakheart interrupted.

"No. At least not right away. He wouldn't talk about what he was doing, but I knew it had him concerned. Then two nights before the accident, he came to bed around one, which was unusual.

Jack always joined me in bed by eleven, and most nights we would snuggle in at around ten."

Breakheart listened intently, sipping occasionally on his coffee. He was thinking of Captain Dunn's special report, but didn't say anything.

"I was asleep when he slid in next to me, and didn't even know he was there. The strange thing was, he shook me awake. He said he needed to talk to someone, and didn't know who. When Jack said he needed to talk to someone, he really meant me and right then. I learned that over the years. He always bounced things off me first. We were close, Dan, very close."

"I know," Breakheart said. "I guess that's why I always enjoyed your company so much. I have always respected yours and Jack's marriage. Maybe it was because I could never find the happiness in a relationship the two of you enjoyed."

"Thank you, Dan. It's true. We were special, and I doubt I'll ever find another man like Jack. I'm not sure I want to try. Anyway, we got up and came out here into the kitchen. I was going to make some instant coffee, but he poured a small glass of sherry for both of us. I knew it was serious when he did that. Whenever Jack got the sherry out, we were going to spend some time talking."

"Do you remember when Jack started drinking sherry?" Breakheart grinned, trying to lighten the conversation. "It was after he and I returned from England. We were there coordinating an air exercise with the Brit air force."

"Yes, I remember, and as I recall, the two of you stayed drunk through most of your visit."

Breakheart laughed lightly. "Yeah, but we surely had fun while we were there. I'm sorry, I didn't mean to interrupt you. Please, go on."

Sally smiled at Breakheart, "I'm glad you're here," she emphasized once more. "We did have some good times, didn't we?" She didn't wait for an answer, but felt better seeing Breakheart smiling at her. "As I said, he poured us each a glass of sherry, and then sat down next to me. He said he'd been working on something which he thought involved officers here at Cherry Point. It was what he had been doing for the past several nights, tabulating cross country requests from every squadron on base."

"I thought it might have something to do with cross countries," Breakheart said.

"Really! Why?"

"Because Jack requested a special report done on that very subject. Unfortunately, it, along with everything else in his desk, was removed shortly after the accident. I can't figure out why, but the Chief, Colonel Keller, requested Jack's desk be cleared of everything, and he also had the captain in charge of tracking the cross country schedule bring all the back information to him."

"Can't you talk to Colonel Keller? I don't know him very well, but he always seemed nice enough." Sally leaned forward in her chair with anticipation, almost knocking her coffee over.

"Yeah, Jim, Colonel Keller, is okay. In fact, he is a darn good Chief of Staff. Unfortunately, he's on leave with his whole family. They took off for someplace called The Other Shore Club in the Bahamas. Please, Sally, go on." Breakheart took a notebook from his breast pocket and began scribbling in a hand only he could decipher.

"Well, it was late, and I had been roused from a sound sleep, but the gist of it all was Jack thought someone on base was operating some sort of smuggling ring. Probably drugs."

"Drugs? You have got to be kidding?" Breakheart blurted before he could stop and think. Sally looked as if she had just been slapped. "I'm sorry Sally, I didn't mean to doubt what you're saying. It's just…well, you know. Marine Officers smuggling drugs, I have a hard time believing what you're saying."

Sally's face softened. "Yes, I know. So did Jack, that's why he wanted to talk."

"Did he say who he thought was doing the smuggling?"

"Not really, only that he thought it centered around the Harrier community."

Breakheart's face fell like a stone. The utter disbelief reflected clearly in his eyes. "Sally, I have been in the Harrier community for almost twenty years. Hell, I can remember when there were only sixty AV-8 drivers in the country. I used to know every pilot by name, and still recognize most of them on sight. Are you sure it was the Harrier community?"

"Dan, I'm as sure of it as you sitting there. Jack said it was the Harrier community, but he thought someone high up was behind it."

"High up?"

"Yes, someone with enough rank to keep things hidden under a pile of paper. Jack even mentioned it could be someone in Washington."

"You mean, at Headquarters Marine Corps?"

"Yes!"

"Whew," Breakheart whistled through pursed lips. "I know you're aware of the consequences of what you're saying. But, if what I've been speculating happened to Double Nuts is true, then it fits. Was Jack planning to talk to anyone else about his findings?"

"That's what our late night conversation was all about. He wanted to know what I thought about him talking to General Geise."

"What did you decide?"

"We talked for over an hour, and never really came to a hard conclusion. We left it open. Jack was going to talk to me again about it later. After all, it was pushing two in the morning by then, and we were both tired."

"What about the next day, did Jack mention if he talked to anyone?"

"No! We had an evening social function to attend. We got back here around nine thirty, and went straight to bed. The subject just never came up. I think he would have told me if he had talked to anyone though."

The two fell silent for several minutes. Breakheart was digesting what he'd been told, and Sally recognized his need to do so. He got out of his chair and started pacing, his head bowed in concentration. It was a cause for sabotage, he was thinking, but who could be behind it all. Certainly, no officer could have rigged the seat. He would have been noticed immediately. No, someone had to be directing the efforts of others. He couldn't imagine Colonel Keller being behind it, though from what Sally has told me, he is a possibility. Certainly, he asked for Jack's desk to be cleared. Still, the jovial good nature Keller always displayed didn't meet the stereotype of a drug smuggler, or murderer, but it was very convenient for him to be on leave right now.

"We have to find out if Jack spoke to anyone other than you about this," Breakheart said, stopping in mid stride, one foot slightly off the floor. "Jack's digging, I'm sure, precipitated this whole tragic chain of events. Did you know one of the captains on my investigating team was murdered?"

It was Sally's turn to be surprised. "What? No, of course not, and no one bothered telling me."

"That's understandable, under the circumstances. Not everyone recognizes what a strong personality you have. Listen, Sally, I have to get going. There are several things which need doing, like yesterday. This information you've given me is invaluable, but please don't tell anyone else." Breakheart's voice pleaded with the woman next to him. "I mean it, no one!"

Standing with Breakheart, Sally looked directly into his deep blue eyes. "Dan, you can count on me. If it means finding out what really happened to Jack I'd cut my tongue out. I won't say anything. But please, Dan, keep me informed. That's all I ask."

Breakheart smiled compassionately. "I don't think anything so drastic as cutting your tongue out will be necessary, just don't tell anyone else." He spoke as they walked to the door. "I'll be in touch," he said, jamming on his cover and taking off at a full trot for his own quarters.

Breakheart was speeding, something he rarely did. He was on his way to the front gate where the Military Police, Pass and Tag offices were conveniently located. Not only did the small building house the multi-duties of the gate, it was also where Major Collins hung his NIS hat. He dialed a number on his car phone, and waited impatiently for someone to answer.

"Cherry Point Naval Investigative Service, Staff Sergeant Leadfoot speaking. May I help you?"

"This is Colonel Breakheart. Is Major Collins in?"

"Yes, sir. I'll get him for you."

There was a short pause. "Colonel, I was just about to call you," an excited Major Collins answered.

"Are you going to be in your office for a few minutes? I'm on my way there now." Breakheart was abrupt.

Collins was slightly taken aback by Breakheart's charged voice. "Yes, sir, I'll be here. Though I have to leave soon. We have had another murder."

"Holy jumping Jesus Christ, you have got to be kidding me."

"No, sir, I wish I were. They found Sergeant Reddock's body early this morning. He'd been pumped full of holes with a large caliber weapon. It looks like someone wanted to make a Swiss Cheese out of him. I just returned from the scene not more than ten minutes ago."

"Okay! Hang tight. I'm on my way. I should be there in about five minutes." Breakheart slammed the phone down and accelerated down Roosevelt to beat the stop light leading to the PX.

In the tiny room, Collins called his office, Breakheart sat heavily on a straight-back chair, noticing the several certificates of appreciation hanging on the wall behind a metal desk. Major Collins sat comfortably behind the desk, though it was easy to tell the younger man was excited.

"Colonel, we have got to call in some heavy artillery from Washington. This whole thing is getting too big for the two of us. Christ, we've had three murders, with no end in sight."

"Yeah, I suppose so, but let's hold off another day or two. I'm getting close to finding out what happened to Colonel Adams' aircraft, and I don't want to scare whoever is behind it all off to some forgotten land. Besides, the local authorities are working on Reddock's death, I presume."

"Sure they are, and I'm going to have to tell them of the connection between him and Hamilton. It is just a matter of time before they begin getting nasty about me withholding information. Do you want to see Reddock's body?"

"No, that isn't necessary. But I do have some information for you. I think I know why all this is happening."

Collins sat forward in his chair with eager awareness. "What are you talking about? What have you found out?"

"I just spent an hour or so with Colonel Adams' widow, Sally. She has been a good friend for years, and wanted to talk to me. It seems Colonel Adams was doing some investigating of his own a couple of weeks before his death. To make a long story short, he felt there were officers in the Harrier community who may be involved in a smuggling operation, probably drugs."

"That's it!" Collins leaped from his chair with excitement. "Of course, it all makes sense, and would explain the series of deaths we've been having. Reddock would have had access to the airplane prior to Colonel Adams' flight. Still, we don't know how he did it, but I'm sure you'll figure it out. Reddock gets blown away because he knows too much, or something like that. But why kill Hamilton?" He sat back down contemplating his own question.

"I've been thinking about that on the way here," Breakheart said seriously. "It's my guess, the captain found Reddock trying to cover his tracks and Reddock killed him. If that is the case, then the answer to the cause of the crash has something to do with the engine."

"Of course! That makes perfect sense. Now all we have to do is find out who is behind it all."

"There's more," Breakheart interrupted. "The Chief of Staff for the Wing had Colonel Adams' desk cleared completely, shortly after the crash. Plus, he made sure all the research done on cross countries for the past three months was delivered to him. I mention this because, it appears Adams thought the smuggling was accomplished during weekend cross country flights."

"Wow! Do you know what you are implying?" Collins was beside himself with excitement. "We have a senior officer involved in drugs. Hell, this could blow the Marine Corps apart, if it's true."

"Yeah! I know," Breakheart said. "The trouble is, Colonel Keller is on leave in the Bahamas. Very convenient. In fact, almost too perfect. Personally, I don't think the Chief has anything to do with this. He may have unknowingly helped someone, but I don't believe him capable of causing the accident or the murders."

"You'd be surprised what people will do for money," Major Collins said, studying Breakheart. "I think we have to consider him a prime suspect."

"I suppose so,…but." Breakheart left his sentence open. "Look, you do what you can with Reddock's murder; meanwhile, I'll be at the NADEP. Hopefully, they will have something for me there today."

"Okay," Collins exclaimed, then paused, tapping his knuckles on his desk impatiently. "Look, Colonel, I have got to say this. If you don't think Colonel Keller is our man, then someone would have had to direct him to clear Adams' desk."

"I realize that, and I don't want to even consider the possibility, but you are right."

"There are only two men who could have given that order… Geise or Blake."

"No, that isn't necessarily true," Breakheart retorted. "He could have received orders from someone higher yet. Someone from FMFLANT, or even Headquarters Marine Corps."

Collins combed his hair with his fingers and whistled. "If you are right, we have a real problem on our hands. For sure we will have to bring an outside Federal agency into action. The two of us wouldn't be able to get on first base if we have to leave the Wing's command structure."

"Let's hope it doesn't come to that. I'll see you later," Breakheart said, standing to leave.

"Yes, sir, you can count on it."

Breakheart climbed behind the Firebird's wheel and fired the big engine over. His mind was adrift with chunks of related and non-related facts. He backed out of the parking space and eased the car forward, stopping at the main gate. A corporal, his uniform as crisp and sharp as a razor, saluted and waved him through. Breakheart returned the salute absentmindedly, but sharply. The car bumped over the railroad tracks used to supply aviation jet fuel and ammunition to storage areas located around the base. The tires' thump drew him back to reality, as he braked for the stop light on A Street leading to the NADEP.

Burns' car was parked on a cant in the "Visitor Parking Lot" of the NADEP. Snake parked his car across his parking space so no other car could use the parking spaces on either side. It was his contention that by taking up three spaces he would keep jerks from opening their doors and bumping his prize possession, a restored Austin Healy. Breakheart silently cussed his friend, as he searched for a parking space. There were no "reserved for colonels" spaces in the lot. Finally, two blocks away, he located a spot, and began the long walk to the NADEP's engine shop.

Sena and Burns were deep in conversation with two engineers when Breakheart broke in on them. "What's new?" he asked.

The four looked up together. "Nothing much, I'm afraid," Sena answered. "We are still waiting for the results from the spectrographic and the electron microscope." She was serious, but let a smile cross her lips as she spoke, thinking of their evening together.

Breakheart couldn't help but return her smile, but tried to hide his feelings. Burns picked up on their overt greeting immediately.

"Listen you love birds, we have work to do," Burns poked.

Breakheart gave him a "leave it alone" look, and Burns backed down. Something he rarely did, but he understood the situation here in the NADEP spaces. "Seriously, boss, what have you got?"

"Well, let's just say this has been an interesting morning so far. I need you. We have some leg work to do, and it is going to take the better part of the afternoon to get it done. Sena, we'll be at one of the Harrier squadrons if you come up with anything."

"Okay, but I don't expect to have information for you until much later today, or even tomorrow morning," Sena advised.

"I'll call you later this afternoon, if we haven't talked before then. Come on, Snake, we have work to do." Breakheart turned and started for the door with a purpose.

Once clear of prying ears, Burns asked, "Well, Cuda, what's going on between you and Sena? Don't tell me 'nothing' because I won't believe you."

Breakheart smiled at his friend. "Yeah, well you'll just have to suffer not knowing. If I say anything to you, you'll give me nothing but grief."

"Hell, I'll give you grief one way or the other, so you just might as well tell me," Burns pressed, as they stepped out of the cool darkness of the shop, and into the glaring morning sun.

"Let's just say Sena and I get along very well, and leave it at that for the time being. Besides, we have work to do." The two walked across the street to Snake's car in silence. "Damn you, Snake, why do you park like this?" Breakheart stated with a trace of anger touching his voice. "You and your three parking spots. Because of your eccentric way of parking, I had to park two blocks away. You can drop me there."

"I'll park any damned way I please. Besides, this way I can piss senior officers off, such as yourself. It's my one way of rebelling against authority. Hop in, and explain to me what is so damn important."

Breakheart wiggled his way into the passenger's side of the Healy, and waited for Burns to get himself settled behind the wheel. "We are going to spend the afternoon reviewing log books. I'll start with VMA-203, and you can start with 231. You'll finish before me because you'll only have about thirty logs to search, I'll have over sixty. When you are done, join me at 203 and we'll finish their logs together. When we are done, we'll hit VMA-542."

"Would it be too much to ask what in God's name we are looking for?" Burns asked.

"Hold your socks, I'm getting to the reason why." Breakheart went on to explain his conversation with Sally Adams and Major

Collins, finishing with the loss of the cross country report Adams' had requested. "What we are going to do is tabulate who is going on cross countries regularly and where. Maybe we can reconstruct the information Colonel Adams was upset about."

Snake looked at Breakheart as if he'd just lost a large portion of his brain housing group. "You really think this whole thing started with drugs, and some of the so called 'good guys' are involved?"

"I know it is hard to believe, but, yes, I think we have a smuggling ring in the Harrier community, and it has something to do with the crash."

"Okay, you're the boss, but your talking about blowing the Second MAW right out of the water. If what you think is true, this will be National news and about the worse publicity for the Corps since that sergeant drowned those recruits at Paris Island over twenty years ago."

"Yeah, I know. But, damn it all, the Corps is nothing more than a reflection of the civilian world. We can't be expected to be without our crooks and bad guys just because we wear the uniform. I know we would like to believe we are pure as the driven snow, but the fact remains, offer enough money and there are those who will put it in their pocket."

"I suppose you are right," Burns said sadly, starting the sport car's engine. "Okay, I'll head to 231 and meet you at the training squadron when I'm through there."

Burns dropped Breakheart next to his Firebird and drove down A Street to VMA-231. Moments later, Breakheart was parking in front of 203. He exchanged several salutes as he walked for the hangar. On the second deck, he went straight for Major Beasly's office, and entered without knocking.

"Major," Breakheart said, walking through the door. "I need your help. I want to review all your log books, and would like one of your troopers to help me."

The abruptness of the interruption startled Major Beasly, who looked up from a stack of paper work on his desk. "Certainly, Colonel. May I ask why and what you might be looking for?"

"No! I just need your help. Let me just say, it has something to do with the ongoing investigation."

"Sure, I understand. Why don't you grab a cup of coffee and I'll make the arrangements."

"Thanks. I would like to set up in one of the briefing rooms, if that's okay?"

"Yes, sir. Give me about five minutes," Beasly said, leaving the room.

Breakheart strolled into the readyroom which was filled with pilots. The talk in the large room was airy with laughter and banter. Filling a cup with coffee, Breakheart spied Major Dyke charging through the door.

"Colonel, damn am I glad to see you," Dyke smiled. "We didn't have our meeting last night and I wanted to tell you we are really moving on clearing the field. Plus, the sifting through the wreckage is going very smoothly. We still haven't come up with anything new though."

"Thanks, Major. I'm sorry I haven't been more in touch with you the last couple of days, but things have been moving pretty fast. Besides, there are some things about the accident I don't want the team to get involved with…if I'm wrong, then I'll take the entire responsibility."

Dyke's face took on a questioning expression, but he did not press for further information. "Do you want the team to get together this evening?" He asked.

"Yes, now that you mention it, I would. Let's say around seventeen hundred if that's possible."

"No problem, Colonel. I'll have to call Captain Evans in from the field, but he'll probably like getting home early tonight."

There was a whoop from across the room. The Acey Ducey table had a winner, and the lieutenant was letting everyone in the room know he'd just whipped up on his opponent. Breakheart smiled, thinking it would be wonderful to be a lieutenant again, with nothing more to worry about than your next hop and wining at Acey Ducey. His scan picked up the eight foot by four foot enlargement of an AV-8A taking off from a road on Camp LeJeune. It was a spectacular photograph at any size, but hanging on 203's readyroom wall it was awesome. The aircraft, with its nose gear just breaking from the ground, was creating a huge cloud of dust and debris behind its hot nozzles. The picture captured the utter essence of V/STOL flight. Burns, the Snake, was sitting in the cockpit, though all you could see was his yellow and black tiger-striped helmet. The picture reminded Breakheart how long he'd been flying the Harrier, and how much the community had changed in those years. His silent reverie was broken suddenly by a call from the duty officer.

"Colonel Breakheart, sir, Major Beasly called to say he has briefing room four set up for you."

"Thanks, Captain," Breakheart said, throwing his cup in the trash can next to the coffee pot. "I'll be right there." He looked again at Major Dyke, "I'll see you at seventeen hundred, and thanks again for all your hard work."

The briefing room, its blackboard erased clean, was located next to the S-3's working spaces. Several enlisted men and women were busy updating schedules and training boards in the large office. The felt training board took up almost an entire wall. Used to keep track of each student's completed training missions, hundreds of little white Xs covered its surface. Breakheart, on a whim, detoured to face the big board. The name, "Adams, J. A. appeared near the top of the board. Scanning the board quickly, Breakheart could tell Colonel Adams had successfully completed his Harrier training through air to air combat. He was, he thought, a well-qualified aviator. He cataloged the information and turned for the briefing room.

A Lance Corporal waited for Breakheart, and introduced himself as he entered the room.

"Okay, Jones, here is what I want us to do. I want to make a list of every pilot who took a cross country in the last four months. I want to know where they landed, where they spent the night or nights and who broke down in route."

The young Lance Corporal looked at Breakheart as if he had just lost his mind, but did not say anything. He just nodded his acceptance as if it were as common as blowing your nose.

The morning dragged on. It was slow eye straining work, sorting through the log of every pilot attached to 203. On a yellow legal pad, Breakheart copied a list of pilots who had been on a cross country and where. The Lance Corporal scribbled on his own pad, working quietly and steadily. Snake joined them later in the afternoon after calling ahead. He knew his friend would not bother stopping to eat lunch, so he stopped by the base Burger King, after taking an order from the corporal and Breakheart for a sack of flame broiled hamburgers with fries.

"Well, did you find anything unusual?" Breakheart asked through a mouthful of burger and bun.

"Hell, I don't know. I found two captains who go on cross countries practically every weekend, if that's what you mean," Burns answered. "One of them, a Captain Lamb, has a girl friend in Nashville, and normally ends up at NAS Nashville for at least one night. The other, well he goes just about anywhere the weather is suitable. Normally, he drops into Patrick AFB for a fueling stop or an overnighter regardless of wherever else he might land."

"That's interesting. Patrick is just northwest of Miami. What's his name?"

"Captain Light! He's been with 231 for two years and is considered an average pilot. He's a bachelor, which explains why he likes his cross countries so well. I asked a few questions about him, and he is well liked, but keeps to himself."

"Hmm," Breakheart gave the information thought. "Well, we have about fifteen more logs to go through here, but one name already stands out." Breakheart turned to the corporal, "Would you excuse us for a few minutes?"

"Yes, sir. I'll be in the S-3 office if you need me," the Marine said, gathering his food together and leaving the two officers.

Breakheart waited until they were alone. "The only name I can detect as taking an unusual number of weekend sojourns is the

Operations Officer, Major Beasly. He takes a two nighter at least twice every month, and here is the catch, he always goes south. Just like your Captain Light, he always finds a way to land at Patrick. He might not spend the night there, but he makes it a mandatory fuel stop regardless of where he might end up. Interesting, don't you think?"

"Not really," Burns replied. "If he is just trying to get flight time, why not stay in airspace you are familiar with?"

"True! That could be the only reason, but with what we know or suspect, I have my doubts. Let's finish here and do VMA-542 and see if anyone there likes Florida bases to spend their weekends."

It was 1530 before the last of the logs had been tabulated. Breakheart and Burns thanked the corporal and departed for 542. They had found no other pilot who made a habit of taking cross countries to a single point. In fact, Breakheart was beginning to doubt his own suspicions.

VMA-542's readyroom was the show case of the wing. It represented everything a readyroom is expected to be. Pictures, some blown up to dimensions which covered ceiling to floor, were placed on the side walls. Over the sliding multiple blackboards at the head of the room was a sign which stated, "EVERY FLIGHT PROFESSIONALLY EXECUTED." Breakheart located the Operations Officer and explained his needs. By 1630, Burns and Breakheart had gone through the 542 logs, finding a major who enjoyed cross countries very well indeed. Major Krump, in the past sixteen weekends, had been on a cross country flight on twelve of them. Every flight had landed at Patrick at least once on a Saturday or Sunday. The pattern, Breakheart thought, was established.

FOURTEEN

BURNS AND BREAKHEART thanked the Commanding Officer of 542 for his cooperation and returned to 203's readyroom for the Accident Board meeting. Burns excused himself to hit the head, as Major Beasly intercepted Breakheart at the Duty Officer's desk.

"My corporal tells me you were reviewing the logs for cross country flights. Mind if I ask why?"

"Same answer as before, Major. I do mind, but it does involve Colonel Adams' accident. By the way, I noticed you're quite a weekend flier."

"Yeah," Beasly fidgeted. "I want to build up as much time in the bird as I can."

"How does your wife put up with it?" Breakheart pressed, trying to reap a reaction from the major.

"Oh, she understands. Besides, I tell her the more I fly the less chance of me having an emergency I can't handle." Beasly smiled. "Regardless, I love flying, and I can pull down ten or twelve hours on a weekend."

"Why do you always land at Patrick?" Breakheart requested the information innocently.

Beasly looked nervously around the readyroom, as if looking for a place to hide. "I just like South Florida I guess," he responded weakly. "They have some great low level routes down there."

"Yeah," Breakheart responded walking away, leaving Beasly to stew on his own words.

Breakheart kept the meeting short, just long enough to detail Reddock's murder and what little the NADEP had to offer. He did not mention his suppositions concerning a smuggling ring. Those thoughts were to be shared only with someone he trusted, and that meant Burns.

After the team left, and he and Snake were left alone, Breakheart asked, "Should I go to Geise with the info we have? Hell, he might be the head of the whole damned thing. I just don't know."

Snake understood the dilemma in which his friend was trapped. Something this big had to go higher on the totem pole than the Wing's Safety Officer, but who could they trust? "I think you have got to trust him. If it turns out Geise is the head mucky muck, we'll know soon enough."

"You're right. I wish I could get in touch with Colonel Keller. I tried calling around noon with the number the Staff Secretary gave me the other day, but he was out diving. I'll try again this evening, but I think he is trying to keep a low profile."

"Have you talked to Sena yet?" Burns asked.

"No, but I thought I would call her from here. I hope she has something for us. I know in my heart the airplane was sabotaged, causing Jack's death, but I still want to know how it was done. I'm sure Reddock had something to do with it. Don't you?"

"Of course, I don't think there is any doubt about that. But I'm with you. I sure as hell want to find out how he did it."

"Right! Look, why don't you head on home. I'm going to see if General Geise is still in his office, and I need to make a few phone calls."

"Yeah, right! A phone call to Sena no doubt. Just a warning pally of mine, don't let your little head start thinking for the big one. She is a great gal, but don't you be getting serious about her. Just remember, you have only been divorced for a relatively short time, and you don't want to get all tangled up with a house mouse again. At least not so soon. I know you, you'll be mooning over her until she falls in love, or something equally stupid. Just have some fun. Ya hear?"

"Yes, I hear, and bow to your infinite wisdom of worldly matters. Now get the hell out of here and let me alone for a while."

"I'm gone," was all Burns said, as he disappeared through the door.

Breakheart slipped into Major Dyke's office and made two calls. One to Sena, who had nothing more to add, but assured him the final report would be available the next morning. Breakheart excused himself from seeing her, as he wanted to spend a few hours with his sons. Though he knew it would only be in front of a TV set. Sena understood, and told him she would see him the next day. The second call was to General Geise's office. He asked Staff Sergeant Gilbert, who had answered the call, if the General was in. She told him he had been out of the office all day, and they didn't expect him until the next afternoon. She explained he was called to FMFLANT for a conference with Lieutenant General Hayes. Something to do with the Wing's safety record, and Lieutenant Colonel Barry, Breakheart's replacement, accompanied Geise.

"But," Sergeant Gilbert continued, "General Blake is still here. Do you want to speak with him?"

Breakheart didn't even have to think. "No, that's all right. I'll talk to General Geise tomorrow. Thanks, Sergeant. I appreciate your help." He started to hang up, then thought of his arrangements with 542, "Sergeant, please pass to General Blake that his flight with Colonel Breakheart is set for a 0630 brief Friday morning."

As he hung the phone on its hook, 203's Duty Officer gave a yell. He had a phone call on hold for him in the readyroom. It was Major Collins.

"Sir," Collins began, "nothing much to report. I just wanted to check in with you. Reddock was killed around ten last night. Whoever did the job wanted him dead. The bastard filled him with five forty-four slugs."

"I wish I could say I'm sorry he has been killed, but about the only thing I'm sorry over is that we won't get a chance to talk to him," Breakheart stated flatly. "By the way, I think we can safely assume the theory we discussed this morning to have validity. If you'll stop by my quarters in about an hour or so, we'll talk about it."

"Can do," Collins replied. "I'll see you in about an hour."

It was past six when Breakheart opened his front door, and tossed his cover on the foyer table. The boys were just finishing their desert…mountainous amounts of ice cream, leaving little more than a couple of spoonfuls for their father. By the time Collins knocked on the door, he had poured himself his second cocktail, and consumed a peanut butter and mayo sandwich.

"Come on in the kitchen," Breakheart instructed his guest. We can talk while I finish the dishes. Go ahead and pour yourself a drink. The rum is on the table, and you'll find the Coke in the 'fridge."

Collins poured himself a drink, retrieving ice and Coke from the reefer. "What have you got, Colonel?" He asked, once he'd settled himself at the dinette table.

"I'm sure we are talking about a smuggling ring. Colonel Adams was right, it appears to be centered around the Harrier community, but I can't be sure about that until we look at MAG-14's log books. I'm almost positive Patrick AFB is the pickup point, and there is at least one captain and two majors involved."

The excitement on Collins' face was evident. "Can you believe it? We are going to solve the biggest case of my career."

"Hold on, Major," Breakheart interrupted. "We are still working on an aircraft accident, everything else falls out of my realm."

"I know, sir, but not mine. Can you provide me some names?"

"Yeah," Breakheart shook soapy water from his hands, and began drying the dishes he had neatly stacked neatly in a drain rack. "Before I do, I want you to promise you won't take any action until I say so. Agreed?"

"Sir, we have two murders, maybe three counting Colonel Adams. I can't just sit on this sort of information."

"I know, but I have an idea. So far we have the possible names of the carriers, but not the head man. Plus, someone has to load and unload the goods from the air plane. Until we have more information, I don't think we want to stir the pot too heavily."

"I hear what you are saying, and perhaps you're right. What do you suggest?" Collins asked, and took a long pull on his drink.

"Tomorrow morning, bright and early, I want you to pick up Captain Light from VMA-231. I'm sure he's involved. Once you have him in custody, interrogate him like he was caught red handed. Use the cross countries he's been flying and the fact he always lands at Patrick. Put real pressure on him. I don't know if he can tell us who the ring leader is, but he might be able to give us the details on how the smuggling is accomplished, and who is doing the unloading here at the Point."

"You got it, sir." Collins paused for a long moment, and finished his drink. "Colonel, do you have any idea who is behind this whole mess? I mean, do you really think it goes beyond the Wing level?"

"I've got no idea, but I hope not. I'm praying we can keep things at a local level, but who knows? Do you want another drink?"

"No thank you, sir. I think I'll head on home. Do you want me to call if I find out anything from this Captain Light?"

Breakheart looked at the Major with astonishment. "You have got to be kidding! Of course I want you to get in touch with me."

"Yes, sir, that was a stupid question. It is just that this is really getting big, and as an agent, I'm pretty excited about the whole thing."

Breakheart smiled, "Go on, get out of here. I'll talk to you tomorrow."

For the remainder of the evening, Breakheart sat and watched TV with his sons. Conversation was light, with occasional comments about the utter stupidity of the program they all watched. Still, they were together for a change, and that was satisfaction enough.

FIFTEEN

MAJOR COLLINS WITH two enlisted agents in tow, walked swiftly into VMA-231's readyroom. Stepping up to the Duty Officer, he pulled his badge from his left hip pocket. The captain's eyes manning the squadron's radios registered surprise and lack of understanding.

"Yes, sir, what can I do for you?" The captain asked.

"I would like to speak to Captain John Light," Collins said flatly. "Is he here?"

"No, sir, he hasn't come in yet. He should be arriving around zero eight hundred."

Collins glanced at his watch, noting he would have to wait for better than thirty minutes. "Gunny," he spoke to the Gunnery Sergeant at his shoulder. "Check his locker. I'm sure the captain here will be happy to show you where it might be located. Wouldn't you, Captain?"

"Sir, I think you had better talk to the CO. Don't you need a search warrant or something to break into Captain Light's locker?"

"Will this do?" Collins unfolded a legal document.

"I guess so, sir, but let me call the CO. He should know what's going on." He picked up one of the three phones in front of him, pushing a single red button. The Commanding Officer, Lieutenant

Colonel Reese, immediately answered. "Sir, we have some NIS agents here in the readyroom, and I think you should talk to them."

Moments later, Collins quietly spoke to 231's CO, and convinced him, without divulging any real information, the need to examine Light's locker. The Gunny followed a First Lieutenant out of the room, which by now, held a knot of curious on lookers. Collins wanted it that way. He wanted curiosity to build among these pilots. All of his actions were carefully orchestrated to cause questions. His rationale was to create a situation provoking surprise, confusion and disbelief. He hoped to smoke anyone else out who might be involved in smuggling. By the time the Gunny returned, not finding anything other than PT gear and a change of flight suits, Captain Light was walking through the door.

"Captain Light," Lieutenant Colonel Reese said quietly. "This is Major Collins from NIS. He has some questions for you."

Major Collins flashed his badge once more, and immediately began reading Light his rights. The speed at which Collins was moving had Light in confusion, and he looked frantically around the readyroom at his friends. No one was coming to his aid, yet there were expressions of disbelief in all eyes. Before action could be taken in his behalf, Light was escorted swiftly out of 231's spaces, and placed in an unmarked Military Police car.

Breakheart drove slowly from his quarters to the Hancock Marina. The cooling breeze of yesterday had turned into a near gale overnight, and he wanted to check the dock lines on *Dreamer*. With the sunrise, the wind had abated to less than twenty knots, but the remnants of the night's blow were evident. Small branches and leaves covered the winding road to the marina, and he had to dodge several downed limbs. Leaves and twigs audibly crunched under the Firebird's tires, breaking the morning's stillness. There had been no rain, but yesterday's reprieve from summer's humidity was short lived. Already Breakheart was perspiring under his NOMEX flight suit.

Dreamer sat comfortably in her slip, rolling slightly under the creek's chop. He examined her dock lines, which were still holding the boat securely after the blow. Pleased at how well *Dreamer* had laid to the wind, he started back up the dock. As was his nature, he checked his friend's lines as he walked. He noted *Silver Sides'* sparkling topsides and thought the boys had done a great job cleaning her for the upcoming race.

"Morning, pally," Burns said, his red Healy coming to a stop at A-dock. "Did you check *Rainbow's* lines?"

"Yeah! They're fine. Looks like everyone made it through the blow all right."

"What's on the agenda today? Did you get a chance to talk to General Geise?" Burns asked two swift questions.

"Geise wasn't in. He was called to FMFLANT for a meeting," Breakheart said, leaning on the roof of the Healy. "As far as the agenda is concerned, I think I'll head for VMAT-203. I want to put a little pressure on Major Beasly. I won't be long there, just talk to Beasly and check in with Major Dyke. After that, I'll see you at the NADEP. By the way, I did call Major Collins. He came by the house last night. He told me Reddock was filled with forty-four slugs."

"I'll bet he was excited about what we found in the log books."

"Almost too excited. I had to practically hog-tie him in his chair to keep him from running off half cocked. He wanted to arrest everyone in sight. I got him convinced to hold off for a day or two, but I did tell him to arrest Light. Maybe we can scare a rabbit or two out of the brush."

"That's a good idea. Well, I'll meet you at the engine shop," Burns said, shifting the Healy into reverse.

"Yeah! And stop being a prick by taking up three parking spaces."

Burns stuck his hand out of the window and waved. "Fuck you…SIR!"

Breakheart shook his head and laughed. The irreverent SOB, he thought, climbing into his car.

The 203 office spaces were humming with morning activity. Students, instructors, and enlisted men moved through the passageway in a hurried, business like manner. Breakheart went straight to the S-3's office and knocked. There was no answer, and he let himself in. Paneled in light oak, the cheap fiberboard type which could be purchased at any retail lumber outlet, the office was none-the-less neat and orderly. Several pictures of Harriers adorned the walls, along with an array of family pictures on the desk and hanging on the wall behind a cadenza. Two phones sat on a side table, with a base phone book, and a rotary number indexer. The only thing missing was Major Beasly.

Breakheart was greeted by enlisted and officers alike, as he moved to the readyroom. He asked the Duty Officer where he could find Beasly, and was told he had not arrived for work yet. Which, the captain offered, was unusual. Major Beasly was always one of the first officers aboard every morning, he explained. On a hunch, Breakheart returned to Beasly's office and picked up the phone book. He dialed Beasly's residence.

"Major Beasly's quarters," a pleasant feminine voice answered. "Sarah Beasly speaking, may I help you?"

"Good morning, Mrs. Beasly," Breakheart said in a pleasant voice. "Is your husband home?"

"Oh, hi, Colonel. No, he left for work early this morning. Why, is something wrong?" Her voice held a hint of fear. This was normal for an aviator's wife, particularly when a senior officer called for no apparent reason. There was always the chance there had been an accident.

"No! Nothing is wrong, I just needed to talk to him. I'm sure he's around the squadron somewhere. Thank you, and I'm sorry I bothered you."

"No bother, Colonel. Anytime," Mrs. Beasly said, in a more relaxed manner.

When he had finished his call, Breakheart sat down behind Beasly's desk, and started rifling through the major's phone file. The numbers were standard for a staff officer…listed were friends, Group and Wing numbers of importance, and the like. One number caught his eye. It was unusual for a major to have a general's home and work number at his finger tips. Breakheart rubbed his forehead, as if to force a hidden fact from between his ears.

Still puzzled by the phone number he had seen on file, Breakheart walked down the stairs to the hangar deck. His Accident Board was busy at work, sorting and laying out the remains of Double Nuts. Though burned and battered, you could now tell the charred mess on the deck was once been an aircraft. He flagged Major Dyke's attention and joined him near the blackened ruins of the airplane's left wing. Actually, he thought, it was more like small pieces fitted together to appear like a wing. No chunk of disfigured carbon fiber could have been more than three feet square.

Breakheart explained his agenda for the day to Major Dyke, who was beginning to understand why the team's boss was not grubbing around in the debris with the rest of the board. Normally, Breakheart would have been as dirty as the rest, but Dyke rightly calculated there was something the Colonel was involved with, which was very much out of the ordinary. He had served with Breakheart on earlier boards, and the man standing before him explaining the need for him to be elsewhere, was not the same individual. He said nothing, but wondered what the hell was going on, as Breakheart excused himself and headed for the door.

Sena was waiting at the entrance to the engine shop. Her normally radiant features were even more so. Her blond hair was done up in a bun, which accented her finely sculptured face. Bright, blue eyes sparkled with excitement as she waved at Breakheart walking toward her from the parking lot.

"Dan! I've got it. The report from spectra and the electron microscope. I think you're going to like what they came up with," Sena bubbled with exhilaration.

Breakheart hurried across the street, holding his cover on his head against the wind. "What did they find?"

"Come on in and have a look for yourself." She smiled and took his hand, oblivious of what her co-workers might say.

Entering the shop, Breakheart was immediately struck by the number of engineers surrounding a large worktable. The same table they had used to inspect the F402's engineering specs several days before. Burns looked up as they walked to the table, taking note of the hand holding.

"We've got the bastard dead to rights," Burns said. The God-damned creep might have got away with it if you hadn't insisted on having the throttle quadrant scrutinized."

"Well, what is it?" Breakheart asked. He jostled his way to the table, and looked questioningly at the throng around him.

"In short," one of the engineers spoke, "the throttle linkage was modified by someone who knew just what he was doing. Look here," he pointed to a set of electronically produced photographs, "do you see the break in the throttle linkage?"

Breakheart studied the blow up. "Yes, but I'm not sure what I am looking at."

"If you will remember, I suspected the break wasn't normal. At least it wasn't caused by the plane hitting the ground. The break was too jagged. Well, I was right. This break was caused by a very intense explosion."

"Hell," Breakheart exclaimed. "The damned bird blew sky high when it hit the ground. Couldn't that have cause the break?"

"Not from what you told me the other day," the engineer continued. "Remember, you said the aircraft exploded behind the cockpit. Further more, you thought the cockpit was probably already buried in the mud when it blew. If we assume that to be the case, then the linkage would have shown elongation. We have no stretching indicated. Plus, when we ran the rod under the electron microscope we were able to identify traces of what we now know to be plastic explosive. Probably C4!"

"Holy shit," Breakheart interrupted. "Your telling me someone rigged the linkage to blow in flight. But how?"

"It's my guess he used an altitude sensitive device. A detonator which was activated by a pressure differential. If you listen to the Twilight tapes again, you might get some idea at what altitude it actually went off, but it makes little difference. I'm positive an extremely small amount of C4, or something similar, caused the break in the throttle linkage."

Breakheart looked around at the faces in front of him. They were excited about their findings and were right in being so. "Okay! What you have described would have cause a throttle disconnect, but we all agreed a disconnect would not explain the engine going to idle and staying there. We are back to square one."

"Not quite, oh mighty boss of mine," Burns smiled in response. "These boys did one heck of a job. Listen to what they have come up with."

"We thought the exact same thing," the engineer continued. "The Dual Wound Resolver, DECS, and FMU all appeared to be in working condition. However, when we discovered what happened to the throttle linkage, Glen here, he indicated the young engineer who had done mostly leg work earlier in the week, "had an idea. His guess was dead on the mark."

"Well!" Breakheart pleaded. "What was it?"

"If you will look at this photo?" he slid a blowup of something totally unidentifiable to Breakheart. "You'll notice several gouges and scrapes here." His finger traced an outline of two areas.

"What am I looking at?" Breakheart asked.

"This is the throttle linkage where it enters the Dual Wound Resolver. Do you see these marks?"

"Yes!" Breakheart agreed.

"Well, there is your answer. A spring was attached to the linkage, then fed back to the Resolver's housing. It was fastened with fast drying epoxy. Now, we don't have the spring, but there was definitely something attached to both the throttle and the Resolver. It makes sense it was a spring because that would force the engine to go to idle when the linkage break occurred. The explosion and fire after the crash caused the epoxy to melt and disappear to the naked eye. Whoever did this knew exactly where to go and what to do to make it practically impossible to find, unless you were specifically looking for it."

"I'll be a son-of-a-bitch," Breakheart whispered more to himself than those around him. "It had to be Reddock. He would certainly have the access and the knowledge."

Burns beamed at his friend. "You did it again. I don't know how you do it but, for sure you are the luckiest slob on the face of the earth. Congratulations."

"I didn't do anything, you all did, but thanks."

The entire group was slapping backs and applauding each other. It was right they did so. They had just solved another accident, and it did not have anything to do with pilot error, aircraft malfunction, or the involvement of maintenance men making a mistake. It was the best of all worlds.

"Murder!" Breakheart said aloud. "This was all out, no holds barred murder."

His outburst subdued the congratulatory attitudes. True, they had solved a difficult quandary, but the realization a Marine had murdered another was sobering.

"What do you want us to do now?" It was the senior engineer who questioned Breakheart. "Do you have anything else you need to have examined?"

"No, at least not for the time being. However, I wish you would have your full report on what we have seen here written up for me by the end of the day. I know I'm not giving you much time, but we don't have much time to mess around with right now. Do you think you could do that for me?"

The aging engineer ran his fingers through his greying hair, "We'll get right on the job, but it won't be in the smooth. Not, at least, by this afternoon. Stop back around 1630, I'll have the report waiting for you at the front desk."

Breakheart sincerely thanked the entire NADEP crew, especially the senior engineer. Then he asked Burns and Sena to join him separately. The team broke up into smaller groups, and the three walked to the desk where the phone was located.

"Snake, I want you to join the Accident Board on 203's hangar deck. Don't let on to what we have found. In fact, if anything, make it look like you are still desperately looking for a cause. Tell them, when they ask, the NADEP didn't come up with anything concrete. I want to keep a lid on this for just a few more hours."

"Yeah, I can do that," Burns said. "I'm gone. See you later."

Breakheart watched his friend disappear through the shop's entrance. "Sena, if you will just keep tabs on things here, that would be the biggest help you could give me."

"Sure," Sena returned. "What are you going to be doing?"

"I have some rocks to turn over and trees to shake. I don't know who is behind this, but I'm beginning to have a gut feeling. I've got to make a couple of phone calls, then I'll see where to go from there. Regardless, I sure would enjoy having you come by for supper and some TV, if you're available tonight?"

"I would like that very much," she said, taking his hand gently. "I'll see you later." With those words, she followed in Snake's footsteps.

Breakheart let his eyes follow her out, admiring the natural beauty of the woman. He was definitely feeling a stir in his heart, which he had safely tucked away years ago. Just as quickly, his mind shifted gears, and he picked up the phone and dialed the base operator. He placed an overseas call, and talked to the Chief of Staff for over fifteen minutes. The smile on his face, when he placed the phone down, was more a leer of confirmed pleasure, than a grin of mirth. He made two more calls before leaving. One call to VMA-542 to confirm his flight the next day, and the other to Major Collins' office. He told the sergeant who answered he'd be showing up for the interrogation of Captain Light in a few minutes.

When Breakheart entered the small, makeshift, interrogation room located adjacent to Major Collins' office, he was greeted solemnly by the Major. Nothing adorned the space, with the exception of a metal framed table, topped with dull colored plastic. Two chairs graced the room, both straight backed and uncomfortable looking. There were no glaring bare bulbs shining in Light's eyes, only fluorescent tubes giving off a soft glow. Collins sat across the table from Captain Light, his elbows planted on the table, and his head resting in his cupped hands. The Captain looked up, as Breakheart entered, casting sad, and slightly frightened eyes on the Colonel.

"Come in, Colonel," Major Collins exclaimed, a smile crossing his face. "Welcome to the world of 'I don't know anything'." He paused, then yelled, "Hey Sergeant Leadfoot, get the Colonel a chair, and not one of these back busters we've got in here now."

Breakheart took the chair brought to him, which was plastic, but provided a modicum of support. "Well, Major, from what you just said, I guess the Captain, here, doesn't have any idea what we are suggesting. I'll bet he is as surprised about the current state of affairs as we are?"

"Dead on, Colonel. Captain Light doesn't know a thing about anything. Isn't that right Captain?" He faced the young man.

"Honest, Colonel. I don't know what you all are talking about. I just like to take cross countries, and I got in the habit of stopping for fuel at Patrick. I sure as hell don't know anything about any smuggling going on."

There was a knock on the closed door, and the same sergeant who had brought Breakheart his chair entered, and handed a slip of paper to Collins.

The major glanced at the note, and passed it to Breakheart, who whistled softly.

"Captain," Breakheart began sternly, "I'm not going to beat around the bush with you. I want to know right now how you got involved in dope smuggling and who your contacts are. I'm not kidding around here. We have three confirmed murders on our hands, one involving the sabotage of a Harrier with one of my best friends aboard. So if you think I'm going to sit here and listen to you whine about having nothing to do with it all, you are very sadly mistaken."

Before the captain could answer, Collins said, "I guess you got the information we were looking for from the NADEP?"

Breakheart nodded an affirmative, and glared at the captain.

"Sir, really, I don't know anything about this whole thing. I don't even know why you picked me to lean on."

Collins smiled at the younger man. "Captain, I'm giving you one last chance to tell us what you know."

The silence filled the room, with only the ticking of a clock in the outer office breaking the stillness.

"I have here," Collins began, "a recent tabulation of your bank account with First Citizens Bank of North Carolina. Care to comment?"

The shock of what Collins had implied registered clearly on Light's face. He went pale, gawking at the men across from him like a caged animal.

"From the information I just now received, you have over two hundred and fifty thousand dollars stashed away in your bank account. Quite a lot of money to have socked away in your short career. Do you come from a wealthy family, or did you just win the lottery?" He paused. "Careful of what you say, because we will check out every word."

Captain Light's face fell. He seemed to age twenty years under the scrutinizing gaze of the two men watching his every move. Tears began to roll down his cheeks…great wet rivers freely dripping from his chin to the table. "How much trouble am I really in?" he asked in a whisper.

"More than you can handle, I assure you," Breakheart said flatly, and without emotion.

"I want a lawyer," Captain Light said. "I'll tell you everything I know, but I want a lawyer here."

"Why, do you think he'll be able to swing a deal for you?" The gravel in Major Collins' voice rolled with disgust.

Hours later, deep into the afternoon, Breakheart excused himself from the questioning and made his way for General Geise's office. Earlier, he had Collins' sergeant make an appointment with the

General for 1600. Geise had returned to the Point earlier, and was now expecting him.

"Come in Cuda, come in," General Geise boomed, his voice resounding off the walls. "I understand you have some pretty exciting news for me. Here, sit. Do you want some coffee?"

Breakheart, for all the years he had known and enjoyed Major General Geise, still had a hard time keeping up with the blasting verbalization and rapid fire questions. He sat on the couch, waving the coffee away and gave his greetings. "Good to have you back, sir. I trust LANT didn't eat you alive?"

The big man laughed. "No! Even they couldn't open their mouths that wide." He sat down in the over stuffed winged chair across the coffee table from Breakheart. "Still, they are getting antsy about Jack's accident. Let's hear what you have."

Breakheart started to speak, when the side door opened, and General Blake stepped into the room. For once, it did not bother him to have Blake present. In fact, he was counting on the Assistant Wing Commander joining him and Geise. "Good afternoon, General," Breakheart said, smiling. "I'm glad you'll be able to hear what I have to say along with General Geise."

Blake nodded his hello, but said nothing. He crossed the office, and took a seat in an adjacent chair to Geise.

The room settled, as Breakheart began to speak. He spent the next twenty minutes explaining what he knew to the generals before him. He told of the smuggling ring, or his suspicions of the probability of such an organization. The deaths were each clearly enumerated in detail. How Reddock rigged the throttle and the use of the spring. Full credit was given the engineers at NADEP, and the outstanding work they had accomplished in such a short time frame. Details were presented on Reddock's murder, and how it clearly tied in with the evidence surrounding the existence of an illegal drug alliance operating within the Harrier community. Breakheart laid everything on the table for his superiors to digest. Everything he knew to be true was articulated, with the exception of his conversation with Colonel Keller, the arrest of Captain Light, and the ongoing interrogation, and finally he left out the possibility that Major Beasly had gone AWOL. When he finally finished, the room remained deathly silent for several moments.

"This is unbelievable, Cuda. I can't believe what you are saying, nor will I even give the notion a try. Drug smuggling in 2nd MAW, you must have lost your fucking mind," General Blake stated with determination. "You really don't expect General Geise and me to believe what you have just told us, do you?"

"That's up to you, sir," Breakheart said quietly. "I'm just presenting you with the facts as I see and understand them. Nothing more and…er, nothing less."

General Geise stretched his big frame, sticking his legs straight out before him. He sighed. "Christ, Cuda, if what you think is true, I may lose my job sooner than I wish. It's apparent someone high in the Chain of Command is behind this whole thing. I don't see how it could be accomplished on strictly a squadron or section level, do you?"

"No, sir, I don't. I believe as you do. Where the individual or individuals are located, I have no idea as yet, but I think we have stirred up a hornet's nest, and there are going to be some very interesting bees swarming to cover their tracks."

"General Geise," Blake pleaded, "you don't really buy off on this story do you? I mean, it's just too preposterous to warrant serious consideration."

Geise turned to glare at his assistant. "Listen, Gene, if Cuda says we have this problem, it's my bet we have it in spades. The question is, what do we do now? Cuda, you have your accident solved, this is a matter now for the Washington nerds. I expect we should call in the heavy guns."

"Sir, with your permission," Breakheart began, "give me one more day. I'm the one who put the fire under the pot, and I would like to see if I can solve the whole thing and present the bastards names to you on a silver platter."

"No way," Blake interrupted. "In fact, sir, if you think this wild story has merit, then I think you should take Colonel Breakheart off the Accident Board immediately, and let me take over. That way, if the story is true, you will be protecting your command by showing Headquarters Marine Corps how seriously you felt about cleaning your own house."

Breakheart smiled at General Geise. "Sorry, sir, I can't let you do that. If you change horses in the middle of an accident investigation, you're going to have the Naval Safety Center down here in the form of some admiral or other, and he is going to tear the Wing's safety program apart, piece by piece. You can't get rid of me that easily."

"I wouldn't if I could," Geise blared. "Gene, there is absolutely no way I'm going to replace Cuda with you. He has done the work, and regardless of how this whole mess turns out, he is going to get the credit. Do you understand?"

The strength of Geise words slapped Blake in the face like a brick. He was not accustomed to being treated in such a manner. After all, he was second in command of the Wing, he thought indignity.

"Okay, Cuda, I'll give you one more day. That is the best I can do, then we call Headquarters Marine Corps and dump this thing in their lap."

"Yes, sir, I understand, and thank you." Breakheart stood to leave. "Oh, by the way, could I speak to you for a moment, General Blake? It doesn't have anything to do with the accident or drugs."

"I guess so," Blake said with resentment.

Once inside Blake's office, with the door separating the two generals closed, Breakheart asked, "Sir, are we still on for tomorrow morning?"

"Sure, why not? But why would you want to take the time for a hop, if you are going to be the master sleuth?" his voice dripped with sarcasm.

"I need a flight to clear the cobwebs from my head. I think getting airborne and tossing a few G's on the body will do me a world of good."

"Okay! The brief is zero six-thirty, at VMA-542, right?" Blake asked.

"That's right, sir. I'll see you there. I arranged the hop so you could lead. See you in the morning."

Breakheart left the office before Blake could say anything else, and headed for the front door. Once in his car he dialed VMAT-203's readyroom. He asked to speak to Lieutenant Burns, who, he told the Duty Officer, would be on the hangar deck with the Accident Board.

SIXTEEN

Darkness was beginning to cast long shadows across the well-tended yards in Officers Country when, after picking up the NADEP report, Breakheart pulled onto his asphalt driveway. Sena's car was parked on the grass, leaving room for him to motor into the carport. Damn, he thought, I forgot all about Sena coming over this evening. He cursed himself royally for his error in judgement. He should never have asked her. As he walked to the door, he heard laughter and loud conversation from inside. Letting himself in, his presence went unnoticed, as he tossed his cover on its table.

"Hey, if anyone is interested, I'm home," he yelled over the din.

"We're in the dining room, Pops," Steve hollered back.

Breakheart walked through the living room to the walnut dining table. Sena and the three boys were in the middle of eating supper. From the looks of the food on the table, his sons had not prepared the meal.

"Hi, Dan," Sena said softly, her blue eyes sparkling from the good-natured discourse exchanged between her and the teenagers. "I figured, when you didn't show up, something important must have delayed you, so I fixed dinner. I hope that's all right?"

"All right, heck yes it's all right. I'm sorry about being so late, but as you suggested, something did come up."

"Hey, Dad, you should be late more often, particularly if you've invited Sena. We've been having fun, and she's a better cook than you are," Bill said, between a mouthful of a warm dinner roll.

"Thanks for the vote of confidence," Breakheart said. He disappeared into the kitchen, reappeared with a chair, and pushed his way to the table. "I gather I am welcome to join this rowdy group of discontents."

Dinner was fantastic, and Breakheart had to admit though, he would never tell his sons, that Sena was a better cook than he. She had somehow whipped up a Lasagna from whatever she could find in the kitchen. How she was able to accomplish such a feat was beyond him. After they had finished with their meal, the entire crew retired to the sink and washed the dishes together. The talk was fast and lively. Breakheart's spirits soared. Dishes done, and the counters wiped clean, his sons plopped in front of the TV, while the adults poured a small glasses of sherry, and took a seat on the screened porch.

It was warm on the porch. A Carolina, summer night, with ten million stars winking overhead. The wind, which had howled the night before, was now nothing more than a moderate breeze rustling oak leaves, and sighing through the stately pines dotting Breakheart's backyard. On the river, not more than seventy-five yards from where the two enjoyed the night air, lights danced… fishing boats moving slowing with the current. They sat quietly. A golden disc began to slice the distance, so bright that moon shadows immediately began to crawl from the bases of the trees. As if on cue, two does walked into view. The deer browsed unfettered by fear…the moon's light reflecting off healthy tan coats.

"Lord, what a beautiful night," Sena said, taking Breakheart's hand. "It makes you appreciate life, when you can spend even a few minutes enjoying this kind of evening."

Breakheart did not respond immediately, he just squeezed her hand lightly, conveying his agreement. "Sena, I don't know how to thank you for tonight. You made it very special, and I know the kids feel the same way. You know, of course, this thing between us could get serious. It isn't anything I'm looking for, but I just feel so very comfortable around you."

"I know. The feeling is mutual, I assure you." She tightened her grip on his hand once again. "I'm not going to fight the feeling, it's too natural and warm."

They each took a sip of their sherry. Breakheart wondered if he should tell this woman next to him of his plans for tomorrow, then thought better of it. She could never understand his motives, nor the exhilaration he was expecting to feel in flight. No! Maybe years from now, if they were still holding hands in the moonlight, he would try to explain the reasons why, but not this evening.

The ship's clock, hanging in the den, chimed four bells when Sena said good night. They kissed deeply under a moon which had risen higher on the horizon, and Breakheart stood motionless as he watched her drive away. When he finally reentered the house, the phone was ringing. He crossed to the kitchen and grabbed the head piece. It was Snake.

"Okay, pally, everything is set. I think you're stupid as a blue fish, but you have always been that way, so I'll not try to talk you out of this crazy stunt."

"Thanks, Snake. I appreciate your help. Did you get in touch with Collins?"

"Yeah, he'll be there around nine."

"Good, make sure he doesn't show his face until I'm airborne."

"Will do. See you at Oh-dark-sparrow-fact. Sleep well! You're going to need to be bright-eyed and busy-tailed in the morning."

"Don't worry about me. See you tomorrow."

SEVENTEEN

Breakheart was paying particular attention to detail as he preflighted his Harrier. Never, in his long career as a naval Aviator, had he ever asked to have inspection panels opened by a plane captain. But under a cloudless sky, the sun already bearing down with intense heat, he stood by as the corporal opened fuselage engine panels on either side of the aircraft. As he waited, he thought of how the day began.

The alarm woke Breakheart from a dead sleep at 0530. He'd been dreaming of sailing with Sena and the clock's stringent bell interrupted the pleasant fantasy sounding like the engine warning horn on *Dreamer*. Unwinding himself from the single sheet covering him, he stumbled into the bathroom. Thirty minutes later, he sat at his kitchen table drinking his first cup of coffee for the day. His flight suit was clean and pressed, the name and squadron patches aligned perfectly on the left breast. He had even taken the time to shine his steel-toed flight boots. This was going to be his day and he wanted to look the part. He recognized the open vanity he was displaying, but, he thought, what aviator isn't unequivocally filled with self importance. Absolute confidence in one's abilities was the corner stone of staying alive in a fighter. There were those who thought fighter pilots were too filled with bravado, self-importance and conceit. They are, he smiled to himself. Yet, it was those very personality traits which accentuated a topnotch pilot. Breakheart felt the best of the best learned how to use their inflated self-image to push themselves and their aircraft to the outer limits of the flight envelope…each testing the other at a regulated pace. Over the years, he had learned to identify fledgling aviators who would one day be the finest the Corps had to offer. Give me a lieutenant who isn't afraid to open his mind to learning, is unafraid to jam the throttle to full and pull the stick to his lap, and you might have the next Red Baron in the making.

Before he left his quarters, Breakheart dutifully banged on his boys' doors. It was still too early for them to get out of their bunks, he smiled, but he wanted them to know he was thinking of them. He drove slowly to VMA-542, savoring the morning air, which was sprinkled with the sweet scent of summer flowers and Azaleas. He didn't bother with the car's air conditioning, though the sun was already warming the humid air. He let the wind waft across his face, and blow the Doral's smoke out the window.

He arrived in 542's readyroom with fifteen minutes to spare. General Blake had not yet arrived, and he took the time to drink another cup of coffee from the freshly brewed pot. The readyroom was quiet, with only the Duty Officer and two other captains who had been stuck with early briefings. Breakheart made casual conversation with the Duty Officer, who was copying Cherry Point's weather forecast for the morning on the plexiglass covering displaying the day's flight schedule. Next to Blake's and his name, the first two pilots written in black grease pencil, were their bird assignments. Breakheart was to fly 02, and Blake 10. Breakheart copied the numbers down on his knee board he'd carried in from his car. Because he was allowed to fly with any of the three Harrier squadrons, a special privilege his position as Wing Safety allowed, he carried his knee board in his car. The kneeboard was simply a metal frame contoured to fit the thigh. It had a clip at either end to hold a pad of paper and briefing cards. His flight gear, the torso harness, helmet, and G suit were maintained by VMAT-203's paraloft. These items he would have delivered to the squadron he was scheduled to fly with the night before his flight. He had made the appropriate arrangements with 203 yesterday afternoon. His flight gear would be waiting for him in 542's paraloft locker room.

When General Blake arrived at 0630, the Duty Officer snapped to attention, "Atten-tion! General Officer on deck!"

The room snapped to attention, which Blake took in stride, saying, "Carry on!"

Blake and Breakheart greeted each other formally. Blake appeared out of sorts…preoccupied with something unrelated to the upcoming flight. Breakheart finished copying the necessary numbers from the schedule board. Blake began doing the same. By the time the two men were finished, they had their assigned aircraft, the predicted outside air temperature, duty runway, and altimeter setting. This done, they adjourned to the first of three briefing rooms, located across the passageway from the readyroom. Quietly, with accomplished precision, they calculated their individual STO figures required for takeoff. Each AV-8 had its own set of engine specifications which demanded each pilot calculate his own take off requirements.

The briefing took over an hour. Blake, as leader, briefed carefully, covering every nuance dictated for a guns at BT-3 hop. He expected they would have sufficient fuel to have a couple of head on dog fights, and briefed air-to-air requirements as well. When they had finished, they returned to the readyroom to await maintenance's call to the Duty Officer that the birds were ready for flight.

During the briefing, and during the interval of waiting, Blake had been cordial, but removed from idle talk. He was not displaying his normal braggadocio so evident when he chided Breakheart in his office. Breakheart smiled inwardly, thinking perhaps General Blake finally was beginning to realize he had bit off more than his big mouth could chew. Also, he suspected the General had significant misgivings about how much Breakheart knew.

Blake waited impatiently for the call from maintenance. He wanted to get this damned flight over with, he thought. The recording in his mind, registered the night prior, played like a broken record. He had again spoken to Raoul Bolivar, explaining to the Colombian the most recent turn of events. Mr. Bolivar was, as he expected, totally unsympathetic, telling him to handle it, regardless. Again, he had been threatened with a visit from several of Boliva's closest companions. He had not slept well, but during his sleepless hours he had conjured a plan. A scheme, which if he were lucky, would stop the whole investigation in its tracks. After all, he figured, the accident had been solved by Breakheart, and if he could somehow get the meddling son-of-a-bitch out of the picture, he could stop worrying for the time being.

"General Blake, sir, your planes are ready," the Duty Officer announced.

"Thanks," Blake said. "Come on, Cuda, lets go fly."

Thirty minutes had passed since then, and now Breakheart was finishing his preflight, and climbing the ladder to the cockpit. The start was normal, as were the following cockpit and plane captain checks.

"Ragged Flight, check in." It was Blake, using his personal call sign asking Breakheart to signal if he was ready to taxi. Ragged would be their interflight call sign. Whenever they spoke to an outside agency, such as the tower, they would have to use the squadron's call of Tiger.

"Ragged Two," Breakheart returned, keying his mike button on the throttle. "I'm ready when you are."

"Roger. Break, Tiger Base, this is One Zero, taxiing with Zero Two."

"Roger, One Zero. Have a good flight," the Duty Officer declared.

"Ragged Flight, go button two," Blake told Breakheart to change his radio channel to ground control.

"Going button two."

"Ground Control, this is Tiger One Zero, taxi two for arming with information Bravo," Blake requested.

"Tiger One Zero, you are cleared to taxi to arming with Bravo. Hold short at the center mat," Ground Control stated.

The two Harriers began taxiing clear of 542's flight line, each pilot saluting his plane captain as he rounded clear of the chocks. Blake was in the lead, with 02 following at a fifty-yard interval. As they approached the center mat, Blake requested crossing to the arming area. Ground Control gave its clearance, and the camouflaged aircraft taxied across the huge chunk of concrete. They entered a taxiway connecting the landing end of Runway 32 and the takeoff end of runway 05. Entering the semicircular taxiway, they were met by 542's arming crew. A taxi director guided them through a ninety-degree turn to face 110 degrees.

Immediately upon stopping, both pilots stuck their hands in the air, and then grabbed the metal frame of the cockpit's windscreen. This way, there was no danger of hitting a switch and firing a weapon while the arming crew was under the aircraft. It took several minutes for the six man crew to arm both birds. Stray voltage checks were professionally accomplished and the safety pins were pulled. With a final thumbs up to each pilot, the crew backed away and climbed aboard a waiting truck.

"Ragged Flight, go button three," Blake directed.

"Button three."

"Tower, Tiger One Zero. Request position and hold, runway three two."

"Cleared position and hold," the tower responded.

Staggered slightly, the two Harriers sat wingtip to wingtip in the takeoff position…each man going through his own pre-takeoff checks and engine run ups. Breakheart finished well ahead of Blake, and sat under the closed canopy with his right thumb extended in the air. Seconds ticked by before Blake acknowledged he, too, was ready.

"Tower, Tiger One Zero, ready for takeoff, flight of two."

"Tiger One Zero, you are cleared for takeoff. Wind, three three zero at fifteen."

"Cleared for takeoff," Blake said, while windmilling two fingers of his left hand to indicate Breakheart should do his final acceleration check.

Everything ready, they exchanged a thumbs up, and Blake released the toe brakes and jammed his throttle to 100 percent. He jumped airborne five hundred feet in front of Breakheart, who immediately followed. Airborne, Breakheart, pulled his throttle back only two percent, allowing the aircraft to rapidly gained airspeed for the rendezvous. He was aboard Blake's left wing before his leader could complete a 180 turn. During his rendezvous, he had purposely accelerated to more than a hundred knots of overtake speed, much too fast for a properly executed join-up for any airplane but a Harrier. Using his nozzles at the last possible moment, Breakheart slowed his bird to match Blake's, sliding neatly under the general's wing.

Blake had his flight switch radio channels to Twilight, and checked in airborne with the ground controller. They were cleared to switch to button nineteen, for clearance into BT-3. It was a busy time in the flight…changing channels, climbing to ten thousand feet, leveling off, and, requesting clearance on the target. BT-3, located to the northeast of Cherry Point, was but a short seven or eight minutes away.

Tiger Flight, with Ragged in the lead and Cuda flying number two, was on their way to Bombing Target Three, more commonly known simply as BT-3. The air-to-ground ordnance range, a massive complex located in the middle of nowhere, could only be reached in a power boat by the men and women who manned the target's control tower. The multiple targets, including a thousand foot and a five hundred-foot bull, a tuck convoy, guns and rocket panels, and simulated bunkers, sat in the middle of a Carolina swamp. There, where the Neuse River dumps into Pamlico Sound, and among the many estuaries feeding both river and sound, lay BT-3. The large bull was used primarily by Cherry Point's A-6 community, dropping Mark-76 practice bombs in fabricated nuclear attacks. The smaller bull, its center marked with a school bus, was used by Navy and Marine Corps light bombers practicing both high dive angle bombing, as well as low level close air support. Open six days a week and used from 0700 until midnight each day, BT-3 had hundred of thousands of pounds of practice and high explosive ordnance dropped within its confines since being constructed during World War II.

"Target Control, this is Tiger One Zero, requesting clearance on to BT-3," Blake said into his oxygen mask.

"Tiger One Zero, you are cleared on target. Say position, pilot names, time on target, and weapons aboard," a clear feminine voice filled the airways.

"Roger, Target Control. We are presently five miles out. In Tiger One Zero, pilot Blake, I spell, Alpha, Romeo, India, Charlie, Kilo. In Tiger Zero Two, pilot Breakheart, I spell, Bravo, Romeo, Echo, Alpha, Kilo, Hotel, Echo, Alpha, Romeo, Tango. Thirty minutes on target with guns."

"Roger, Tiger One Zero. Call target in sight and the break. You will be using the gun panels to the left of the small bull. Do you copy?"

"Roger, Target Control. BT-3 in sight. We'll call the break in approximately one minute."

The two Harriers, glued together as if they were one, passed the target to the south. Breakheart could not see the bulls, as he remained on Blake's left wing, his view monopolized by fuselage and wing. Blake set his power for 350 knots, and allowed the target area to pass to his seven o'clock before starting a gentle left turn to intercept the target run in heading of 270 degrees. During the turn, the sun was directly in Breakheart's eyes. He squinted through his visor, trying to keep his lead in sight. It was momentary, and the blurred silhouette soon reappeared as Harrier One Zero. Blake leveled his wings on a heading of 270 degrees, and held his arm up with a balled fist to Breakheart. It was the signal to cross under, and take up a position on Blake's right wing. Breakheart executed the maneuver in short order, purposely tucking his nose close under Blake's tail plane. The air pressure from such immediate proximity, caused Blake's nose to buck downward slightly. Breakheart knew it was childish, but it was the little things in life that made living so special, he smiled.

"Target Control, Tiger One Zero in the break," Blake called.

"Roger, One Zero, I have you in sight. Cleared to break."

Blake looked over his right shoulder at Breakheart. Taking his right hand from the stick, he touched his fingers to his lips and gave his wingman the kiss off signal. Then, suddenly, Breakheart was looking at empty air space, as One Zero rolled into a sixty-degree angle of bank, and slammed on four G's for the turn downwind.

For proper downwind spacing, Breakheart counted seven seconds and then pulled his stick aft and to the left. Zero Two, turned to follow its leader into the gun pattern. As the G's took their hold on Breakheart, sweat poured from under his helmet and into his eyes. He was expecting the wet, and after leveling his wing on the downwind leg, he took a chamois from his G suit pocket, raised his helmet visor, and wiped his face clear of perspiration.

Breakheart took up a proper interval downwind from his lead. They were level at four thousand five hundred feet and maintaining three hundred and fifty knots. The interval between aircraft had to be sufficient to allow one aircraft to complete its firing run prior to the second diving for its turn at the banners. The banners were nylon meshed panels stretched between two poles. Three of these orange and white nylon sections were stationed at a right angle and to the left of the multi-ringed five hundred foot bull's eye.

"Tiger One Zero, your designated target is the panel closest to the bull. Make your first run cold."

"Roger, Target Control. First run cold," Blake answered, indicating he understood which target was in use, and that his first pass was to be a cold run...no shooting. Seconds ticked by. "Target Control, One Zero, in cold."

"Cleared in cold," Target Control came back.

Blake's aircraft rolled up on its left wing, and the nose dropped. His throttle pushed forward, he rapidly accelerated to four hundred and fifty knots, where he pulled it back to near idle to hold that airspeed. The windscreen filled with brown earth, water, and an orange panel. He sighted the center of the banner through his weapon's computer controlled sight reticle. The computer generated green dot, displayed on his HUD, showed the exact point of impact his 30 millimeter bullets would make on the target. The small dot moved rapidly from a six o'clock position on the banner to one directly on its center. He was at nineteen hundred feet, where, if he wasn't on a cold run, he could have pulled the trigger on the front of his stick, but this was a cold run…no firing.

"Tiger Lead off, cold," Blake called, as he pulled the stick into his lap, and twisted it to the left, climbing for the downwind leg.

"Off cold," Target Control answered.

"Tiger Zero Two, in cold," Breakheart keyed his mike to broadcast his intentions.

"Zero Two, cleared in cold."

Blake did not pull his throttle back after his pull off target and turn for the down wind. He was accelerating to over five hundred knots, screaming for the roll-in point. His face was a mask of intense hate. Slamming the Harrier into a five-G left turn, he switched his guns to hot.

Breakheart leveled his wings in the ten-degree dive for the target. The run felt good, with the pipper planted at six o'clock to the banner, and his airspeed solidly set at four hundred and fifty knots. He passed twenty-five hundred feet, and though his guns were safe, his finger tightened on the trigger. At nineteen hundred feet, he pulled the trigger, wishing it had been a hot run, because his pipper was dead in the center of the target. Suddenly, flashes of orange-white light streaked by his canopy on the right side.

"Simo run! Simo run," the woman's voice screamed from Target Control.

"Knock it off, simo run!" It was a cry filled with excitement and fear.

Breakheart knew immediately what had happened. Blake was in a gun run with him, only Breakheart was the target. He smiled in his mask. "You miserable cock sucker," he keyed his mike and grunted over the pressure of the G's, "I knew you would try something like this." He was pulling seven and a half G's when he spoke, trying to raise the AV-8's nose above the horizon. More thirty millimeter slashed by him, this time, to his port. He threw the stick to the right, and the plane rolled rapidly onto its starboard wing. The fiery balls of death passed behind him.

"Knock it off, simo run," Target Control pleaded.

"Roger, simo run," Blake broadcasted. "Off target, and returning to base."

Breakheart was now passing ten thousand feet, with Blake at six o'clock, but way out of gun range. "Well, I guess it's going to be you and me," he spoke to Blake. "Lets switch to 333.3 and get on with it."

"You miserable bastard," Blake's voice dripped with hate, "switching 333.3."

Breakheart, his throttle fire walled, was in a hard climbing turn to port, having reversed his heading to drag Blake over the Pamlico Sound, and away from land and habitation. "Well, we know who the bad guy is, don't we, Ragged? Do you want to give up now, or do I have to shoot your slimy ass down?"

Following Breakheart's every move, Blake felt cocky. "You're forgetting who's at your six, Breakheart. You're dead, and I'll blame it on the simo run. Lots of questions, but the accident board will believe it was just a terrible mishap, and you died on the way back to the Point."

"Fat chance, asshole," Breakheart responded, dragging his opponent into a tighter circle.

Blake tried to pull inside Breakheart's turn, succeeding slightly, but slowing his aircraft in the process. Breakheart reversed rapidly, dumping his nose for the deck. Blake rolled with him, but was slower, and could not build airspeed as rapidly. Passing five thousand feet, Breakheart leveled his wings and drew the stick back, loading the bird up to four and a half G's. As the aircraft clawed for altitude, Breakheart screamed into his mask and tightened his whole body, forcing blood to his brain, delaying the onset of a blackout.

Blake, saw the move coming, but not having the airspeed, he could only draw the nose through the horizon, and hope he could follow…he knew he could not cut the distance between them.

Breakheart held his nose in the vertical, allowing the airspeed to dribble away like a forgotten promise. He contorted in his ejection seat, fighting against the restraining straps cutting into his shoulders, trying to keep Blake in sight beneath him. Sweat poured down his face unnoticed. Blake was several thousand feet below, his nose trying in vain to stalk the Harrier above. At seventeen thousand feet, Breakheart did a rapid scan of his instruments; his airspeed was down to one hundred knots, still he held the nose straight up.

Below, Blake was running out of airspeed as well. He was getting nervous, thinking he could stall or go into uncontrolled flight if he didn't ease the nose. He eased the nose. The Harrier's nose started to drop through, and no matter how much pressure Blake put on the stick, which was already in his lap, he could not stop the nose from seeking earth.

Breakheart watched with a knowing eye. He had seen it a thousand times before, while fighting F-18s, and AV-8s alike. Someone with experience would know better than to try and follow a Harrier into a vertical climb unless he had an overwhelming advantage in airspeed. But Blake was not experienced, nor was he a very accomplished pilot in any arena.

He waited patiently for several seconds. When Blake's nose was hopelessly committed to a dive, he yanked the nozzles to the breaking stop. The aircraft reacted immediately with the violence of a horse suddenly whipped across its rear with a piece of barbed wire. One second the nose was pointed straight up, the next it was straight down. Breakheart slammed the nozzles aft the moment the "flop" occurred. He was momentarily out of controlled flight, and the Harrier's wings wagged back and forth without command. Once the nozzles were aft, the plane settled down in his hands, and fell like a stone. The airspeed built from eighty-five knots to three hundred in a wink, and still it accelerated.

Beneath Breakheart, Blake knew he'd made a mistake. He had to get his nose up to meet the demon flying down from above. He'd lost any advantage he might have had only seconds before.

His airspeed was climbing, but not so rapidly as Breakheart's. At four hundred knots he slapped the stick to his lap, putting six G's on the bird. His oxygen mask slid down on his sweaty cheeks, and the world around him narrowed…his peripheral vision tunneling as the blood supply to his brain fell short of its needs. He was greying out.

Breakheart saw Blake pull his nose up, trying to meet him head on. He grabbed the throttle and pulled it back to idle, slowing his breathtaking run for speed. Blake's aircraft passed three thousand yards in front of his nose. He pulled back hard on the stick and dumped the nozzles to thirty degrees. The nose pitched violently up. Breakheart slammed the nozzles aft, and continued to pull. The sudden boost in the reduction of turn radius the nozzles had given him put Blake directly in front of him. He was now the hawk and not the rabbit.

Blake strained against G's and the seat restraints, trying to see Breakheart. He was now in a hard five G left turn, hoping to cause the faster Harrier at his six to overshoot in the turn.

Breakheart, sweat streaming down his face and back, grunted loudly as his G-suit inflated against his legs and mid-section. He loaded the bird to six G's and turned inside Blake. He saw the overshoot developing and eased the G's, slammed the throttle to full, and pulled the nose into a high yo-yo to reduce the overtake.

Blake reversed his turn to the right the moment Breakheart went into the yo-yo. He pulled with all his strength to force the nose in the direction Breakheart was moving. His airspeed plummeted, as he increased the G's in the turn. He had to release pressure on the stick and extend away from Breakheart. He needed airspeed, something Breakheart appeared to have more than enough at his command. He was getting scared. The man flying the other aircraft was toying with him, pushing him into making one mistake after another.

Breakheart pulled his throttle to eighty percent and stomped on the left rudder. The plane skidded with the rudder turn, and the nose fell onto Blake's tail. Breakheart laughed silently to himself.

You're dead ass hole, he thought. This time he eased the throttle forward just enough to accelerate at a moderate pace, and fell into Blake's six o'clock as if he had a rail guiding him there.

"Well, General," Breakheart keyed his mike and broadcast over the airways in a voice filled with contempt, "do you want to tell me why you had Jack killed, or should I just go ahead and shoot you down right now?"

Blake was in complete panic. His threw his aircraft back and forth in desperation, trying to shake the certain death hanging on his tail like a magnet. "What do you want?" he whined in fright.

"Tell me you gave the order, and we'll go home. I just want to hear you say it," Breakheart asked. He was following the ineffectual gyrations of the aircraft in front of him without thinking. His instincts flew the aircraft as if it were an extension of his own personality.

"Okay, you bastard, I had Reddock set up Jack's airplane. Is that what you wanted to hear?"

"That's all." He paused. "Hey Snake, you got this on tape?"

"Cuda, me lad, it is safe and secure in the readyroom. Plus, we have Major Collins, two Federal Agents, and General Geise here enjoying the commentary. You okay?"

"Never been better in my life," Breakheart replied. "I've always wanted to have a 'real' dogfight, and today I got one. The only trouble is, this jerk couldn't fly his way out of a wet paper bag."

"Cuda," it was General Geise, "bring the little rat fink bastard on home. You've had enough fun for one day."

"Yes, sir. Can do! Blake, I'm going to stay right on your tail. You make one false move and I'm going to fill your cockpit so full of lead you'll be lucky not to be mistaken for a Swiss cheese. Do you understand me clearly?"

Blake had stopped jinxing his aircraft the moment he heard Breakheart calling Burns. He was finished, and he knew it. "I understand," was all he said.

"Then take up a heading for a straight-in approach to runway three two. Switch to button three, and do exactly what I tell you."

"Switching button three," Blake said, completely defeated.

Ragged Flight turned for the Point. Breakheart remained at Blake's six, varying his distance from fifteen hundred to a thousand feet. His guns were armed and sighted on the Harrier before him. He had meant every word. If Blake so much as wagged a wing the wrong way, he fully intended to fill the small airplane with 30-millimeter rounds. As Blake slowed to two hundred and fifty knots and punched his gear down, Breakheart slowed with him, using his nozzles to give him the stability necessary to follow the bird now in a landing configuration. If he were to put his gear and flaps down with Blake, then his guns would no longer fire. In the landing configuration, gear down, an armament safety solenoid would engage electrically, rendering his guns useless. The nozzles gave him the edge he needed while he followed Blake to touch down.

When Blake's wheels hit the runway, Breakheart rapidly accelerated a way, and made a hard three hundred and sixty-degree turn. He flew over the Blake's Harrier low and fast, as it taxied down the remaining six thousand feet of landing roll. Breakheart maneuvered in this manner twice. On his second pass he saw three trucks surround the AV-8, and knew Blake would now be escorted the remaining distance to 542's flight line, there to be met by Collins and his Federal Agents.

"Tower, Tiger Zero Two, at the one eighty, gear down, stops clear, for landing on the South Pad," Breakheart called on his third and final turn downwind. The 'stops clear' call was unique to the Harrier. It told the tower the STO stop was clear, and therefore, the pilot could use his nozzles without hindrance.

"Tiger Zero Two, clear to land South Pad, wind three three zero at ten."

"Cleared South Pad," Breakheart answered.

The bird turned off the one eighty to a heading of three two zero, and began decelerating. Breakheart double checked his gear and flaps down, the STO stop clear, and duct pressure. With dexterity, he brought the bird to a hover over the South Pad, reduced power slightly and sat it down with a gentle bump.

"Tower, Tiger Zero Two, clear South Pad," Breakheart broadcast once his wheels cleared the metal outline of the pad.

"Cleared to taxi, and cross the Center Mat. Contact ground," A Marine tower operator said.

Ten minutes later, Breakheart was completing his shut down check list. VMA-542's flight line was buzzing with activity. Military Police cars, unmarked vehicles and men surrounded Blake. The general was just climbing out of his cockpit to be hand cuffed and escorted away with little more ceremony than a common criminal. Which he was, thought Breakheart, as Zero Two's engine unwound, the throttle having been brought around the horn to the cut off detente, He unstrapped and began climbing from his cockpit. He was met on the ground by General Geise and Snake.

"That was the craziest stunt I've seen in years," Geise said without anger. "Only the Cuda would come up with such a harebrained scheme."

"Yes, sir, but it worked, and we got the bastard dead to rights. He tried to kill me on BT-3, and then I forced him to confess. I don't see how any miserable, self-righteous lawyer can get him out of this one."

"They'll try," Burns said, slapping Breakheart on the back. "Good job, pally!"

"Couldn't have done it without you," Breakheart smiled at his friend. "Thanks for the help."

"I wouldn't have had it any other way," Snake said.

The three started to walk off. Breakheart turned and walked up to the nose of the AV-8B he had just flown. He patted the nose cone and said, "Thanks girl, you done good."

EPILOGUE

D*REAMER* DUG HER rail down, heeling on a starboard tack. The wind, blowing from the south at twenty knots, stretched her Genoa and main taunt. Breakheart eased the helm slightly, reducing the heel angle. It was a perfect day to be riding the Neuse. The Fall sun was warming to both body and soul.

"Well it's finally over," Sena said, her blond hair streaming with the breeze. "I have to admit I'm glad, though I don't believe he got what he deserved."

"Life in Levenworth without chance of parole isn't what I would call a piece of cake," Breakheart answered, putting his arm around the woman next to him. He smiled at her vehemence, keeping an eye on the waves and white caps pounding *Dreamer's* bow.

"I wish he'd gotten the chair. It was what he deserved."

"Yeah, maybe, but he did provide enough information to arrest that creep in Miami. Of course, Bolivar will probably buy himself off with a slap on the wrist, and if that becomes the case, I wouldn't give you a plug nickel for Blake's life, in prison or not," Breakheart stated flatly.

Blake's Courts Martial had ended the day before with his sentencing. The military tribunal had taken little time to deliberate after the evidence had been given by Breakheart, Collins, and others. He was caught in his own trap. Breakheart's testimony was the clincher, as was the recorded tape Snake had made in 542's ready room the morning Blake had tried to gun Breakheart down on BT-3.

Colonel Jack Adams' accident report had been completed shortly after the arrests; and Breakheart, along with the other members of his board had each been awarded The Legion of Merit medal for their efforts. In the end, two captains from VMA-231, Major Beasly from 203, and Major Krump from 542 had been arrested as the pilots involved in the smuggling ring. Each Harrier squadron had at least one enlisted man, all sergeants, who acted as the agents who stripped the returning cross country Harriers of their valuable cargo.

The whole affair had ripped through the Corps like a knife. National newspapers and TV went out of their way to make it sound as if the Nation's finest could no longer be trusted. Fortunately, the vast majority of the men and women reading and hearing this journalistic trash, realized the most important fact of all…the Corps cleaned up its own messes, not asking for favoritism. The Corps would survive.

A gust of wind caught Breakheart off guard, and the boat dipped its toe rail beneath the foam speeding by the hull. He spun the wheel into the wind and *Dreamer* righted herself. The two were on their way to South Creek, a tributary on the south bank of the Neuse. Breakheart knew of a secluded anchorage where they could spend the night alone, without people or other boats. The boys had seen them off at the dock, telling them both to have a great weekend, and that was just what Breakheart had in mind.